"Carolyn See captures all the tacky charm of that Los Angeles world and all the diversions it offers, and does it well."
Chicago Tribune

"I've always admired Carolyn See's novels."
ALICE ADAMS

"Carolyn See is quite mad, in both meanings of the word, and very funny too."
ANNE LAMOTT
AUTHOR OF *Rosie*

"See has a sharp eye for the California scene."
Library Journal

"She explores human values and the nature of women's ties with startling clarity."
Booklist

THE REST IS DONE WITH MIRRORS

Carolyn See

FAWCETT CREST • NEW YORK

For Richard and Joan,
with love

Although some places in this novel are real, what happens in them is fictional. I'm sure nothing untoward occurs in the music rooms of UCLA; the confines of the Surf Rider are not only chaste but unphotographed; and (especially) there aren't any spies at the Self Realization Fellowship.

I

I'VE SAID BEFORE that Lorraine made every minute, every encounter, the beginning of a myth. That's pretentious but she did it every time. With her, people became symbols; they were elevated, in spite of themselves and to their usual delight, to vast effigies depicting greed or lust or gluttony (with Lorraine, it usually was the baser emotions); they changed from ordinary dun-colored human beings to life-size projections.

We lived on myths anyway, and it was a seller's market. A poor pimpled unfortunate in one of my freshman composition classes once remarked in a paper that he often walked about campus and drove the freeways with his mind filled with "thoughts of copulation." Thoughts of copulation! For months afterwards, any incipient paranoia he may have had was fed by fifty or so teaching assistants in different departments, clearly adults, falling sideways to the wall, clutching each other, tittering disgracefully as he went by. (This was later, after we became teaching assistants, but things hadn't changed in that aspect.) Thoughts of copulation. Our world, so trimmed, so graceful—gardeners caring for acres of expensive landscape, earnest students hugging trees so that they could write about them accurately—was populated by desperate men. We had seen it in ourselves when our husbands slammed out of the house dyspeptic from underdone oatmeal, furious, deprived of their morning screw—but those undergraduates seemed at a distance to

1

live in a downy bed of sex, grinding on it and in it, as it were, fucking themselves silly in the new co-ed dorms, then trooping noisily down to community dining rooms to eat huge dinners with seconds of everything, so that they could run upstairs for seconds of sex.

Years before Juan Ramirez had been a part of that apparently self-indulgent undergraduate army (we all were). He wandered the campus, swarthy and grim, swathed in heavy Pendleton shirts even in hot weather, his long, turkey neck wrapped in scarves against his perennial sore throats. His mind was filled with those thoughts. As president of the Newman Club, an easy post to be elected to, certainly, he spent hours in earnest conversation with the university chaplain, and served at mass, the tallest, sickest altar boy ever. He pinched pimples, which plagued him even at twenty-five and after two sleepwalking years in the Army, and thought long and hard of the base joys of the flesh.

What I retail now, a lot of you will know and long remember anyway. I've heard the story with a different cast, a different setting, even different crimes including burglary, larceny, and what we call, in California at least, the crime against nature. It's been set in a darkened bakery among the rising loaves of bread, or inside the Griffith Park Zoo in broad daylight behind the lion cages. And the only way to tell its authenticity is to collate texts in the manner of German philologists. The words, "Is that you, Louie?" remain unchanging and the same, hallmark of a myth of violence and sex, our own atrocity we all could understand and shiver to; much worse than Caryl Chessman's fumbling outrages in Barnsdale Park, because it happened to one of us. All the charm in the world couldn't put a good face on it, and, because we saw the results for years, it convinced us more than all our childhood-heard FBI programs or adventures of Mr. District Attorney that crime doesn't pay.

At that time Lorraine was a senior majoring in art, thin, crazy, beautifully dressed, living at home with her parents who fixed diet custard and truffle sandwiches to put in her elegant box lunches. She was the center of a group of raffish, trash-talking young people in their early twenties, who lived, like jazz musicians, off day jobs and their mothers' munificence. Like Lorraine, they dressed beautifully (their good taste was a wonder in the thriftshops), and got high, free, on terpin hydrate they cadged from the Medical Center to treat their non-existent illnesses. I had lunch with them about once a week as they reclined, supine, in the elegantly fading grass outside the Art Center. I hated them then; they told long stories that didn't sound like jokes but were, and I never knew what any of them were even talking about. Loneliness drove me there, an uneasy twelfth of eleven spiffy people. The best I ever got out of them was when once an older, stout man said that I had a medieval face. I brightened; surely that was an OK thing to have. They all turned to look. Lorraine said, "With that chin?" They all looked away and went on talking.

Through all this, Juan Ramirez stalked through the library, took the elevator down to the fifth level underground and waited heron-like among the old volumes. When a girl came, unsuspecting, to find a book, he would reach a long, eczema-covered skinny arm through the stacks and clutch at her buttocks like a querulous crab.

At that time the Art Center was surrounded by a group of temporary buildings left over from World War II. (Like a mother hen with her chicks, one of my freshmen later said in a paper, and got a C— for his pains.) Too small to be used for regular classes, too shabby to conform to the image of effortless wealth which all the humanities cherished (because they had no money at all), these architectural sores were an inconvenience. At that time the problem was solved by the administrative genius of some associate professor. The buildings were divided, and each half given to two of the more promising art students to use as studios. That guy was sorry later.

Lorraine had one of these studios, which she shared with another student, much older, named Louie Lambretta. They worked harmoniously (Lorraine, through everything, worked), and generally at night, since in the day the rooms were dark and uninviting, and in the night those long fluorescent bars did something crazy to the colors.

Lorraine, one Wednesday night, stayed late. It got to be twelve-thirty, one. Beside her fluorescent-lit cabin, the bright lights of the new Art Center glittered emptily, no one was around at that hour. She had two middle-sized decorative paintings going—one of a back porch, the other a chicken with a piece of flank steak in his mouth. She sold paintings like these to her mother's friends for pocket money. She would mix a color she particularly liked and dish it around a bit, first on one canvas, then the other. Then, behind her back, the door opened, the fluorescent lights went off. "Is that you, Louie?" she called.

It wasn't. What follows I received from Lorraine, from a hundred secondary sources, from Ramirez himself. The stories are different but they're all the same. Knocking down lions, wading through bread dough, tipping over jars of expensive oils and tripping on easels, a dark specter advanced. Lorraine found herself smothered against a bony stretch of rib bones, against wool that smelled overpoweringly of Vick's Vapo-Rub. Since only weeks before another art student even more beautiful than she had been raped down on Central Avenue by a seven-foot Black who had threatened to put out her eyes, Lorraine knew better than to struggle. "But he certainly never screwed anybody before," she said later. "You just hoped he could get through it without embarrassing himself or he'd have to kill somebody." Juan Ramirez, for that's who it was, naturally, pulled out his prick and held it against the only part of Lorraine he could find, her upper stomach just under her barely defined breasts. "I didn't know what I was supposed to do," she said, "and besides, I couldn't do anything because he was holding my arms so tight and bending my ribs." Finally, after a stymied minute or so in the dark, she bent down her head to give a tentative lick. Ramirez took that badly. He slapped her, he ordered her to take off her clothes, he lifted her up until they faced each other, though her tiny feet barely reached his knees, jammed himself into her hospitable cunt (I don't think I've ever known Lorraine to turn down anyone under any circumstances), and strangled her with his tongue—which was coated with one of the worst cough medicines Lorraine had ever tasted. Even then he plainly didn't get the hang of it. "He wouldn't move," Lorraine complained later. "How is anyone going to get to do anything if you don't even move?" One reason he didn't move, of course, as Lorraine made sure to tell us, was that he was so small. "I mean I never figured it meant much to be small, short and thick does it quick, right? and a stiff prick hath no conscience." (Let me say here that since we all were going to be specialists, we borrowed from each other's fields. We knew about art history from Lorraine, nineteenth-century English novels from me, Australian languages from Walter, the decline of the drama from Mr. Goodman, and Jorge Alphonse furnished us all with medieval proverbs he was collecting for his doctoral dissertation. When a tire went flat, we'd say, "The world is as round as a ball," and feel obscurely comforted. Don't laugh or put down the nostalgia; I fell back on proverbs when after seven years of marriage I found my husband screwing someone else in a vast bed of morning glories.) "So," Lorraine said, "I moved a little, just to give him the idea, and he fell out. He slanted *down* or something. I *know* now, there's just that one angle you can deal with him at all."

Lorraine moved; Ramirez slipped out. He swore viciously in Spanish; she giggled. It had become in the dark another sleazy undergraduate hotel room; she was at home and not terribly afraid. There was just that one project she had to do, like always; given the situation and a disgruntled male, she had to make it work.

OK. There they were in the dark room alone. Ramirez has dropped her and is thinking murderous thoughts. "If I'd killed her then, we'd all have been much happier, God forgive me," he said later. His rage, drunkenness, apprehension, had taken away his erection. He'd turned to leave when Lorraine, blindly in the half-dark, reached for his thigh, turned him half around, and once more found his diminutive prick with her narrow, gossipy tongue. "It was better than that mouth, and easy to get to, at least." But why did she do it? Why not let him run away to lurk again among the stacks? "I couldn't let him go off like that. It would have been too sad." She licked, sucked, bit, just like in a pornographic novel, while Juan Ramirez, in a fit of lust and rage, swore and called her dirty names in Spanish. Then he grabbed her, pulled her up as before. Even then it was mighty strange because he still refused to move. Lorraine tried a little something again; he bruised her lip with one of his chapped, rawboned hands which (she saw later) was covered with cheap New Mexican rings. So she waited, and waited, and furtively shifted her weight, without destroying that all important socket and joint, and leaned her artistic head upon his scratchy Pendleton shoulder, and suddenly in motionless, industrial, university silence, he managed to do it. "Have you ever had someone come when you were hanging in the *air*?" she asked us next day.

It was done. He flung her to the floor and began to sob. What was he anyway? Just some spic from the East Side who had happened to luck out—maybe one of only thirty-six Mexicans in the whole university. He fell to his knees—not neglecting to fold himself back into his clothes—and covered his face with his hands. He wanted to die, he said, and I believe him, for on the other side of all those thoughts of copulation were a big, cheap-but-fancy wedding, with him and his love-eyed wife strung together in a giant five-foot flower rosary.

Lorraine put on her pants and slipped her blouse over her bony, seductive shoulders. She went over and turned on the lights. Juan didn't run, poor bastard. "What's your name?" she said. He told her. "You want to see my painting? I got one girl friend to pose as a maenad, suckling this cat. What do you think? What's your major? Do you like it? Here's one, a chicken with a piece of flank steak, I love it. And one of Barney Ross." She sleeked around the room, pestered him with questions, leaned in and stared nearsightedly at him, complimented him on his nose—which he blew without saying anything. She giggled, went on painting, told him to make coffee, laughed at him. They left at quarter of four in the morning, but she made him take her out for coffee, where she voraciously consumed a patty melt and spent his last money. It was dawn by the time they got to her house and he walked her to the door, suffering, probably, because she wouldn't kiss him goodnight. She giggled instead, patted his prick, and went inside to sleep until ten-thirty. It was all one to her.

The next day—in eighty-degree heat—I took a pastrami sandwich over to the Art Center lawn. A new person was there, a dark bony man in steel-rimmed glasses which cruelly punished his nose. He unwrapped a copious lunch and offered it around, but no one wanted any. (We didn't know his mother's incredible style with tamales stuffed with raisins and spices, or those crusty almond cookies, or her blue tortillas. If you showed us a blue tortilla then, we'd have thought something was wrong with it.) He sat straight up on the dry grass. He ate. He got up to get coffee for Lorraine, came back and sat again beside her.

"He raped me," she said, "you can't put it any other way. I was painting, and all of a sudden it was dark. I said, 'Is that you, Louie?' But it was this lunatic *madman*," and she snuggled in against him, and looked up past his crinkled-acne chin to his desperate eyes. He nodded, he tried to laugh, he nodded around the group and blew his nose. He had cachet from my point of view, he was socially accepted as I'd never be. I didn't necessarily believe her chat, but I believed him and his out-of-place, beyond-words face. It was true, all right. There had been rape and mayhem in the night, and I had been out with my in-laws to a flower show.

I've always hated the first person; I think anyone with any sense does; there are people who know how to blow up the whole world at the AXEL Corporation and it takes them all day to write a halting, childish letter to their mothers. It comes from an aversion to the first person. The passive voice was invented as a cover; no matter how much we explain to kids in class that the passive voice is bad, they cling to it, either imperiously, as to a fur coat, or pitifully, like one of those ragged babies in a foster-parent ad. I think it's because we always look *out*, we see everything but ourselves, we talk about sensitivity and forget to listen to what people say because we're too busy seeing them. When our marriages break up, we offer various interpretations of our husbands' behavior; sometimes we are spiteful, more often magnanimous, but in the night we strain our faces toward the bathroom mirror (clichéish yes, but we see ourselves in the most primitive clichés) and think, Was it this, was it that? Did I nag? Did I . . . stink? Was I a bad lay? Was it the sound of my voice? But we can see nothing, nothing.

You see already why I hate this voice; it shows more than I care to describe. You might already know why my husband didn't mind leaving me as much as he might have, and I'll never figure it out. I am, or was, at least, a little plodding, a little dull, very smart, oh very smart, but poor, and sort of sad, and very eager to please.

I've always assumed an unhappy childhood for myself because they told me I was having one. My father, a glittery-suited sport, left when I was eleven, and my mother cried from then on. There was a general feeling of unutterable deprivation in my middle youth but no particular evidence to back it up (except that my mother, in a fit of masochism after Daddy left, bought some paper drapes for the living room; textured, cloth-like, printed in garish flowers. Once we'd put up those horrid strips we could never have anyone over at all; we sat in separate shame on the couch and my mother cried some more). Mostly, however, the windows were open in our little house, my mother planted nasturtiums; I played with other children on the buckling sidewalks of one of Los Angeles's middle-class, old-time, in-town suburbs.

I grew up determined to find the good life, believing in it with the openhearted naïveté people used to save for family or the church—and only an authority on how it *wasn't* done. My little sister who still lives at home came recently to visit me: when it was her turn to cook dinner she plucked a carton of Chef Boy-ar-dee spaghetti from the grocery shelf. "No, baby, that's how it's *not* done," I told her in my thirtyish old semibopper dialect, and she allowed herself to be propelled to the garlic, clams, the celery. I showed her real spaghetti and cloth curtains on the wall. By which is meant, I've spent *all that effort* just to get to where everybody else started from.

Tacky, commonplace, cluttered with details, with an overfondness for nouns (because they lock you safely in the world); that's what my mind is; that's my first person. I'm unathletic, used to wear dark colors and now wrap up in the brightest I can find. I'm colorless, I think, and what moves me most in a man are useless gestures and lots of style. Because I never was beautiful and never knew how to even begin, I've always been a pushover for an aquiline nose or a lavender shirt. Shall I tell you about my husband?

I grew up Spartan and rigid, toughing it out, my emotional life predicated on those exotic times when my stepfather—he didn't hold office long—came home drunk to throw up on the flowered rug, or sat smashed in our Grand Rapids easy chair saying, "Fuck, fuck, fuck," out *loud*. For dinner I ate a single apathetic lamb chop soaking into a slice of white bread, and pined for something better.

I got two things into my mind early: (1) that all men are beasts. I learned that from my mother, which, considering my stepfather alternately puking or sobering up on Bromo Seltzer and turning the most appalling shade of powder blue, I found it not hard to believe; (2) that sex was dumb, because people were so dumb when they sidled up to it. They lost their humor, they lost their style: "Añd dón't yōu thínk thāt wé míght háve ā líttle kíss gōōdníght?" an imbecile named Arnold Katz asked me when we were both sixteen. Had I known then that he spoke in poulter's rhythm which nobody has used to communicate in for a cool five hundred years I'd have fallen into his arms; but I said, of course, no, and slammed the door, trailing up the stairs of our dark and dusty walk-up, to the tender mercies of my mother's powder-blue consort.

When love came to me I was unprepared. It was the authentic Renaissance affliction; a bad sickness with rather more nausea than fever in it. My last year of high school I met Walter Wong, ah, even now I smile and bow to what he was. He was twenty-one, he drank, he was half-Chinese. Into my life of dry lamb chops and paper drapes he came, positively dripping style. His caved-in, sallow chest was usually covered by a lemon-yellow dotted swiss shirt—this in the fifties when they didn't do such things. He wore knee boots which laced and drove a lopsided car; all his friends were Chinese and he didn't date. He had put in a driveway for Elizabeth Taylor, was asked in one night for a drink, lolled back with his dirty shirt against the cream-colored sofa, scuffed his knee boots on their millionaire carpet, criticized the paintings of her current husband, drank too much, threw up on the carpet. And when the love goddess herself was patiently helping him down the hall to the bathroom he peed on her.

There's not a single right-thinking girl, I believe, who wouldn't respond to all that in some way. But I thought he'd scoured thriftshops for that shirt, or borrowed his sister's blouse in a fit of eccentricity; when what had really happened was that his mother had lovingly stitched it up for him because that's what she thought everyone was wearing. And that is basically the story of our life together.

We went out—never to those parties where all the boys and girls necked themselves into a mass impasse and rested, glazed-eyed, like crocs on a muddy riverbank—but to parks and Chinese restaurants. Walter never touched me. What style. He wrote me letters when he went on camping trips, he gave me my first beer to drink. He took me to my senior play. (I was embarrassed for his necktie, a yellow, woven atrocity with a fringe which was a wonder in the thirties

when it came into existence, and would be great now, but
sure wasn't then.)

He drove me home, I had been in the play and was ar-
rogantly pleased with myself. I had the upper hand; whatever he had in being a college man and playing poker with
Anna May Wong was cut into seriously by the old newspa-
pers strewn in the back seat, not to mention his half-slanted
eyes. Walter never knew how to go on a *date*. When we
drove home, instead of copping a high school feel, he explained the lyrics of "Two Sleepy People" to me—"I've
always felt there was something cogent about that song"—
and talked about why he didn't like to neck: "If you touch
someone, you should touch her completely." I listened to
him, a snotty virgin in a borrowed cashmere sweater, fas-
cinated by his eccentricity, now that we were alone, but
immensely superior because I wasn't like that.

We drove home by a shortcut, past raw foothills which
had just been bought by Forest Lawn to form minority cem-
eteries for Jews, Mexicans, Chinese. There was nothing out
there then but vast black vacant lots of thigh-deep weeds, a
dusty culvert, those bleak and barren hills. Walter stopped
his filthy car, and stared ahead. I noticed with childish ex-
pertise how his lips hung a little slack in the machinery of
his face. I didn't like full mouths very much. I smelled the
dry weeds, and the aromatic, insistent smell of geraniums;
it was all familiar, dry, pastoral, that wide dusty Los Angeles landscape. Then he reached for me. He said, believe
me, "Where do the arms go?" I thought, Oh, *brother*, and
then was lost, literally lost, in an embrace which was more
like being in a wind tunnel than two people embracing.
Later I wondered why it worked that way; at those parties
I've mentioned we toted up french kisses in our prissy little
minds, or bare breasts, even, maybe, more. Then how come
it worked like that? There was no pleasure that I remember,
or intimation of it, nor did he seem pleased. But it was a
soul kiss I guess, because his soul came out of where it
usually stayed, and informed me that it was unhappy and
needed me, and put me under an intense, permanent sense
of obligation.

Walter turned sourly back in his seat; he didn't say boo,
he started the car. I would have screwed him right then in
pure astonishment, but he drove me home, let me out of the

car, didn't walk me to the door. I was outraged by that time.
Everything in me revolted and drew away. No wonder he
acted so weird all the time. Because he was just so weird,
that's all.

When he called the next day and the next and the next,
my mother told him I wasn't home; she was just as pleased
since his all-Chinese friends who sometimes came around
with him constituted an eyesore and he knew it and brought
them around anyway. She thought I'd had my liberal fling
and looked for me to go to secretarial school and marry a
man in an office, since she and her husband couldn't put me
through school. But Walter had tainted me. I enrolled in
City College and made arrangements to move into a seedy
boardinghouse nearby.

Walter wrote me letters, didactic and full of passion.
When he stopped writing I began thinking, alone now in a
little room in the middle of the city. I called *him* and he
scornfully put me down, or gave me numbers to call him
back where the only voices which answered were a gabble
of Chinese. Then he went into the Army and I began to
suffer. Through my romance with a salad man named Or-
lando S. Hungerford, through my first affair and my second,
I thought of that one embrace. I cursed Walter Wong, I
wished him every misfortune. I cried for him and recon-
structed his every word, his not so terribly winning ways.
It seemed to me that if there was any happiness in the world
it had to be with that half-breed Chinaman.

In my sophomore year he came back from the Army on
leave. When he wrote he was coming to see me I had a
terrible sense of doom. I'd been running absentminded
through my life, picking up ways of thinking that I'd thought
might interest him. I'd held exclusively to the thought of
that elemental passion. But on the front porch of that shabby
boardinghouse, with a girl friend who was privy to all my
thoughts saying, "Oh kid, oh kid, oh kid," I read and re-
read his letter, and began to sweat.

He came back the next week, out of sorts and ill at ease
in a badly fitting uniform, his cheeks beginning to puff out
under the bones from liquor. (Walter will always be the bad
drunk of my life.) The first night we listened to jazz and
went home and went to bed. It was OK, I guess, but we
walked through it as though we had contracted to do it, it

was what we were supposed to do that's all; remember, we were in our early twenties. I lay awake in bed and listened when he slept. He ground his teeth horribly, and it took me months to realize he did that only when he was in misery or pain or very sick. We were married three weeks later, the Wongs despising me for a white middle-class drag, my own folks goggle-eyed at a tremendous wedding display which must have included every Oriental in this big town. Well, he had style, and I married him for it; he had soul, and I married him for that. Our troubles began.

To begin with, we'd overlooked the Army. Walter went overseas right away. I lived for a year packed up with my wedding presents in a spare room of the Wong house, and kept on with school. Then Walter came home after a year and we took an apartment while he worked for his folks another year and I graduated. We had in our minds we wanted to go to Europe and saved for it with no idea what we'd find when we got there. Walter belonged for a long time to that great society of young men in this country who can't decide what they want to do in life and keep everyone on tenterhooks waiting for the verdict. (Meanwhile your twenties slip away.) The feeling was, in both our families, that during a year spent in Europe the real Walter Wong might float to the surface.

We went tourist class on the *Queen Elizabeth*, of all the square ships, me already pregnant and so *drug* with everything within and without that no kind of riches or Lucullan living could have reached me anyway. Twenty-three years old and my life was over. There isn't any older age, I believe, than the fourth month in the life of your first infant, when your stomach pops a little, and it dawns on you.

Walter *drank*, as I've said, but was only warming up to what he would be later. If anyone in the world felt more wretched than me it was him. We got off the boat (disembarked, right?) in cold cloudy weather. Lorraine and a friend of hers named Margaret who I barely knew were living in Europe. They'd read the boat schedules and rode to meet us in some great friendly gesture. We were too weary to be grateful (in the first throes of our own Great Depression which would bug us for the next four years).

Some hours later we were in the Gare St. Lazare. We followed the two girls in dumb misery through customs past a giant hand-drawn picture of a penis between two breasts which made Walter brighten momentarily, then down in the métro for our *hebdomadaires*, and into the métro car itself.

We came out—I had red high-heeled shoes on, and the navy-blue maternity jumper I'd wear for the next five months—and there was the Arc de Triomphe glittering in the sunset. There it was and all I could drum up was a mental *oh shit*, and then to our red velvet mirrored hotel room which we were to share with Lorraine and Margaret and some man, and then to dinner. I ordered an *escalope milanaise* because the name sounded so great, and you know what I got, then afterwards *zabaglione* and threw up.

Well, everyone has their Europe stories. We stayed a year and studied and toured around; our blameless baby was born and came to live in that velvet hotel room. (On a happy racist whim we decided to name her China.) We learned to like Paris a lot in our morose way, but it was, really, no life at all. We were so sad, Walter and I. Locked in our own corporation, we stared at Lorraine.

An American took her out (for instance) in a tiny foreign car, together with a large police dog. Once alone with Lorraine and the dog, the American remarked, "How long since you had a romp in a car, baby?" Lorraine started to laugh, and that was the end of her, yet another end. She drove to Cherbourg on a motorcycle with a Swede and got a bladder infection; her urine was bright orange for months after. She got TB, almost, and the first of many infected teeth. She worried about venereal disease.

Lorraine, ah, Lorraine, screwed Nigerians with tribal markings. She screwed a flock of Algerian wine salesmen, oh my God, unwashed cheerful gents who brought presents for the baby and preserved figs for us; a string of swarthy men our age who treated us as parents when they came to pick up Lorraine. She dealt with one Arab while another squatted close by on the floor making *couscous*, and then came home, pale and pleased, to tell us about it. She screwed wealthy Siamese who wore imported clothes, hand-printed ties with cowboys on them from Sears Roebuck. And more.

Our own travel stories and adventures aren't pertinent here—we went to Yugoslavia where Walter got drunk and drove down a steep medieval flight of stairs and I hit him in the head with a baby bottle. I had a nice talk one night in a little town in northern Italy with a tall, corpulent, middle-aged man with a scarf, and had a strong desire to spend the night with him; that was my erotic adventure in Europe.

Through our defeat and funk, which lay like smog about us, and like smog you didn't always notice it—oh, I remember Walter staring out of our window into an eventless gloomy street—we still had this great vision of bright, intense life. We knew already that suffering doesn't ennoble one; suffering, as an English lady one cloudy day said to us over tea and *pâtisserie*, ''Suffering makes one cross.''

Lorraine went home after six months. We stayed our full year but when we came home Walter's identity was as much a mystery as ever. He worked for a while while I stayed at home with the baby—I can't even talk about it. After a while Walter went back to graduate school. He had decided to become an anthropologist. There was some hope to that but it was canceled by our all-around poverty and sense of defeat. During this time we lived again with Walter's folks. A sense of shame kept me from calling my friends. I lived in a Chinese world and it wasn't so marvelous.

At the start of Walter's second year—that would be September 1959—we decided to move on campus. Graduate school takes a long time. After almost five years of marriage we'd have our own home—at the princely sum of twenty-six dollars a month. (Also we would find people in our same slow-motion boat.) For twenty-six dollars a month, the university let you live in Vets Housing—some already old, falling-down barracks from World War II. For that modest sum you got a long envelope of an apartment, with a couple of niggardly windows at each end, a kitchen and bathroom in a hellish no-man's-land between. For years—maybe forever—the ideas of ''interior decoration'' of an entire subculture have been and will be influenced by this simple plan: living room→kitchen→bathroom→bedroom in one long line. For years mommies and daddies slept in living rooms with their children in that dark little jungle at the back. The battle for light and air was primary to most of us, but you could see that lots of couples had given in right away, had painted the walls green or brown and elected to live like moles for five years or seven or twelve, whatever it might be. (And it was that many years for many of us. The ex-wife of Steve Rader—who will be a Romeo in this story—lived in her cardboard twenty-six-dollar apartment for seventeen years, until her daughter was in the tenth grade and she herself in graceful, cultivated middle age. The best years of her life were spent in the shadow of a great university—a sports arena on one side and a series of luxury co-ed dorms across the street which proliferated like cancer and were just as distasteful to the respectable married unfortunates below.)

Because we tried to do it. The twenties are the oldest time of all, because you get married and try to do it. Every one of those apartmental slits was filled, crammed, overflowing with either the ideas and artifacts which our mothers had handed down to us, or the exact opposite of the ideas which our mothers had handed down to us, which amounts to the same thing.

I remember in the late fifties a bar opened in Los Angeles called Jack's Rack, where the bar itself was divided from a few booths by an ingenious construction of household string. How many kitchens in Vets Housing were separated from how many living rooms by screens of string I'd hate to think (and yet they looked OK).

The afternoon we moved in, Walter's car—which was pulling a rented trailer full of furniture—broke down. While he was trying to fix the motor a policeman came by and gave him a ticket. By the time Walter got to the apartment where I was washing windows and cleaning up the last spots of paint on the floor he wasn't too jovial. When Walter got mad he drank. Sometimes this stimulated him to a feverish, unattractive gaiety, but generally his anger not only spread but increased in depth. He lurched inside with one piece of furniture after another while I timorously told him where to put things. The baby was already—in one of the few real blessings of that place—out digging with a spoon in the wide fields of dust which separated the barracks each from the other. Walter drank steadily through the afternoon and laid down our newly acquired furniture; he arranged our mattress and springs which would serve as a couch, our coffee table made from a door. I cleaned around him, and even as I did, a fine dust settled over all. Walter began to brood, to tally up the insults he had received and the injustices of the day.

"You dumb cunt," he said once, as I offered to help him. Even now I have no idea of how we talked or what we said, of how our arguments started or finished. I remember pictures in the stop-frame way a child remembers his first home. Walter put his clothes on fast when he was truly, really angry, and he moved fast—I remember that. Once when he got out of bed and put on his pants in about four seconds flat I was afraid for my life, and once in Venice, Italy, we argued in the parking lot by the canals, and he got out of the car on my side, with me sitting on my side. Do you understand? Walter, so fluggy, so generally drunk, so lethargic in his ways, had *flown* out of the car. I sat there terrified, waiting for the Venetian earth to swallow me up, because I'd gone too far. I don't remember what happened after that. He must have gotten back in the car by his own side—or I'd have remembered him crawling and heaving over me—and we must have driven off, because here we are now.

Outside of those flashes—the only time I saw him as a man who could beat the shit out of me, and didn't only because of his mercy and common sense—I by and large considered him a drunk, and ragged him when he was sober, while he bitchily retaliated when he was drunk. We could sustain either of those conversational states for hours. No wonder I don't remember.

"Oh, Walter," I said, when he called me a cunt, and started weakly to cry. He muttered after that, he lurched about, he even knocked down a lamp. But he wasn't that drunk. He sat down heavily on the couch.

"Don't I get my lunch?" he complained, and still wailing a little I got up to make him a sandwich.

The last two or three minutes had been observed by a young woman in her middle twenties, thin, small, chic but shabbily dressed, who hesitated by our open door like someone in a play. It was Lorraine, our friend, married now—as all of us—and living next door. I'd talked to her on the phone from time to time, but we hadn't seen her since Europe.

"I've just had my tooth killed with arsenic," she said, by way of a greeting after two and a half years. She crossed to the bed where Walter had loutishly spread himself. She sat by him, she laughed, she opened her mouth.

"Right here."

Walter appeared not to recognize her. He thrashed convulsively; he turned away from her to lie on his side. Then, since her mouth was still open exposing two lovely crescents of even teeth, a small, narrow red tongue, a cave of pinkish, pearly tissue, really a kind of cunt that could talk, he heaved himself up on an elbow and gazed into it.

"They drop in arsenic and *hot wax*."

"Shit!" Walter said with feeling.

I came over and looked. The gum around the offending tooth was black and swollen.

"Does it hurt?" I said.

"I couldn't tell you, my dear, it's unspeakable." And she crooked her hand, faglike under her chin and closed her eyes. I gave her some wine and Walter tried to sit up straight. I brought a tray of sandwiches. She took one and began dithering away, peering closely into our faces. It was just the same as before.

"They *looked* at the tooth. I wanted it out. I begged them to take it out but they said, 'Save the tooth!' My husband sends me to the East Side, they're all greasy pigs over there. They love to do it, they put the arsenic in a little silver pitcher and they *pour it on your tooth*." Walter got down on his hands and knees. He bit her knees and licked them. "Want to fuck?" he said, and smeared her lap with mustard. My anguish was intense. But Lorraine said, "Oh, Walter, for heaven's sake," and giggled. And he gave her a truly charming smile and rubbed his loosely hanging lips against her skinny knee once more and flopped back on the floor smiling at the ceiling. He closed his eyes. Lorraine touched his shoulder with one bare toe and we talked, drinking, while her babies met mine outside and it was pretty cool; we had progressed from an empty cardboard house to a sad bad quarrel to a regular homey time in less than three hours.

"I'm so glad you're going to live here because everyone else is a *lunatic*," she said to me, and batted her eyes. "Juan is looniest of all . . . I mean, sending me to a Mexican dentist. Of course, it's quite neat. They have mariachi music blaring in the waiting room and a toothless crone

dying of typhoid in a corner and a hand-tinted photograph
of the Sacred Heart . . .''

"Oh, Lorraine."

"And a jungle of potted plants, they reach out at you as
you go down the hall, and a dentist playing the guitar, and
some slick greaser in a white jacket and he says, 'Wa yoh
mou,' 'Rin yoh mou,' you wouldn't believe it.''

Half-asleep, Walter smiled at it all, that infinitely toler-
ant, infinitely amused, grateful smile we kept for Lorraine
and her orange urine and her black, pitted lovers.

Then the light at the open door was blotted out, as they
say, by the gaunt stooping form of Lorraine's husband. I'd
known she'd married Juan; indeed, it was the kind of thing
that contributed immeasurably to Lorraine's myth; like beg-
ging on the streets of Paris with a yoghurt jar she'd stolen
from a student restaurant. She went home and married her
rapist. But with Juan you had to forget how bad, how far
beyond exotic he was and back into the realm of down-and-
out ugly. Juan was like a prism, by his reflections you got
another idea of the girl Lorraine; between "she married her
rapist,'' and that tall lank scratchy body, there was a no-
man's-land of something where Lorraine quietly lived.

Yes, yeah, I'd forgotten how *bad* he looked. He was beyond any joke. Maybe she'd forgotten too, in Europe, and
thought to come home to a real Don Juan, only to be terrified or demoralized into submission when she spotted that
sepulchral stork waiting at the airport, a ghastly chaperone
for her nervous parents. Why do you do anything when
you're young? They'd been married now for almost three
years. He would have about two more years in graduate
school, while Walter was just starting out.

We sat on the bed-couch and looked at him. The light
around his head in the open doorframe blotted out his features—which was all to the good. His glasses glinted; he
slouched. His hair was all different lengths; he had something wrong with his scalp, and had clipped his hair to get
to the large ringwormy sores. I didn't know that until later;
but his hair stood up and fell over like a bean field during
a drought.

"Well, Juan," I said, getting up and going over to him,
vaguely embarrassed for Walter, but conscious even then
that I wouldn't trade his drunkenness for Juan's lack of style,

"how *are* you? I haven't seen you for years. It's so *neat* that you guys are married, and like neighbors . . ."

I went on at some length. He didn't speak to me or look at me or look at Walter, and finally, I quit. Lorraine lay back on the couch, not moving a muscle, her legs primly crossed.

"Come home," he said.

"Can't you stay for dinner? Everything's fixed up around here, and Walter's parents gave us a pot of Chinese pork and noodles." I've always believed in good manners, I guess, but I can't say, on reflection, that they've ever done me much good. Because in the places where people need them, that's right where they aren't using good manners.

Walter suddenly sat up. "Hi, Juan," he said.

Then we all waited around for a couple of minutes and Lorraine got up and left with Juan without either of them saying good-bye.

"What's wrong with him?" Walter remarked.

I went to put my ear against the wall but I needn't have bothered. From their apartment came, clearly, perfectly encapsulated, the sounds of a violent argument. It might have been the rape all over again, except that carrying on was the one thing you could swear they weren't doing. Juan didn't yell; he spoke, but in a voice that literally brought up gooseflesh upon my arms. I went over to the bed and lay down, Walter climbed up and lay beside me. We held hands and listened to the chanted chains of Spanish, and then he began to hit her. Even then it had that touch of theatrical grotesquerie. We soon found that you couldn't take anything in those housing units seriously because the setting simply wasn't up to it. Juan Ramirez must have picked up Lorraine and thrown her against the wall. We heard him grunt, we heard her cry out, we saw the wall move and buckle in toward us, it was just too bizarre, and my indignation was divided from then on between that sleazy spic belting my oldest friend, and the fates which ordained that we had to live in such a badly constructed house.

Since we were lying down, Walter put his hand on me and began in his dogged insistent way to make love. I felt a wave (one thing about clichés, they're true), a *wave* of revulsion, but let him go on of course, and it's an ill wind that blows no good—the distraction of those bumps and

Spanish epithets kept my mind off it enough that I was able to give a passable account of myself, while Walter went on with his loutish (to me) task; and only once did we stop: when after a series of slaps—he really was beating the shit out of her—we heard Lorraine laugh, tremendously, tentatively, that thin clear sound which had carried us through simple boredom a thousand times. She probably, as she was sailing through the air, said something silly, and laughed along, prompting him, hoping he would get the point. What made it worse was that the Spanish voice went on, he wasn't having any, he was intent on his own scene and didn't want to be entertained.

One thing about Walter, he always took a long time—he'd read somewhere that was cool. There were times when I dug my nails into my arms and broke the skin hoping he'd finish or stop or quit. By the time he'd figured out I didn't like it, of course he made a point to last as long as he could—his friends called him Two Hour Walt, which—though an exaggeration—was remarkably apt. I only say this as a way of measuring time, we were still doggedly doing it when Ramirez's voice broke or changed. Then there was silence. From what Lorraine had told me years before, I realized that meant they were doing what we were, and that while our section of the barracks was gently rocking, theirs was in that tension-filled stillness, that agony of waiting which was sex for Juan Ramirez.

We finished all together, and Walter said it was bad enough trying to have an orgasm at the same time as your spouse without having to do the same for your neighbors. When he said things like that I loved him, I thought I could stay with him forever. We talked in hushed, outraged tones about the atrocities next door, but I'll tell you, after a couple of weeks it didn't seem to matter much, we were in such a concentration of life and confusion—it was like one of those tour de force etchings with a thousand scenes which you have to examine with a magnifying glass to appreciate. Because the people on the other side of us had a life filled with passion and discontent too, and so did the people on top of us, and on either side of *them*, and so on down the line. If a husband found himself in the bathroom without toilet paper and called to his wife we all came running with a roll; and if someone sneezed, someone next door might say God bless you. The husbands at their studies were unhappy and unjust, and in the mornings we sat blowsy in the sun and rehearsed their wrongs, while pretty little girls and boys twitched by us from the co-ed dorms and saw what was in store for them if they neglected contraceptives or yielded to the sweet temptations of romantic love.

This is not to say we didn't get along with the Ramirezes. With coaxing, Juan could act like anybody else, and at times, flushed with wine, he'd lean back and talk with the first baby beginnings of what you'd have to call self-confidence. We had them over for dinner and they had us; if you remembered not to talk religion he was OK, and his occasional violent rages compared not unfavorably with Walter's continual drunkenness or my sulks or Lorraine's bitchiness. If this gives the impression that we were all consciously unhappy, that's not true. We felt lousy, I believe, but didn't know any better. We thought that was the way most people felt. (They do, right?) With it all, I reiterate, we did the right things. Walter, drunk or sober, read two stories to the baby every night. I cooked the lousiest pieces of meat and came up with a good dinner almost every time. Lorraine and I soon took some graduate classes and had something else to think about. For us and all our friends, the next two years went by in domesticity and concerted hard work.

II

In June of 1961, about two months before he was to receive his doctoral degree, Juan Ramirez sat at his mother's kitchen table, eating an enormous home-cooked meal. He ate alone. His mother stood near him in the bright, shabby, clean room, her arms folded. He felt her staring at him, but in the kind of impersonal way that didn't demand acknowledgment. She was thinking of something else. She had made him tamales (which took hours of time spent bent double over a bucket of corn, a parody of those "hours over a hot stove" which American women talked about, but of which they knew nothing, nor did their mothers), and tacos made with homemade tortillas, and *atole*, a thin cereal or a thick drink, depending on how one thought of it. Juan ate heartily, ravenously. He sipped the *atole* with the liquid sound of Chinese drinking soup. His mother had made all this, this symphony of corn, from a blue grain which his relatives had grown in the New Mexico fields, and then sent to his family in this wicked town as a talisman against white, pale, rootless city life. His mother ground the corn, moistened it, patted it into tortillas, molded it into tamales, boiled it up into *atole*. He believed in it too, and so he ate, and thought on the other hand that it was too late for such naïve safeguards, and hated himself for his maudlin thoughts. He loved the food and loved his mother—not in that incestuous way with which the white world tainted love, or giggled about it as a dirty joke, but—he sighed at his own banality—as a peasant loved the mountains, or a fisherman cared about hills of silvery fish banked up in the bottom of his boat.

"How has it been with you? How are you?" his mother asked in Spanish. "We never see you."

"*Así, así,*" he answered, his mouth full. He never told them anything, not because he thought they couldn't understand, but because a man must have privacy if nothing else; his life is his wealth. His father never asked him a thing. When Juan was young they had sat night after night in the clean little living room, decorated by a garish portrait of the Blessed Virgin (which Juan would have never thought of as garish if he hadn't met his wife; science left room for religion, but not his wife). They sat, and sat, while his mother told her rosary in the kitchen, or spoke in mournful Spanish on the phone to her friends. Juan and his father sat like two storks in an aviary, his father deep in a book of political science, or hunched over by the radio listening to the news, or reading the Bible, while Juan read or studied, his mind disembodied, in pain, working. For nights and nights, they never said a thing, but lived together.

The blue corn tasted just like any other kind. The linoleum he looked down at—he never looked *up* when he ate— was frayed or scuffed to a patternless limbo in the middle of the room. The oilcloth on the table was new; a pattern of Pepsi-Cola labels and ivy leaves which Lorraine would have loved and laughed at, and bought some herself if she had seen it. She rarely came over, and he rarely brought over the children. Lorraine seemed to like his family well enough, and his parents said nothing about his marriage— it was *his* after all. But Juan had come into the kitchen on the afternoons of those few married visits to find his wife with her glasses on, looking suddenly Jewish, talking to his mother. He couldn't do it! He couldn't stand it! His wife and mother ceased their conversations as he came in, his mother folded her arms and gazed out at the backyard; patch of grass, clothesline, Spanish-style garage, a stand of gawky poinsettias, the *East Side*, and Lorraine would cross quickly to him, tripping lightly across the worn linoleum, place her bony hip against his thigh, pat him on the chest and titter. He came alone to see his parents, as much as he could.

Juan finished his meal and pushed away from the table. He picked himself up and stumbled heavily out to the living

room. His father listened, alone, to the radio. *"Padre,"*
Juan said, "Papa." "What is it?" his father said. Juan said
nothing. Then he said, "How are you?" His father considered and said, *"Así, así."* Then Juan said, "How is the
job?" His father looked up with the sardonic gaze of one
who knows he is being patronized. "Fine, my son, and how
is yours?"

Juan answered without sarcasm. (He never noticed anything.) "I think it will be all right. They'll let me do what
I want. I'll have freedom. We can swim at lunch if we want
to. I'll be the only Mexican there. I can *wear* what I want.
My office looks out on the ocean. They like me there and I
can do the work. The work isn't difficult at all. . . ." His
voice had lowered into a perfect, preoccupied monotone.
When he looked up, off the rug and into his father's eyes,
he found that he wasn't listening anyway.

Juan got up and went back to the kitchen. "I'm going
now," he said.

"So soon? We never see you. We never see Davey or
Jennifer or Lorraine." But his mother crossed the room and
hugged him good-bye. Over her stubby coarse body he
looked outside; the *green* of the grass he saw, the *white* of
the garage, and then he remembered his manners and patted
her back.

"Lorraine says hello to you. She wished she could come
but the kids have a little cold." His mother looked up at
him, then out the window.

"I'm leaving now. Take care of yourself. Be good to
yourself."

His mother took his arm, she was as short as his wife.
She looked up at him. "Are you all right? Are you sick?"

He shook his head and blinked. I ought to be able to
laugh, he thought. Or she ought to. He bent down to her
and hugged her, picking her up, sniffing her neck, her hair,
a decent, touching smell. He held her not as hard as he
could but very hard, and sniffed that good smell of his early
life, his earliest memories. *"Mi hijo,"* his mother said, and
pushed against him with her arms. "You're hurting me."
He gazed straight up into the light, and pulled his arms
tighter, then put her down and let her loose.

"You're too strong for your own good."

"Good-bye. I'm leaving now."

"Adiós."

Once in his car he felt in his pocket for a rosary. My God, forgive me for whatever it is I'm doing.

He had a job all right, two of them, but he wasn't sure who he was working for. During the past months he had visited several ceremonial recruitment interviews, clad in his best suit, exchanging amenities. He learned, too late, what he had been training himself to be. It was something that many "educated" people did. They studied, and loved what they knew, and only later, when the question of what they knew had to be tied to what they could do in the world, did they realize, finally, what it was they had become. For Juan, who loved the way things grew, who loved to plant flowers or gaze at his own children and note down in what minute ways they changed, who had dissected numberless animals, but with a prayer, always, of apology, it came as a shock to find that he had been training all along to kill people. And it was a shock to his interviewers that he hadn't noticed. "What else do you think you know how to *do*?" a pleasant man had asked him after a forty-minute talk in which it had taken thirty-eight minutes for Juan to figure out that the company dealt, really, *really*, in germ warfare. "What did you think I was *talking* about? We sell insecticides, we advertise in the national magazines, but what did you think we *do*? God knows, *you* ought to be smart enough to know what we're doing. We're prepared to finance any project you're interested in—any major communicable disease. You'll be doing good work for yourself, for the country."

"But you don't want to stop those things. You want to start them."

"Look. We stop them over here. Maybe someday—I don't even say we will have to, but then we can start them over there, yes. Or, even, if *they* start—say, encephalitis—over here, then maybe with the help of your work we can stop it. You'd be helping *our* kids, our world, it's not a bad thing. We have a saying—it's a joke, but there's something to it. We say the good guys are boring from within when they work at places like ours. You'd be doing that."

Juan looked at his interviewer. He was clean, yes, well groomed, yes, white-Protestant, yes, but he was OK, it was obvious. He wasn't a bad man but on the other hand he was some kind of crazy killer.

"What you're asking me is to work for some crazy killers. I won't do it. I can't do that."

"What'd you come around for? What makes you think you're not working for us now? Where do you think your department gets its money? Half the teaching assistantships in microbiology are paid by our company or its affiliates. How'd you get the equipment to work with, the new rooms, the tissue bank, the cages, the animals?"

"This is a state university, it's, it's, we have . . ."

"Where did you get that three hundred dollars at Christmas?"

Juan stared at him.

"The anonymous award for the most deserving student? The most deserving *of our attention* is what that letter meant."

"I'll, I'll . . ." He wanted to say that he'd give it back, but it had gone for inexpensive presents and a new carburetor and crates of canned peaches for the kids, and a new dress for Lorraine. "I can't tell you . . ."

"This is your—not your last but your biggest chance. We have a good company, we do good work. We're not fascist warmongers or whatever you think. We do the work and it hasn't hurt anyone yet. And, uh, you ought to remember, we're an equal opportunity employer."

Juan stood up. He reached up to rub his eyes and his fist cracked into his glasses. He took them off and polished them with a dirty handkerchief. Later he would assemble insults, leaving the man to say *this*, while he countered with *that*—adolescent dreams; while he, Juan Ramirez, was thirty years old now, a man with a wife and two children, and the only one of his Ramirezes to finish college; a man who said, "Ah, ah, ah," and bolted out the door—clumsily, because he still held his glasses in his hand.

Someone else got the job, a worse student than he, but someone enthusiastic and eager to get ahead. And as in those rushing rites at the beginning of college—which he had watched, dismayed, knowing he could never be dealt in to go to one beerish dinner not only because he was Mexican, but because they didn't know he was there—Juan listened to his friends exult as they got their good jobs, as they saw for the first time in five or seven years an end to high-carbohydrate dinners, an end to Care packages from hated in-laws.

By the middle of May he had turned down four offers. Two other company representatives had said that they paid for his deserving student money, which made him wonder. He meanwhile looked on his world with new eyes and saw that if the men from the corporations lied in particulars, what they said was generally true. Those classes where he had been swept up in the joy of finding out things, where students spoke, in spite of themselves, in hushed excited tones, where they saw things through microscopes which no one had seen before, or, at least, knew there was something on a particular slide which no one in the world had seen before—all that excitement was basic training, nothing more; mad scientists studying to drive bayonets through children they didn't even know. Juan took to reading medical books; he read of swollen livers and damaged brains, of groins filled with pus and throats choked with blood. He thought of teaching, but he was too shy. He prayed, sheepishly, ashamed for having been so unbright before; he was ashamed of his race and felt that God thought he should have known better, that whites would have known better. Indeed, they did; they took to those jobs like happy little ducks.

His fifth interview—to work for a corporation whose name, like the others, was a demented alphabet, AXEL—was like the others. Again, a really nice man explained that conflicts in this world were inevitable; that even if the educated class didn't believe emotionally in a Communist menace, still there were those billion or how many Chinese, and the United States, whether it wanted to or not, had to think of something. "That's our job. We don't make hardware. We don't blow up people. We try to *think of something*, and a man in your position can underwrite that power of thought, insure its place in the power structure, right? You think for us, that's all we want."

Juan knew enough to say, dragging on a cigarette, one hand hooked on the inside of his thigh, "I prefer something a little more harmless, if I can find it. I doubt if I can. Perhaps—like Brother Mendel, I can find a cloister. . . ."

His interviewer laughed heartily. "Keep in touch," he

said. "Celibacy isn't worth the price you have to pay for it."

During the days of recruitment interviews, Juan avoided the graduate student coffee room. It had been only the year before that he had conquered his shyness enough to go in, get some coffee, sit down at the one long table and study so intently that no one with common decency would talk to him. But his colleagues, his fellow students had been indecent; they had slumped up, closed his books, asked him questions, picked his mind, vilified their professors, talked about movies. Juan discovered, to his joy, that he could talk as well as the next, not as an eccentric, or even as an ethnic type, but as that particular kind of colorless student who was first of all a scientist and who left the culture, the frivolities, to women and to fags. He was a microbiologist who detested small talk because it got nowhere. He wanted to know things; how viruses multiplied, how to take their picture. His classmates—whether the sons of lawyers or private detectives or liquor store salesmen—wanted to know too, and that's what they talked about, endlessly, philistinely, in their fluorescent-lighted coffee room, spooning quantities of Preem into bitter coffee and strong, unpalatable tea.

This year maybe ten graduate students had their PhDs almost in hand. Now, they talked like mushy girls about who liked them, who liked their work, whether their children would have ballet lessons or go to the dentist free. He was alone again, scorning and alone.

He didn't know what to do. He had grown up in decent poverty, he didn't notice it particularly; but he knew his wife regarded each day as an endless imposition, a real-life Monopoly game where you always missed your two hundred dollars. She didn't complain, but he felt keenly that it was only her strong character and good manners which prevented it. He was thirty, it was time, God knew, to be a man. But his life in the future, the barest thought of it, made him sick. He knew about violence in a way his school friends didn't. A night didn't pass that he didn't beg God's pardon for his conduct to his wife, and wordlessly try to make his wife know that he was sorry, sorry. At night while she slept he stared at her pinched, animal-like little face, so giddy when it was awake, so helplessly intelligent and sad in sleep. Wordless with emotion (and besides she was asleep), unspeakably touched, he felt each time the side-by-side desires; to violate her and to protect her from violation. He brooded over his children, Jennifer and little Davey—he would be one of those bad fathers, he knew, seeing an adventurer in every Sunday school boy who came around, and he prayed, hopelessly, that his boy would grow up to let *live*, that he wouldn't envy every scrap of life, and in that classic outlaw way barge in on women the way boors crash parties. He knew that God never listened to his kind of prayer, that God was like a woman; vain, preferring compliments above everything else, and not particularly apt to do favors for anyone, but who else could he ask? His children wouldn't get any help from him.

Knowing, then, what it was they wanted him to do, inserting germs in helpless little bodies, causing them death, of course, but first pain, a pain which saluted the virility and power of the attacker, and made them *know* before they died, who was boss, he saw what made his boyish, hemmed-in colleagues do it. Knowing what it meant, and knowing, too, how sometimes it worked out, he said, no, God, I really can't.

The next morning in the department office Juan Ramirez picked up his fellowship check (which had kept his family from starvation for a year, and which was ending in a month with no more to come). The secretary only nodded to him instead of saying hello—a bad sign. A professor brushed by him without a greeting. Juan knew that by now he was a bit of an embarrassment to his colleagues—not a disgrace, but an embarrassment. He embarrassed his superiors because he wouldn't find a job, he embarrassed his equals because they took jobs which he had already turned down. A note in his mailbox said that yet another interview had been arranged for him. He didn't recognize the room number or even the building where the interview was scheduled.

"Pardon me," he said formally to the secretary (after five years he was too shy to call her by name), "where is this room?" She didn't know and had to call up another girl.

"It's over in the *music* building, one of the practice rooms downstairs. Where'd you get this anyway?"

"It was in my mailbox. I thought you did it. Don't you . . . do . . . those things?"

"That's not our stationery, Juan. And I didn't type it, I

promise you that.'' It was true, the note was on plain blue paper and there was one misspelling. ''Maybe it's a joke, honey,'' she said. ''You better not go. Someone's having fun with you.''

Juan moved off without saying thank you or good-bye. It was the kind of thing that made him unloved. There was no question but that he would go. A joke played on you meant you were in someone else's thoughts.

He went home for lunch to tell his wife, but she wasn't there. The people next door were quarreling, he could hear Edith Wong cry. He grimaced in distaste and went in to shower and shave. All he had to wear was the black silk suit in which he had graduated from high school. He couldn't see much wrong with it, and he would have worn the embossed tie he had first bought to complete his outfit, but his wife had lately thrown it out, replacing it with a tasteful paisley. He had seen by her look of frantic regret that it made his suit look more disreputable than ever. He was dressed for a gaudy Catholic wedding on the East Side.

Walking down the long fluorescent-lit halls of the music building basement, he began to wonder and be sad in advance. Was he really so disliked that someone could play that kind of a trick on him? Each cubicle door had a tiny glass window in it like the cells of a madhouse. The windows were there to cut down lasciviousness—the tiny rooms and endless disconnected music had an erotic effect he could understand. To be down here, in a little room with the door shut, was to think of pleasure, illicit, childish pleasures. Hence the windows. But couples huddled against the doors out of the line of sight, or musicians hunched over their instruments with backs to the door, and masturbated with scholarly application.

So Juan Ramirez speculated, and thought of his years on this campus with incredulity. While his mind learned, his body had explored each corner of these clean buildings. He had been in these rooms, yes, and in the library stacks, and watched the girls undress for gym at some danger to himself, and loitered at the bottoms of stairways between classes gazing casually upward at babyish bare thighs and clean underwear. Once in a day or a week he'd seen a glimpse of brown, a furry bush, and beside himself he would follow the girl for an hour or two, intercepting her on stairs, brushing against her arms or hips or breasts, even following her into class and listening to the lecture while he looked at how she sat, and waited to see if she surreptitiously touched herself in any way. Because the women who didn't wear underwear often thought of those things too. Then, too, there were days when he stayed too long in men's rooms, watching as men came in, lobbed it out, used it, stuck it away—*everyone* had one. But when they put their pricks away they stayed docile, folded up, until the next time, or until the man was out on a date, when, like a trained dog they came out—barked, rolled over, did their tricks. Juan's was something else; like a spoiled child it had tantrums in front of company, and when it was supposed to give its recitals, legally show off, it sulked and shrank, and once more showed him who was in charge.

He found his room number and went in without knocking—no one could have heard him knock against all those clarinets and bassoons and sitars. The room was occupied by two Africans in full tribal dress. They sat, legs apart, facing each other over a square stringed instrument which they strummed together, each with tiny bones or ivory picks.

Juan blushed. Thirty years of being out of it were once more confirmed. He hated himself for being gulled, for being slower than the white man and less impressive than the Black. "Sorry," he said.

The Africans, for their part, went on strumming. While one of them hummed alone (to keep the melody) the other said, "You the man Ramirez?"

"Ramirez, Juan Ramirez."

"My good sir, we hear you are looking for a job. We know that to be true."

The joke was more complex then. "Who put you up to this?" Ramirez said. The muscles in his face felt stiff and pulled away.

"Put up? Put up?" The sleek faces looked suddenly lost. The fatter man, dressed in violet and gold draperies, dropped his bones in a pocket of the stringed table. He picked up a small leather-bound book. "Put up," he read hurriedly. *"Put up.* 'To sheathe one's sword or stop fighting. To pay down or stake money. To take lodgings, lodge.' Do you mean put up? Do you tell us that?"

Juan stood impassive. What were they doing?

"Look," he said, "can't you tell me that? Enough is enough. I suppose it's funny, but then give me my turn, that's fair."

The boys in his department made a tradition of practical jokes. And they had had a recent transfer from Cal Tech who told of filling a classmate's room with great chunks of ice from top to bottom which at once melted and welded themselves into an ice cube eight feet square. "It's just that you have to give me my turn now."

The fatter man stood up with dignity. "I tell you good-bye, Ramirez. Welcome and good-bye. I tell you both two good-bye."

"Wait," the other man, slimmer and in an old rose caftan, said. "Wait. We stay together and talk."

"I tell you good-bye." The fat one slipped past Juan Ramirez into the hall.

The slim African shrugged and addressed Ramirez. "Sit down, sir. I can give you a job for my country and I know you need it."

"What are you talking about? Why don't you work through the department? You're a student anyway. I tell you, buddy, I don't think it's funny at all." Juan turned to leave.

"Sit down buddy yourself," the Black man said. He reached into a deep voluminous sleeve and pulled out a gun. Then he reached under the stringed instrument and a record of what the two had been playing before sounded through the room. "Pick this bone up and strum this instrument. This is not our national instrument at all, but a made-to-order ethnic camouflage. Our country is too backward to have a national instrument at all. All we have is the drum, and that can't get you a music fellowship. So we hire the instrument made in Switzerland, they send some samples to us together with a Swiss teacher . . . strum the instrument or die to your surprise! . . . and we are so good that we win a fellowship to an American university. Everyone has been very kind here."

"I'm leaving."

"Sit down or die. Everyone has been very kind. I'll tell you your job. In our country we have leprosy, we have anthrax, we have—still—to our chagrin and horror, the plague. We have what one of your friends is working on—the harmless-seeming flu, where you sniff (he demonstrated, noisily, then blew his nose on a silk handkerchief), your bones are down and aching like crazy in the night, you say it is the flu, and in a year you are dead of cancer. Our country has these things. You work for AXEL and take money, you tell us what you find and you work for us too. You save children and families, you work hard, you help us. We have so much money for you to take. In a monthly salary, because it is a job we give you.''

Juan shook his head. He couldn't believe it. And yet his wife had a friend in Saigon who was a spy, and the husband of a friend of his from the French department was in Paris for a year now, his fare paid by an American agency of finance. He audited income tax forms of prominent Frenchmen while working overtime at night, and went to the opera and had a nice apartment.

"You mean it," he said. "You really mean it. Well, that's interesting. But nobody's giving me a job in one of those places because I can't do those things, I won't do it, I've already said no.''

"Do you want to be dead?''

"No," Ramirez said, "and I admire you. I'd like to work for a small country the way you do and know that what I'm doing helped my country.''

"You see, man, you can work for us.''

"How did you get a job like this?''

"My father is in the government.''

"I want to thank you, but I don't even have a job to spy from.''

"We know your feelings, your thoughts. You could cancel out the bad work by good. What you learned by working for the war you would give to us in the name of peace. It is not a betrayal. It merely keeps your country from killing our country. And if not these lethal diseases, you work in children's diseases, a mumps vaccine, a measles vaccine.''

"But we already have that. You just write to the Department of the Interior.''

"Do you know that of the last shipment of measles vaccine we ordered and paid for from your country, half of our vaccinated were struck with the disease? We were made into guinea pigs, I fear. Your country used us for an interesting experiment.''

"I don't believe you.'' But fresh from conversations with

four eager murderers who loved their jobs and wanted him to try it, Juan knew better.

"We can get you a job at AXEL on any disease you wish."

The music stopped, the Black leaned under the box and put in another tape of ethnic music.

"You earn about fifteen thousand from your country, and eventually about ten thousand from ours. You aren't worth any more. I'm sorry. There are reasons we haven't spoken of why you must take this job, this assignment."

The man, who until now had looked so confident, who had held his gun at such a professional angle between himself and Ramirez, seemed suddenly nonplused. Ramirez realized that the Black was about five years younger than he.

"They picked me for my job because of my good English."

"It's very good."

Again the Black looked puzzled, floundering. He's nervous, thought Ramirez, he's just another poor bastard.

"I learned it in Paris."

"Oh?" It was worse than a cocktail party.

The boy smiled helplessly. "They want this work done, they need it. They wanted you. You see, they did a lot of work already. They know that I, I'm sorry, I, I, I knew your wife in Paris, you see, and they make this connection. They want you to do this for me."

They were both suddenly stricken, embarrassed beyond words. "I'll do it," Juan mumbled. "I'd, uh, like to do it. I can see doing it."

He did it, he thought later, to ransom his wife, to ransom his mother and father, to do his job. And everyone was a spy—the women in his housing unit, the secretary in the department who monitored phone calls, everyone. The Black must be threatening to kill his wife, but it seemed unlikely; the gun was unlikely, the box with strings; even the national costume was implausible, a bedspread.

"Where did you get your costume?" he said.

The Black looked pleased. "My mother made it," he said. "They start to weave the cloth the day you are born, and on your seventeenth birthday they give you the robe to wear." He hesitated. "I know your Lorraine well. She was a good woman. The good wise woman that I knew in my life."

"I'll say hello to her for you."

"No! You must not know me. Why do you do this? Do you do this for your wife?"

"Yes, primarily, yes. I think so."

"Are you afraid for her?"

"No."

"Ah."

"Was that what you meant before?"

The native looked straight at him, smiled, looked around, hugged himself, shook his head no. "You shouldn't ask me that, my friend," and there was no gangster-like irony in his cultivated English at all. Around them the music droned, kids shuffled by outside in humping, adolescent steps, slowing sometimes to look in. "No. Never. No."

III

THE FIRST MORNING of his new work, Juan Ramirez went to school as on any other day. From now until the end of the summer he would be dividing his time between AXEL and the university. There were a few details left to clear up about his dissertation (some members of his doctoral committee were—as usual—either on vacation or couldn't bear to read his work and pass it), but he hoped that his degree would come through by the fall. Until then, even four hours of work a day would give him more money than he'd had for years. He spent the morning in the shiny labs and endless halls of the medical sciences building where patients, supine and suffering, occasionally shared elevators with old students, young doctors. Ramirez couldn't concentrate on his work. He went into the coffee room, where students ate doughnuts and talked about their futures, and mentioned the coming afternoon. Gill Arvin, one of his old classmates, a nonfriend, said, "You'll be working for the Air Force, right? I worked for the Air Force once. There were a lot of generals in this room, right? I was a kind of public relations man. I spent a whole week making this giant cigar out of papier-mâché with an electric fan in it. And there were crepe paper streamers on the end of this thing, right? Then I got up, because I was supposed to introduce the program, and I turned on the electric fan and the streamers floated out. Guess what I said then? I said, "This, gentlemen, is the Nike antimissile missile.''

"I don't think that's what I'll be doing."

"Wait. You'll be surprised what they'll have you do. That's where they have those war games, right? All the bosses play tennis in one room and the secretaries play pool in another room, and the winners in each league get to— no! they all play with themselves and that's called isolationism."

Ramirez stood up to leave, but Arvin went on. "Those war rooms are actually motel rooms in miniature, each complete with wall radio, built-in TV and one of those finger massagers you buy for a quarter. Also a fake looking glass with generals behind it. If one of the secretaries doesn't love her country enough, they let her have it. The finger massager is really a laser beam, see? And she gets it right through the gut. It comes out her back and turns her nylon blouse to paste."

Back in the lab Ramirez gazed at slides of germs, of diseased cells. They were silent and beautiful, they minded their own business. He loved these hours alone when Lorraine rolled off the stage of his mind, and the secretary of the department, and those furry cowlike women, and . . . his new involvement, everything. His life was those cells and God bless them, clean in their disease, harmless in their harmfulness, obeying certain laws as immutably as the sun. They lived and died under those microscopes in florid, silent dignity.

At noon he washed up and drove out Pico to the coast. Still it was not particularly different; he and his friends often drove out to the beach for lunch. It was a hot day, the early summer sun slanted down into the car and made him sweat. The traffic was heavy. He slowly passed the drapery shops, laundromats, Mexican restaurants that made up so much of semidowntown Los Angeles. It was the same as the East Side only uglier. In spite of everything he felt heavily elated. It was a job he was driving to, and they were going to pay him money for it.

Once he got to AXEL, he wasn't allowed in the building. No one had arranged to meet him in the lobby, there had been a minor administrative mistake. He talked to the policemen at the desk (his guts a mass of jelly, they had already found him out). He heard his own voice, colorless, ordinary, droning on about his department, the nature of the job. But everyone upstairs was out to lunch. No, he certainly could not go up to his office alone. No one was allowed past these doors without a security clearance or a companion who worked for the company. Their cop voices implied that they'd never heard of a Mexican getting a security clearance. You worked here for weeks or months—didn't he know that?—without visiting your office except with an escort. The people who waited for their clearances were paid all right, they had a job, but they couldn't even be trained until it became clear what they could be trained for, the size of the secrets they were allowed to know.

Well, what did those uncleared men do? Ramirez talked simply to hear his voice, to test it for defects. There were three policemen, two behind the counter, one at the door with a portable tape recorder. All three were fully armed. He listened to his voice for slur, for stereotyped accent. There was none. He was as flat, as Midwest, as his colleagues in the coffee room. The police were loquacious; they had nothing to do. "What they do with those guys, is, they shoot them straight to the top of the building in an elevator. They sit there for weeks and read magazines. *We* even had to go through it. They keep the secretaries in another room. You can see them through glass but you can't touch." Ramirez thought of his friend in the coffee room.

"What you need today, until the papers get straightened out, is a badge. What's the name of your department head? You put his name on the badge and this afternoon he'll be with you at all times. Where are you from? What do you represent? For a second Ramirez didn't understand. He looked up, he had been gazing out of the glass doors while the guard talked, into the middle distance of the parking lot. Six American opaque and stupid eyes sized him up. Here I am, he thought. A spy, can you believe it? And a scientist. And a man. And with a family. He thought of his father and the second-hand bookstores, tamale factories, greasy garages which had made up that adulthood, where his father had been a man. Outside a limpid sun warmed the asphalt of the parking lot, a window in the lobby had been opened, probably so that the expensive potted plants could have their dose of air. It was fresh air, for Los Angeles, a little damp, smelling of the sea. A thermometer on the wall registered seventy-two degrees.

"My name is Dr. San Juan de La Cruz Ramirez," he said to the police, and put on his glasses. "I am a microbiologist from the university, from UCLA, and I am to work in Chemical and Biological Warfare. My supervisor is James Joyce, an odd name, don't you think, for a scientist? I was told to report to this lobby and was assured that someone would be here to meet me, to . . . brief me." He turned a quarter around and gazed again at the parking lot. One of the guards meekly typed out his card. The card was slipped into a plastic holder striped in green. "Just pin this on and be sure it's plainly visible at all times. We only ask you to do this until everyone in the Security Guard knows you by appearance and name."

"How long will that be?"

"Twenty-four hours. And if you'll just say your name into the tape recorder over there . . ."

"But I'm not going in until Mr. Joyce arrives."

"We study your voice. We take voice prints. We listen. It's possible for a spy to duplicate your appearance in every detail, but no one can duplicate another person's voice." Outside two or three secretaries walked up the stairs to work. They looked like students at UCLA, maybe prettier, but with that same touching, youthful sweetness. "Juan Ramirez," he said into the machine.

He sat and waited in the airy, well-furnished lobby for another half hour, leafing through this week's *Time* and *Life*, while across the room the policemen played his name again and again, a businesslike whisper in the afternoon, Juan Ramirez, Juan Ramirez, Juan Ramirez.

"Ramirez? I'm sorry I made you wait. Those lunches . . . sometimes I think those lunches are too much of a good thing."

Juan stood up, shook hands. It's amazing, he thought, how I get so I can really do this. "Mr. Joyce. Yes, I know what you mean, though at the university we can rarely afford it."

"Ramirez, now you'll begin to learn the meaning of decadence. Decadence is the number of cocktails one consumes in the daylight hours."

"And the evening?" Ramirez blushed for himself; under stress his voice turned coy, he sounded like Miss America.

"Liquor in the night is wholesome, it's the backbone of the nation."

"I'm afraid with school I haven't even had time to explore that."

Joyce took him by the arm, propelled him past the guard. "Jimmy Joyce."

"Ramirez, Juan Ramirez."

Joyce was to be his supervisor, not his immediate boss. He had met Joyce only once before in a dark restaurant, at one of the recruiting lunches which AXEL regularly held. He recognized the voice; absent, fatuous, thick with alcohol, but had never seen his face in the light. Joyce's face was good-natured; his mouth puffed out like a baby's. His eyes were red and vague, but the overall impression was OK. Joyce looked human, bumbling, reassuring. Ramirez remembered that the administrators didn't have degrees in bacteriology or physics or engineering. They were in the difficult position of being bosses while being paid maybe two thirds the money of the people they supervised.

"I want you to meet someone you'll be working with, Harry Ino, pronounced *I know*. You met him at lunch, remember? He'll be two offices down from you."

Ramirez stared at a young Oriental, small, fine-boned, young man. He stood only a little taller than Lorraine. In fact that's who he was, some friend of his wife.

"Aren't you a friend of my wife?" he asked.

"What's her name?"

"Lorraine, Lorraine—"

"Oh, yeah, I went out with her for a while. Excuse me, but aren't you that guy?"

"What guy?" Jimmy Joyce said. "What guy is that? Didn't you both meet at lunch?"

"I wasn't at that lunch. Aren't you that guy though?"

"Oh, yes, so they say. I guess so. My wife exaggerates, you have to remember." Everywhere I ever go, he thought, everywhere I ever go, they'll know me, or I'll do something like that again, they'll know me. He thought of the penniless Africans, their borrowed instruments, their poor little language, their clothes. How could I have fooled them? How could I fool anyone?

"It's a romantic way to meet, and you don't spend much money on the preliminaries."

"What's this about? What is it, Ino? Didn't you two meet at lunch?"

"He *raped* my girl seven years ago, that's how we met. It doesn't matter, her mother couldn't stand me anyway. See you later, Ramirez." Ino went back into his office.

That's how we met, Ramirez thought. He remembered a young Oriental then, standing outside his office while an ebullient Lorraine explained, "He *raped* me, he *did* that, it was too bizarre," and Ino saying laconically, "Yeah, I know, I'll see you later."

"*What* did he say? *What* did you do?"

This was one thing Ramirez knew how to do after seven years. "It's a family joke. My wife insists I raped her. I take it as a compliment, that's the only way I can take it."

Joyce laughed loudly, his florid face congested. "But didn't you meet Ino at *lunch*? I was sure I'd introduced you."

I'm a rapist, Ramirez thought, but you're a drunk, OK? He looked at Joyce carefully and laughed along with him. He put his hands in his pockets and somewhere, below his ribs, began to relax. He looked around him and saw that the halls, the fluorescent lights, the drinking fountains, the formica tile were a duplicate of the medical sciences building at UCLA. "May I see my lab?" he asked. "Do I work in a lab or just in an office?"

"There isn't a lab here. We don't deal in hardware, remember? Our only product is paper. You'll do your lab work, if you have any, at UCLA, we have an arrangement with them. All we really want from you is publication. But for a few weeks you stay on the top floor until you're cleared. The view is great up there, you can see the ocean all the way from Palos Verdes to Point Dume. Didn't we talk about that at lunch?"

"But isn't there anything I can do while I'm waiting to be cleared? I don't like getting paid for nothing."

"Listen. One of the best documents we have around here is something Russian intelligence wrote up about AXEL. They say we're the Doomsday elite, you know why? Because we all own cars, and can buy gas with cards, and have charge accounts at the surrounding department stores. You know the only department store around here? Sears Roebuck. You see what I mean? AXEL gives you six weeks to read magazines, meet some girls, get to know people. I'll be up with some unclassified material for you to go through, to get the feel of what we're trying to do. Meanwhile, finish your dissertation, try to get that union card. You probably know as much about what we're doing as anyone in the department, certainly more than I'll ever know. But we have to wait a couple of months before we can trade information. Relax and enjoy it.''

Joyce's flushed, kindly face wrinkled up, looked grave. "The one thing they care about around here is security. Police tour the building day and night looking for security violations. Two violations you're warned and the third one you're out. You'll be briefed on security all next week." He lowered his voice. "We've had a lot of trouble lately. We've had two defectors, and as far as we knew there was nothing on their record, nothing. So you'll have to wait while they check you out. Everyone goes through it."

Evidently, after this glimpse of CBW, he was to be shunted up to his proper place. They stepped to an elevator. Across the hall through glass doors he saw another area of the parking lot, a few palms, a patch of ocean. The doors were marked ALARMED EXIT. "Never go through those doors," Joyce said, "or the guards will gun you down."

"How do I get *out*?"

"In the west wing the exit is Room 304, in the east wing the last men's room on the right."

They stepped out of the elevator into a large airy office with fifteen or twenty desks. Picture windows on all four sides showed the ocean, the mountains to the north, and inland all the city that the smog would allow. A few men sat at desks reading magazines. Through a glass partition he saw two girls in cotton dresses and sandals doing their nails.

"I'll leave you here, Ramirez. Stay clean. I'll let you out at five o'clock. Ha ha. And let's have lunch tomorrow."

Jimmy Joyce pressed the button in the elevator, was gone. His suit had been rumpled, his breath musty. And yet he wasn't like Lorraine's friends, you could talk to him. Ramirez again had the feeling of an amateur tightrope walker who had once more made it to the other side, umbrella, bicycle, bowling pins, oranges and all. It wasn't altogether the spy business. He was a Chicano in drag, none of it was real. Maybe his germs, maybe. AXEL, the Africans, never.

By the end of the afternoon Ramirez had struck up a couple of conversations with some bland-faced engineers, a pudgy political scientist. It had been like a four-hour coffee break. As he drove the San Diego freeway back to school and his barracks home, he could only think that he'd earned thirty dollars for four hours of conversation. He'd do the same thing the next day and the next, the next; it was amazing. In his teens he'd earned money as a box boy in a grocery store, or stacking cases of beer in an East Side brewery. Thirty dollars had been a week's wages. They always asked you in the beginning English classes he'd never gotten beyond to write about how college had changed you. What changed was where you *went*, and sitting in his motionless car on the northbound lane of the San Diego freeway, he thought with awe of his slow but steady trip from the ghetto westward to the sea.

When he got home the house was empty; Lorraine had taken the kids somewhere. He sat down in his clean living room, looked, out of habit, for some work to do, when he realized once again that his schoolwork was nearly done, and at AXEL his work not yet started. Besides, as a workingman, he'd put in his time for the day. It was still light outside. Children stumbled and ran in the rosy dust, there were seven or eight hours to be lived between now and bed. He went through the single-file rooms to the refrigerator for a beer, opened it, and remembered what Jimmy Joyce had said about drinking.

His house was so clean, so empty without Lorraine. Instead of being punished for his sins he'd been rewarded. He'd found a jewel, a statue of decency, a girl who combined all the love of cleanliness which his mother had with all those niceties of homemaking which *her* mother had; little pleated children's dresses with hand-crocheted collars, and his boy in short pants because they were suitable, a thriftshop vase—but a beautiful one—filled with weeds and pussy willow. And yet there was nothing arty about her. Lorraine's house gleamed, the closet was full of his ironed shirts.

Juan couldn't stand it. He went next door to the Wongs. Edith met him at the door, unkempt and cheerful, relaxed as a sloth on a tree. She was cooking spaghetti sauce, the whole apartment smelled of it. Walter sat in front of the television, a glass of Red Mountain Burgundy (the very cheapest brand money could buy) in his hand, a gallon of it beside him on the floor. In the back bedroom children played; in fact he recognized his own children's voices.

"Come in, how was your job? Is it too weird out there? Did they make you do bad things on your first day? Walter finished a seminar paper and handed it in today so he's taking the rest of the day off." Ramirez listened politely while she talked, remembering she was, after all, a woman, the object of Walter's passion, a mother of children. He tried to think—or thought of himself thinking—of a woman's body under the jeans and shirt, but it didn't work. She was more sacrosanct, more remote, than his mother. A house full of children, without passion, without obsession. He stepped inside. Walter said, "Yeah baby, have some wine," and he answered, grinning, "Yeah."

"Lorraine's at the dentist. You know how they make you wait there. I've got the kids. She's got the worst teeth, you know? You want to stay for dinner? *Do* it, it'll be nice. If Walter doesn't drink up all the wine before we eat. Afterwards you guys get to watch the kids, I've got to work in the bedroom after dinner."

"No thanks, Edith, Lorraine will be having something, I know."

Edith was quiet for a second. He knew she loved company, people in the house, a lot of voices and guests. He guessed she didn't much like to be alone with her husband. You either fight loneliness, he thought, or you lie down with it. And he had a moment of half-pity, half-contempt for that girl. But he'd come over here, hadn't he? He walked back to the bedroom, said hello to his kids, got a jelly glass from the kitchen (their house was his house in more than architecture), and flopped on the mattress beside Walter.

"How's the job, Big Money Man?" Walter asked.

"Full of shit."

"That's how Big Money Men talk." Walter grinned. His teeth were stained permanent purple from the cheap wine, and his wife said—exaggerating of course—that they were as loose in his head as any second grader's. And yet he worked, night after night, on his language cards, on some enormous project.

"You know, you might get a job at AXEL. They hire linguists."

"I'm on the side of life, Juan. I'm too good a guy to murder people for money."

"Well, where *will* you get a job? Aren't you going to get a job before the PhD?" Juan recognized, with not unpleasant shock, the intonation, the rhythm, of his former colleagues in the coffee room. He poured himself another glass and snuggled down among the pillows. The Wongs' bed had belonged to a famous Chinese movie star of questionable morals. It pleased Walter to recall Oriental nights of debauchery, perfumed nights, which, from his point of view, more than justified sleeping on this matted, lumpy shell.

The late afternoon passed pleasantly. Juan and Walter watched the early show from among the cushions and pillows. They left the front door open to catch some poor breeze from the bedroom window in back. Lucille Ball and Bob Hope did their part. Edith put up an ironing board in the living room. The wine (after the first couple of terrible tastes) lay gently in Juan's mouth and stomach, he didn't get drunk, but after a while the twin enormities of being a spy for someone and having a genuine job faded somewhat, and it was a long time until tomorrow afternoon.

He saw the poverty; in some ways he and Lorraine and the Wongs and all the hundreds of their compatriots in this two-story string of shacks were poorer than his parents. How lunatic to have, as a general thing, less money than an East Side Mexican. And he and his friends had no "morality." His mother would never go to the dentist, for instance, in the late afternoon when the family would be home, waiting for dinner. Well, in fact, she would never go to the dentist except to have her teeth pulled.

His family had a sense of place. They'd loved their stucco house in New Mexico (painted electric blue, with fine purple bougainvillea and some chickens scratching in the yard—he'd seen a picture, he knew). But when fate brought his grandfather to the East Side, they'd lavished their love impartially on another stucco house (painted lemon yellow and white, with a garage). Now, lying next to a half-breed drunk, who by necessity and circumstances seemed to be his best friend, smelling the odors of spaghetti sauce and ironing and dust, hearing his children's clamorous voices, waiting for his wife; already marked, himself, by a salary which would push him out and away from the university, a PhD greaser with a brand-new house waiting for him in some cheap but upwardly mobile West Side suburb, yes, yes, with all that, he lay there and took deep breaths and contemplated the last few years of his life: I don't want to leave here, he thought, hugging his friends in his mind, I don't. Only lethargy and shyness kept him from going back in the bedroom again to look at his children.

So he felt fine for fifteen minutes or an hour, but then this afternoon and the next and the next weighed on him, lay there, like a series of qualifying examinations. Do I get my spy salary if I'm not cleared? Will it take long to be cleared? Will I *ever* be cleared? What can I possibly do for them, how can they expect me to work for them when they don't even know what I'm supposed to be doing, when *I* don't even know what I'm going to be doing? How will they know what they want me to do, if they don't know what's going on? He despaired of working for such a cheap outfit. Do I just drag out everything? He had a single clear thought of what he'd signed on to do, and immediately cut it from his mind. He thought of the people up in Preclearance. The women, oh God. Would he disgrace himself here as well? He had a terrible, physical pang of fear. They'd check out the rape, his habits in libraries and theater lobbies. He'd never be cleared, he'd lose both jobs, Lorraine would leave him and take the children. Ah, Lorraine.

He almost did have dinner with the Wongs after all. It was seven o'clock, the kids had been fed and were in their pajamas. He'd helped Edith set up three TV tables in front of the mattress, he'd helped Walter to the bathroom to wash. The local news was over, the national news just starting and for an hour and a half Juan hadn't said a word. He knew they thought of him as a crank, a bat, but then look at them, *look* at all of them. Friends in misery, friends beyond misery.

He'd just started on his dinner when Lorraine came in and did what she always did, brought that sense of cleanliness and excitement and the world outside. He listened while she described the dentist, the tools, her teeth, the nurses, the other patients. He docilely peered into her mouth and tried to find yet another filling in all that glitter. He watched while Edith, stolid, noncommittal, cleared his clean plate and folded up his table. He allowed himself to be led away, hardly saying good-bye. Another evening which he had lived through, sometimes enjoyed; and left behind him nothing but relief at his departure, taken away with him nothing but misery.

He laid the already sleeping children in their beds, pink from their baths, sweaty from sleep, strange invaders in this clean little nursery. (Next door he felt the effort, saw the litter that neither his mother nor Lorraine would put up with for a minute.) He stood watching his children in the half-dark while Lorraine pulled plates out of the refrigerator.

She called and he came into a charmingly set stage. On the delicate, low table in front of their mattress, set with Mexican glass plates and bright napkins, there was cold tongue and potato salad with capers and white wine, all light, delicious, perfect food for the end of a hot day. Lorraine left the front door open and put on a record; she had changed into pants and lolled about on the bed as he sat silently in front of his food, moving her thin legs here, there, chattering as he crouched and ate.

"I'll never be able to chew on my left side again. They're too insane. They peer at your teeth. You *submit* your teeth to them. It's obscene. I went to the grocery store today and they gave me an immense picture of a *peach*. I'm putting it up in the kitchen. I really like it a lot, it's too bizarre. . . ."

He listened, dumbly, but by the end of the meal, she had poured wine in his mouth and words in his ears, had allowed her thin hand to wander across his stiff and nervous neck while she gestured with the other hand to make a point, or lying suddenly down behind him, had hugged his left side with her knees, and giggled up at him from under his right elbow, while he blindly, sadly, went on eating. Sitting up then, she patted his thigh, or his face; and she went on with it until he finally, against his will and better judgment, smiled. Then she asked about the job, coaxed him beyond monosyllables into a stumbling imitation of the cadences of her speech, and he found himself, poor Mexican orphan, able to make a joke or two, and she laughed at them.

He followed her to the kitchen when she cleared away the

dishes, and stood there, talking, while she quickly washed up. And followed her, still talking, when she went into the bathroom to cream her face. "They wouldn't even let me in, they've got tape recorders you say your name into, I wanted to say my *full* name, but I didn't, even the San Juan de La Cruz part made them nervous, I think I'm the only Mexican there, can you believe that?" He wanted to tell her how lonely he felt, how always out of place, but he couldn't. "They say that Preclearance is the best office, it's on the top floor. The ocean is beautiful, all you do is read magazines. Some guy told me they won't even let you work on your own stuff because you might be a security risk to even know what you already know. Can you believe that?"

She zipped out of her clothes and into the shower.

"I was thinking what would happen if I *didn't* get my clearance. That happens sometimes. I signed a couple of petitions when I was an undergraduate, and my father is kind of a radical, you know that. Where do they draw the line, do you think? Do you think they might object to that kind of thing? Or just being *Mexican*? I don't know. . . ."

"What about your lurid past?" she yelled, and as he tried to answer, crestfallen, terrified, with some joke, some pretense at one, she came out and hugged him just as she was, naked and wet.

"I'd *always* give you a reference, they need criminal types," she said, and smiled up at him, totally fresh, totally sweet.

Later, in bed they acted out their same play. He was hot, hasty, probably too violent, he always remembered beforehand not to be, and remembered, after, that he had been once again. It was that way, he thought, because they were mismatched in every way. His enormous hand tried to pin down her tiny breasts like elusive little fish, she laughed when he was serious and surprised him then with passion which sometimes still offended him. He liked what she did but didn't approve of it, couldn't, in fact, even say it to himself; she knew it made him nervous and did it anyway, delighted in it, and he was again the prudish boor. Once aroused (as they say) it was another story. He was blind with lust and rage. Although it was a sin to go down on her, he did so violently, at length, with a delicious, ghastly sense of sin, and she was an animal, a sharp little animal, a ferret, a fox, a rat. She came with lustful little gasps of laughter. Then he climbed, *locked* himself into her, transfixed, while she whispered him to a violent, shuddery end.

Afterwards he lay, dumb again, terrified, disgusted, amazed that anyone would have him around, would keep him voluntarily. And thinking then that Lorraine was as great a monster as himself. But Lorraine was up already, in a bathrobe, giggling, and brought back a carton of ice cream with two spoons. They lay together and finished off the ice cream, getting spots on themselves and on the sheets, and then she cleared it away, came back to him, put her arms around him, gave him a kiss, and as, partly comforted, he began to fall to sleep, she looked at him and smiled, and lay her head down on his bony chest, his sad heart.

IV

THIS IS HOW Juan and Lorraine broke up, or began to. Sometime in August, almost two years after we moved into Vets Housing, Walter and I gave our first big party. While it was an excellent party in almost every way, it was remembered not only for its food (which was great), or its implications (the first of the great parties which marked the start of a long metaphysical vacation in our lives), but for the specific fact that it was the end of Juan and Lorraine and the beginning of Lorraine and Steve. Lorraine's breakout meant the end of a lot of marriages, the end of that particular state of mind.

Poor people all over the world have cool ways to deal with their poverty; Italian food is upstart peasant fare, Mexican food is a whole cuisine of improvisation, right? The women I knew took pride in keeping better houses than their mothers at a third the cost. We already had our ways, our traditions for giving a party.

A week before our own effort Walter and Juan and Mr. Goodman (my best and new friend, an earnest scholar from the English department) drove down over the border to buy liquor. They drove all the way to Arizona in the desert night in a Volkswagen (to save money) then crossed to San Luis del Colorado and bought tequila at a dollar a bottle and two-liter bottles of rum at two-fifty. They took a gallon each across the border, and put it in lockers in the bus station in Yuma, and then crossed again to Mexico to the same town

50

and bought up three gallons again, and brought them across ten hours later, and the guard said, "Say, didn't I see you boys a few hours ago?" They shook their heads gravely no, and put their three gallons in the bleak locker room, crossed the border again in the foggy spring night, and got drunk and watched the strippers in San Luis's terribly silly night-clubs. At about four in the morning they lurched out of their last club, and thought about the next three gallons. But they didn't have the nerve, and so drove chastely across the border and as the dawn came up raced back into California all the way to San Diego, had breakfast, put their bottles into a naval exchange locker and then went across the border again to Tijuana, that bustling wholesome brothel, totally different from the bleak cribs of San Luis. In T.J. they bought gifts for their friends; so *cheap*, everything, and one item in ten really something you'd want to buy. They went into more liquor stores, buying a quart here, a quart there, a perfect symphony of illegality; peach brandy, *rompope, mescal*, more tequila and rum, some gin, some Kahlúa. Then, bristling dopey bottles ingeniously stuck into piñatas, under cartons of beans and hominy, under the back seat and in the dashboard and under the front seat and under Mr. Good-man, plus a large jar of bennies tucked into Walter's crotch, they drove across the border, saying they had nothing no, just these few little tourist goodies, and then were waved through, madly laughing, back to the navy locker for their six other gallons and home to LA half-drunk on cheap bar tequila and the other half drunk on their adventurous trip. For the three scholars it must have been like the semiannual forays of pioneers off the prairies and into town. They were hicks, sure, but they came back laden, and dazzled their women and children with all those things and more; Mexican chocolate and little toys; the toothbrushes they bought were made of genuine pig bristles imported from New Zealand.

So, OK. The ladies stayed home and cooked. When I think of that onion soup dip that we all made so often I blush, but it was good. We boiled up stewing chickens and made fillings for enchiladas and tacos, and marinated pots of vegetables in oil and vinegar. It was pretty good, all that food. The party when it came lived up to it all. Walter made an excellent punch and unbelievably didn't get drunk. It was a night he took seriously; professors from his department were there—he ladled out punch—I don't know, Mr. Goodman had his camera and took pictures, maybe that's why we all remember it. A sweet wife of a graduate student, usually very sedate, came in, had two glasses of punch, sat on the kitchen table, began to sing along with the guitars of several friends, was overcome with joy, swung her feet in the air, cried, "Whoopee, whoopee," a couple times, and then got sick and passed out for the rest of the evening. But the picture still lives, Sherie kicking her pretty legs (which she usually stood on all day in a bank, so that her husband could first learn and then teach about Victorian novels) singing Whoopeee, whoopee.

There were a hundred people in and outside of our tiny apartment. The lights were bright, people danced. People sang Mexican songs execrably in the kitchen (while Sherie kicked and giggled), and in the living room very early rock 'n' roll records played (Little Richard talking about Adam: "He got what he wanted but he lost what he had.") This, again, like the liquor-buying trip, was poignant and sweet because of what it compared to; innumerable long and lonely nights spent on so-called scholarly pursuits; or for the women, those afternoons in the dust outside with the kids; or waiting in free clinics for shots for the baby, or fixing rice for dinner, just plain rice, because all the inventiveness in the world couldn't conjure up a celery stalk or half an onion to turn it into at least, *fried* rice.

Lorraine and Juan came late, though Lorraine had been there early, of course, helping. Marriage had done to Lorraine what rape couldn't; it had given her a sense of disaster, I think; it had showed her she wasn't immune to much after all. In the same way giving birth did what a couple of lousy little abortions couldn't. Lorraine toughed out catastrophe handily; what she couldn't stand was daily life. Which isn't to say she didn't do it well. She looked great these days, she dressed plainly in blacks and browns, she did her duty, she'd had those two babies.

So they came, and Lorraine met Steve Rader, posed negligently against our wall of string, flicking cigarette ashes on the rug. Steve was a cinematographer; that is, a theater arts major who had raised to an occupation the vice of living one's life out of the movies. He continually got in fights and then was delighted to find that his scars made him look like Jean Paul Belmondo. He constructed theories relating American gangster movies of the thirties to the French love of violence to the entire theory of existentialism. He'd made love the first time with both of his arms in plaster casts—or so he said—and even now courted ladies by showing them X rays of his former broken bones. He was some friend of a friend, an elderly juvenile delinquent, just over his first marriage. Ten minutes later, some guy came and complained to me that it was too embarrassing to go to the bathroom because a couple was necking (and more?) in the shower stall. It was Lorraine and Steve of course; I went right in there and was going to even pull back the curtain—whether jokingly or in a temper I really don't even know, but as I went in the bathroom, I heard that great sound, Lorraine's *laugh*, starting low and chuckling around in a kind of a circle, and someone's elbow jutted out between the curtain and the wall. I thought oh, shit, and walked right out. They could do anything they wanted because what made Lorraine happy made us happy and made the world happy.

Lorraine and Steve spent about two hours in the shower, told each other their life histories, laughed themselves silly, turned on the water once by accident as they lurched against the faucet, and for two hours (it was sad but empirically true) everyone who had ever known Lorraine or Juan pressed Juan in against the kitchen wall with bits of cold chicken and conversation; they asked him leading questions which had to be answered in lengthy paragraphs, and others who didn't know him at all—full professors invited for the most blatant political reasons—sensed that something was going on, and gathered without knowing why in the semicircle around that ugly Latin gent. Juan expanded, he stretched himself, how many times before had he talked to ten or twelve people at a time? His face flushed, he gestured awkwardly, he told about New Mexico, the little town where he was born which was full of poverty and beauty; adolescent girls in curlers, little savage boys in hand-me-down clothes without buttons or snaps, those boys running after each other, throwing bricks in a fight, but keeping one hand on their ragged Levis to keep them from falling down. Lots of people listened, and liked Juan either at first sight or for the first time, but while they liked him half of them knew that his wife was going away, away in the bathroom, and that while they cheered him up, they were doing him in.

I have to say that I didn't even notice too much of this. I was having a good time, a genuine good time. I had my eye on somebody—what a difference it was then to be so securely married, to be able to blamelessly flirt, to idealize some poor but honest young man, to exchange soulful looks and to take for granted that nothing would happen. A friend of mine once said that she'd rather hold hands than screw any day of the week, and even now I have to say I know what she means.

People danced out in the dust in front of our house, neighbors we'd never met came around. Jorge Alphonse, the medieval scholar, went into the backyard with a meditative look on his face, threw up in the daisies, then lay down on our little patch of lawn while people clustered around to chat. Like Juan, he was the center of attention for maybe the first time in his life. He lay back and looked up at the stars and talked until the sun came up. (About half of everyone went home around two in the morning, but there was a solid noisy hard core which stayed until four and an elite which stayed until breakfast.) We approached good times with such wistfulness then, we wanted good times so much, and I don't think we were very disappointed.

About one-thirty there was a scuffle in the back bedroom; Lorraine and Steve literally jumping out the window, and Juan (having gone to the bathroom and discovered them) followed in hot pursuit. The three were gone for some time. Juan chased them around the Sports Arena, around the archery field and co-ed dorms, even up to the regular school buildings. Lorraine and Steve ran, laughing. The times they could have gotten away altogether they didn't. They'd stop for a technicolor kiss under a pine tree, but if they didn't hear Juan's heavy steps after a while they'd talk and giggle, and pretty soon he'd get on the trail again. Somewhere along the line Lorraine and Steve conceived the idea of doubling back to the party. They ran in the front door, hand in hand, greeted by shouts and smart remarks (it was the prime of the evening, professors and grown-ups had gone home), and ran to the kitchen where they put together giant tacos and wolfed them down and drank punch and necked openly with grease on their chins. "Watch it," someone said, and poor

Juan came in. He had leaves in his sweater; he'd looked everywhere. He couldn't believe, I guess, they'd come back to preen in front of his friends. Without a word he went to get Lorraine's coat. Steve—with an attack of the cowardice he was to suffer often but inconsistently in the coming months—ran to the bathroom and locked the door. Juan slipped the coat over Lorraine's shoulders. The room wasn't silent; the music went on and people talked to each other— oh they talked—but all to keep the silence away, and Juan knew. You couldn't tell for sure that he suffered because he *always* looked that way—his face had the permanent lines of suffering. But his face, never the real dark of the "typical" Mexican face, was paler than ever, and his eyes were rimmed in red. Before they left Lorraine came up and kissed me good-bye. "It was an excellent evening, an excellent party," she said to me, in a perfect imitation of her up-tight mother. Over her shoulder I saw Juan looking (oh what a look) at me. I couldn't think of a thing to say. Walter said later he couldn't stand it and jumped out the bedroom window to the backyard himself, so he wouldn't have to say good-bye.

We didn't know about strobe lights then, but that was the effect, a disjointed series of tableaux which we reviewed with extreme interest but with dread (if this could happen to them it could happen to us all).

We couldn't eavesdrop that night of course because of the racket in our house—and in an hour or so we forgot, in a way. Some people slept out back, some in the living room, and some of us stayed up and talked all night. What a pleasure and a treat. And no children anywhere. In the morning I fixed breakfast for the dozen or so people who were still there. Then we all got in cars and went to the beach.

That afternoon Walter and I drove home, sunburned, gritty, exhausted. We'd picked up China from my mother's. What dreariness, what wretchedness; it was all over. Walter read stories to the baby while I cleaned up and we looked at each other and cocked our heads to the wall, afraid to talk because we'd be heard. We couldn't hear a thing, nothing, and their car hadn't moved all day. Murder crossed our minds—we said so later—to each other and to our friends, but I will say that, even though this was the first chapter to a long odyssey of "illicit" love, and we retailed as much of it as anyone else, and with as much gusto, we couldn't bring ourselves to tell what happened between Juan and Lorraine that night and day and the next day.

The next morning was Monday. Walter went to school and so did Juan. Lorraine took the car to pick up her own kids and then came over to our place for lunch. She'd already talked to Steve twice that morning and was crazy with joy and filled already with crackbrained schemes for deceiving Juan. But after lunch when the kids went outside again she told me how he'd been. I think I can say that she tried to laugh and she tried to cry; that is, that she tried to have a point of view, in the same way that you might try for a point of view if you had to strangle a cat; you might say you were sorry or decide you were a sadist and liked it a lot: either one would keep you from the facts of that furry throat and protruding tongue. Lorraine said that when they got home she sat on their bed and waited for the beating and the storm of Spanish. Juan asked her to sit in an occasional chair, a straight-backed thing facing the wall above the bed. She said murder crossed her mind too. Then he stood awkwardly on the bed and took the posters off the wall. "I could hear all that noise, I even knew you'd be listening but I knew you wouldn't hear me if I screamed."

"Well, but what did he do then?"

Lorraine's eyes filled with tears. It seemed totally unsuitable, since I'd seen her penniless and after an abortion, and right after she'd broken her arm in Junior High, and heard her through the countless beatings of old Juan Ramirez and never seen her do that.

"He went to the *closet*, and he took out the *movies*, all the old home movies of when we first got married and first had the baby, and he took out the projector and put it on the little table and showed me all those movies, it was the bizarrest thing you ever saw. But I tell you, I couldn't *stand* it."

There were hours of movies. While we danced next door and finally lay down to sleep, Juan and Lorraine sat in the dark next door and viewed their past life: Lorraine in little print dresses as she showed she could rôle-play as well as the next, pushing their first baby in a stroller and wearing white tennis shoes, her hair all curly, very much the new wife—you know all of it, look at your own home movies, or those first married photographs you took, where your faces hang out like brainless stupid moons. Ramirez ran them chronologically, tears streaming down his face, she said, and they streamed down hers as she said it. Sometimes they sat apart on straight chairs, and sometimes he came and put his big unattractive head in her lap—he couldn't bear to look but made her do it. When finally they were finished—the sun was shining outside and we'd already left, he asked her to take off her clothes. By that time she thought it was even-up she'd be killed, but was too tired and too sorry to care. He undressed too and took her on his lap. He held her for a long time and cried in the half-dark of the curtained room. He kissed her and kissed her and finally made love for what seemed like hours—he wouldn't let that last, motionless moment happen. Then they slept and he lay all morning on top of her and she smelled his sour, tired body and listened to him cry in his sleep.

When they woke up he asked her what was wrong, why she'd done it. It was the first time (she said) he'd ever asked her what was wrong or what she thought. "I said I loved him, and that it was just a big silly fling. If Steve calls here, can you take messages without Walter finding out about it?" I must have looked bad, and I never figured out what Lorraine ever did feel about Juan; I didn't have the nerve to ask, it would have been too corny and square. But I asked her about Steve. "He's just the neatest guy, he's just the most *bizarre* person that ever lived on this earth."

It took Juan a little over a month to find out that Lorraine and Steve were carrying on, "having an affair." In that time they did a lot, and I'm not being silly or lascivious. The day after Lorraine and I talked she left Jennifer and Davey with me and went with Steve to a motel. (And I found this all out from Steve, who enunciated all the details forever of his love for Lorraine, but she—while she went on and on about his behavior or his brain—never said what they *did* together, or what they would do, or how they would live or might live.) The truth is that Steve conceived a future from the beginning, a style, a way of life—and Lorraine didn't, plain to say. So it was Steve who told me, on an easy summer school day—while we ate pastrami sandwiches which had sat for so long in a steam table that the crusts outside covered a vast three-inch protean slime within—it was Steve who sat earnestly across from me at a long wooden table outside of the humanities building, and told about their first motel. No, I'm not going into another sex scene, it's *banal*, and not the point anyway. He told how Lorraine had closely examined the ceiling of their ten-by-twelve room, and said she'd never forget it, the square of white plaster: "I think that's a good sign," he asked me, "don't you?" And the conversations he'd had with the motel keeper that Tuesday afternoon, and how he'd never gone to a motel in the afternoon with anyone, but only late at night when he was drunk.

I have to say that it was interesting indeed to hear Steve—who before this story had a wife and doubtless will again—and who had some very formidable good looks as well as style and wit, turn his theoretical mind to marriage. "I know she's interested in a house and needs someone to take care of her kids and I don't mind kids, that's the role of a *macho*, right? She likes money and I don't have any, but there's a thing where you can get to where you don't need much—just bright paint and some cushions and Mexican posters, you put the kids to bed by eight and then you have the whole night, you live your life for the nights, right?" It was difficult to listen to this, *living* that life he talked about—my God, if you make a wall out of a ball of string, isn't that enough? And I knew the flaws, that the kids don't go to bed at eight for one thing, or they throw up on your bright cushions, but that's only a metaphor for what really does happen. But he spoke it all out; he had plans for the next twenty years.

In that first week they were together I went over to Lorraine's house once—at her request—when Steve was visiting. They'd asked me to lunch and Lorraine fed us sliced chicken with a thin and elegant layer of aspic. I was the only one who ate, and what disturbed me, what *disturbed* me, was not that they didn't eat, which they didn't, or that they necked a lot in front of me, which they did, but that they began to talk like Jean Harlow and Clark Gable, or Saint Bernadette and her parish priest; it was so cryptic, so meaningless I can't even describe. I know Lorraine kept saying, "Oh, uh, baby, oh." That's a pretty silly thing to say when you have a friend over for lunch who's known you for fifteen years or so, even if you are in love. Steve would say those things, completely cryptic, like "Where is the blue typewriter?'' Or ''I told you about the, uh,'' and she'd say, ''Oh, uh, wow,'' and there they'd be kissing. I felt like a small boy in the wrong movie and left as soon as I could—I could see that love, however marvelous, had put a crimp in their individual styles, or they were working out a new style together, and until it was set it was better to talk to them each alone. It made me sad and envious too, it goes without saying. Still I was closer than most others to their adventures—and—what can I say? While they were together and present in the flesh they were a bore, but their activities out of range became another myth—a myth that never extended as far as the rape, but was a continuing love story which sustained us all; it was only a drag when you saw it too close, and I imagine God himself would be a bore if you saw Him too close, it may be only speculation which keeps Him in business at all.

Meanwhile they were that myth. They did it in cars, in the ferris wheel at Pacific Ocean Park (Lorraine explained that the wheel was the kind with cages, although to hear Steve tell it in later years, it was out in the open in the double ferris wheel and the hinges were loose). They did it in the Graduate Reading Room. She told me that, and beyond everything you wondered what it *meant*, and then I thought, well, they were saying, ''Oh, ah, uh, baby,'' and with all that education. But it was what they did and not what they said that counted. When Juan started working full time and wanted to move to a regular nice house Lorraine persuaded him to stay at Vets Housing for a few more months; she was working so hard for her master's degree she said, Juan wouldn't want to make her into an ordinary housewife. And if they stayed in the barracks for a while, Juan could pay off some of his debts. In just a little while the Ramirezes would embark on a golden, certified solvent life together. (But meanwhile she didn't want Steve to have to drive very far to see her; he was having trouble with his car and if Lorraine moved away she was sure he'd find a younger, more convenient girl.)

Lorraine and Steve drove the freeways at top speed, laughing, hugging, swerving. He gave her countless presents which she secreted around the house and said were the fruits of her own frugality with pocket money; she told Steve once she liked house plants and he surrounded her with them, their narrow house turning into a kind of clean and witty jungle. By "their" I mean hers and Juan's. Oh, how bad and sad but terribly interesting it was to see it all unfold.

In late September, Lorraine left a love letter of Steve's on the couch, tucked behind the cushion. What on earth made her do it? And yet I find that's the conventional way, a letter left on the coffee table or under the sugar bowl. She was telling old Juan something, what she didn't say after the party, but the way she did it made him pull out the stops: there was a howling and a growling next door which made us remember the early days when we'd moved in. Juan beat her, he kicked her even, he was mad as hell. He said he'd throw her out if she ever looked at Steve again and that was it. She said she'd never see Steve again, that she was sorry, and that she loved *him*, Juan. But the next day she and Steve took the kids to the Griffith Park Zoo and managed to make it somewhere going or coming, as it were, and in the presence of all those kids, and somehow Juan picked up on it, and there was a scene and she said she was sorry, etc., and did it again the next day and the next, and there she was, staying at Juan's house, Juan's wife after all and still.

The fact is, Juan had a funny kind of good manners for nonhuman things—he didn't destroy those plants even though he knew now where they came from, he knew they were alive; and he didn't break the art objects which came to surround him in his house and which were in effect a kind of trousseau for Lorraine's projected marriage to Steve. Juan relied on the *present*, that encompassing thing that says *this* is what you're doing, and, so, this, is, uh, what you're doing. (Whether Lorraine answered back, "Oh, baby," is another question.)

Steve was put out by this new turn in the situation more than Juan; it was he who made the scenes now, he who took on, flipped, who had to know if Lorraine and her husband still had sex, if Juan destroyed his plants, and not only if he threw out Steve's art objects, but if they were placed in the children's bedroom or on the coffee table in places of honor. He raged over Juan's eating habits, his looks, "that acned creep, that sexless creep, that religio-fuck-up!" and was intensely jealous of their whole life together. For a while I can't deny I envied Lorraine on yet another whole plane.

Lorraine lied shamelessly to each of them: To Juan, *no* of course, even if she saw Steve she never carried on, and to Steve, *no,* she lay by that madman's side night after night and they never carried on; they were beyond that, they were in a celibate no-man's-land. Not only that—Juan was in many ways the perfect husband, industrious around the house, solicitous of the kids, a family man. Steve was the perfect lover (a stud from all I heard, a sex enthusiast, he loved it and all connected with it). But sometimes the well would run dry on one or the other of them, and for instance, when Juan had waited three days to fix a soap dish, well, Lorraine would con Steve into doing it (taking an hour to do a ten-minute job, swearing and sweating in the shower stall), and there were rare times when it didn't turn out so marvelous in the afternoon for Lorraine and her lover, when she would come home funky and dazed and fix an astonishing meal for old Juan, and sit on his lap and cuddle and snuggle and dazzle the poor boy in bed, managing one way or another to find satisfaction for herself—he'd do anything for her.

All this was only the second stage of the affair. It was characterized by good appearances continuously in a state of deterioration—the stuff of a hundred Rabelaisian tales and vignettes in *Playboy.* Everyone knew something (Good God, yes) was going on but pretended a lot that they didn't know. Juan every so often would come home early. Steve—in the old style—would leap out of those long narrow windows in Lorraine's bedroom, and leap into mine, so that twenty minutes later, when Juan came over to check, Steve and I would be playing five hundred rummy in the kitchen while children spilled around our feet, surely a domestic blameless scene. A classmate would ask Juan, "Who was that guy I saw on your porch today? You got somebody staying with you?" And Juan would blanch and grind his teeth and race home to find nothing. To his suspicions and complaints Lorraine blandly said he was wrong, that was all. Her housekeeping was impeccable, her lovemaking the same as ever.

If anyone's marriage was hurt it was mine; I had regularly three children to take care of instead of one, and had to listen to interminable analyses of the entire affair, first from Lorraine's side, then from Steve's and in any affair, I think, there just isn't that much that's new. It made me sad and envious and dowdy-feeling, I can't tell you. Plus I had to look at that poor Mexican and sometimes lie, dead-ass lie to him, when Steve, for instance, would be hiding in my linen closet, doubled up, or in my shower stall, and have to feel that mingled pity and exasperation, that rage, really, that Juan would let himself be lied to like that, indeed, that he would encourage it and try so hard to believe. Walter took no side at all, he liked Lorraine, and didn't like either one of the men very much, so on his part, or our part, our toneless marriage went on, the same, the same, the same, while prayers and sacrifices and acts of unspeakable lust went on next door every day. You can see where it might be a trying time.

This second stage went up in smoke after only three weeks. Steve couldn't stand the strain. On a Saturday morning sometime in October, only two months after the whole thing had started, Walter and the baby and I were out doing the shopping. Lorraine was inside her house dressed in a baby-pink duster doing some housework, and Juan was outside watering his flowers. (Have I said that Juan was an inveterate gardener, a worshiper of all, everything, that grew?) While Lorraine turned their slip of a house into something great, Juan made ten-by-twelve square feet of dust into a sweet, ingenuous Mexican garden, with those pink Mexican flowers that look like bells and rosemary and thyme and Mexican zinnias—anyway, he was watering all that stuff about ten-thirty in the morning. Across the street the sporty co-eds, who scorned to live in dorms and inhabited instead immoral single apartments, were dressed in Bermuda shorts, trundling down their clothes and linen to the laundromats, and the Saturday sense of good work being done prevailed. But all that calm was shattered by Steve's green car, which drove up insanely, bent the chain-link fence which separated our barracks from the street, and then old Steve got out. He carried a wooden box with him. He ran up to Juan—they weighed about the same though Juan was much taller—and slapped the hose from Juan's awkward hands. The water kept running and dug a hole in the damp earth, as it will. Juan—while Steve raved—watched as the hose flopped into his zinnia bed and sprayed away the earth, leaving the flowers' delicate roots exposed.

"I've had enough, you dumb greaser," Steve said, or something like that. "We have to have it out *now*, right now. I can't wait for you to decide. I'm in this too, you know." (I've noticed since then that the main fear of the other man is apt to be that he will be left out, that he doesn't have a big enough part in whatever drama.) "It's either you or me."

Juan Ramirez blinked. "I'll tell you what," Steve ranted, while little children gathered around and our unwashed, unshaven veterans of America's most minor and inglorious wars—taking the sun on their weathered slat porches—craned their necks to hear this newest act in a long-running play, "I'll tell you what, you sexless gutless bastard, you pimp . . . Wait a minute." And Steve stopped his tirade and bent over his little wooden box. "Shit. Can you get this open?" Juan had backed off and surreptitiously turned off the water. Now he stood with one long, clumsy foot tamping down the damp earth around his flowers. All this time he hadn't said anything, but his neighbors, who knew his violent ways, were waiting. Juan stood and waited while Steve fiddled and fooled with his box. It had an elaborate and ornate lock, quite difficult to open. Then Steve finally tore back its lid and its contents clattered to the ground. Six steak knives, the kind you get in Blue Chip Stamp stores. Steve reached down and picked one up. Its blade really did glitter in a bad way in the sun. Twenty or thirty children stood around now and watched with interest. Six feet away those interminable coeducational boys and girls paraded up and down the sidewalk, oblivious, but a couple of family men came down off their porches and joined the little crowd. "Come on, you pimp, pimping for your wife, you don't even care, we screw all over your *house* and you don't even care . . . come *on*!" Steve reached out and grabbed another knife. He held it out to Juan, who simply blinked at it. He seemed a little slow sometimes, and people waited. About this time Walter and I drove up with our poor groceries, our cheap cuts of meat. I'd like to be able to say that Walter did something decisive, or even that I did, but we got out of the car and leaned against it, holding the baby and watching. Juan suddenly grabbed up a knife from the ground. He snarled something in Spanish and bent over in a sort to fighter's crouch, *very impressive*, that he must have learned in his youth from the East Side. And Steve's face got the neatest look of incredulous surprise. (Let me say that in all the years we knew Steve, with Lorraine or without her, fighting for her honor or for his bad temper or because he thought it was expected of him or it went along with the advertisements he was currently laying on anyone, he must have been in twenty-four fights and never won one. And each time he was surprised.) Juan began to make quick scary swipes at Steve's face. It was clear he didn't want to really hurt him but (just like in those movie gang wars) to cut up Steve's pretty face. That in itself was pitiful, because Steve's face is the kind—as I said—that the more it gets cut up the better it looks anyway. But Steve clearly forgot that fact. He was scared shitless you could see, but he was going to go on with it. They began to jump around like in a samurai movie.

The door opened and Lorraine came out on the porch. She didn't step between them, she *was* between, simply by opening the door and coming out. "For God's sake," she screamed. "What do you think you're *doing*?" The sight of Lorraine inflamed Steve—he began to fight with more sincerity. And Juan was in that livid rage we all recognized and generally just dismissed as his own little eccentricity. They scrambled around, each man furious, and Lorraine furious, probably with embarrassment. In one way that seemed unlikely, remembering the Nigerians with tribal markings, and her whole style up until this point, ten-thirty on a Saturday morning; still you've got to remember she'd put in more time on that house, that marriage, than she had on the affair; she'd listened to a lot of out-loud prayers; she'd done it all, and now they were both in league to publicly do it in.

So what happened was they both cut *her* up. Juan savagely motioned her out of the way, and cut through the left sleeve of her pretty duster and rather deep into her arm. She turned pale and Steve—I *swear*, I saw it myself—reached out in a mollifying, apologizing gesture, but forgot he held a knife in his hand and cut her on the shoulder. "You creeps," she shrilled. "You silly dumb creeps! Will you come *inside* now!" She was bleeding and we all stood and stared like loons. She turned around and went inside, slamming the door behind her. Juan stood for a minute, dazed, in that funkish way he had. He dropped his knife and stumbled in after her, saying something we couldn't hear. Steve was left, peering inside, trying to hear. He seemed only then to notice us, and looked awfully silly. He crouched down and got his little box, then shuffled crouchingly around to pick up the knives and put them away. Two of the knives had Lorraine's blood on them but he slammed them right in their slots, where they would stick to the sleazy rayon lining. Then he stood irresolutely for an instant and then lumbered inside. It was the first time since the party that the three of them had been (knowingly) in one house together.

Lorraine sat in the kitchen in a straight chair by the sink, while they bandaged her. She called them both every kind of name, not swearing, just mentioning that Steve was a drunk, a boor, a fool, a showoff, and that Juan was slow-witted, could be taken in by anyone, even *Steve* (what an insult she made that sound like) that he was a religious fanatic who was too busy with thoughts of the next world to remember to put gas in the car (this referred to an unfortunate incident the week before), and never even changed his handkerchief. But then, she said, Steve never even brushed his teeth (which was true, although like Walter he drank so much wine he said it worked as a disinfectant).

Altogether, Lorraine didn't leave either one of them with much. I put away the groceries three feet away from it all and listened with a big grin on my face. That's it, I thought. You bet. It's all true and more. That was the first time Lorraine lost her temper with Steve—though they would have some lovers' quarrels later that would make those two long cuts seem tame—and more to the point, the first time in four years she'd lost her temper at Juan. He was evidently killed; he'd never even known she'd thought he was dumb or that she made fun of his private thoughts, his religion. He went to lay down on the couch. Lorraine got tired of yelling; the whole thing began to strike her funny, she went into the bedroom to admire her bandages, and called out to both of them that they could have at least engraved her arms with sentiments of love. Juan sobbed; Steve came in and started to neck. She pushed him away, but laughed. Then she went in and sat by Juan on the bed and apologized for her rudeness. And Steve said, "Hey, man, I'm sorry." Sorry for *what*? I thought, but Lorraine said, "He really is, you know. He knows he was dumb." She put her arms around

Juan and kissed him while Steve watched in a restrained, *noblesse oblige* sort of way (he made a big thing of his good manners later), and there they were.

During the silence which ensued Walter turned the sound of the television up; he'd been watching a football game while I listened next door. Juan and Steve, I suppose, perked up, they both wanted to see the game, and Juan, with a melancholy sigh, heaved himself up to turn on his own set. He and Steve talked in a desultory way about the game, and Steve simply *didn't go home*. They sat side by side on that low bed where they'd both screwed Lorraine (but I doubt either of them thought of it until later), and Lorraine went out for beer and peanuts. Some people came over to our place and asked what was going on; I told them and then we all watched the game. During the half the three of them decided they had to talk things over, and that Steve should stay to dinner. Lorraine sent them out for food and Juan— so they say—asked Steve what he preferred. Steve asked for liver and onions and awkwardly complimented Juan on his wife's cooking. They ate in front of the television and never talked about a thing. Steve didn't go home until after the late show.

That was their fight over Lorraine. They never had another one. Juan lost his rage and his little bit of self-confidence. He knew he'd lost her, although she had absolutely no real plans to leave him for someone as batty as Steve, and he tried instead, between occasional, hollow scenes, to get her back through love, to *charm* her back, poor bastard.

V

Los Angeles has its dog days, real days. Most of the year people live in a dream; this is what they wanted, isn't it? This is what they came for, whether from eastern Europe by way of the Pittsburgh steel mill slums, or Ireland by way of the TB sanitariums at Saranac Lake, or north on a bus from the Sonora Desert, or east on a ship of coolies (each with his own forged papers, a word or two of English—place names, proper names). This is what they came for, a life without hardship, without typhoons, pogroms, famine, hot weather. New York and the East are the Old Country of the United States, you can't get anywhere back there, rats eat your children and the butter comes in long thin sticks. Here you can be what you want to be, the freeways zip you from one side of the city to another in enormous clover patterns through the California night. But September gets a little grim. The temperature goes to a hundred, a hundred and three. It will stay that way for at least a month. The smog is metallic, grating. Edith Wong does the ironing standing in her slip, Lorraine is out on the freeways somewhere, Walter works lethargically up in the Graduate Reading Room where it's stifling. The university, famous in the city for its elaborate gardens, lies sullenly under the hot slate sky. The tops of trees turn yellow, every green bush has a top layer of dried gray leaves. Dead from the smog. A whole city breathes shallowly. Juan Ramirez waits in his air-conditioned penthouse at AXEL, turning the pages of *Psychology Today*.

The phone on his neat, uncluttered desk rang and Juan Ramirez picked it up. "Your clearance came through this morning," Jimmy Joyce told him. "Isn't it a terrible thing to have to start work in the hot weather? And leave those sweet little girls? And stop going to educational movies down in the basement? To have to work for a living, to earn your bread? Want to have lunch to celebrate? You made it fast."

"It seemed like a long time to me."

"Come on. Usually it's six, eight months. Once we had a guy who'd belonged to the Japanese Communist party in World War II. It took him two years to get cleared. Come on down, I'll meet you in the lobby."

Jimmy Joyce waited for him together with two other men from the department. In the AXEL style they wore sport shirts and desert boots and hair rather longer than the business standard. One of the fringe benefits of the Corporation was the privilege of dressing casually. Only Ramirez looked out of place, storklike, his glasses punishing his nose, his feet encased in black shiny leather lace-up shoes. As they went outside a wave of air hit them from the asphalt of the parking lot. "Christ," one of them said. "Christ, it's hot."

Earlier Edith had called Juan to remind him of the evening ahead. Walter's nephew, a full Chinese, was going away to school, and the elder Wongs were giving him a traditional banquet, a going-away party. As the only other college-educated Wong, Walter was second guest of honor, and encouraged to bring guests of his own. The Ramirezes would be perfect guests; Lorraine was brilliant and cheerful, "and besides, Juan, they'll like your swarthy skin. The only white folks they can stand are women. So you guys will do fine. Please, you have to come. Otherwise, I'll have to talk pidgin English with the old ladies. God, I really hate the Chinese now that I think about it."

Ramirez had asked where Lorraine was, why she hadn't phoned, and Edith said vaguely, "Oh, isn't she at her mother's? I think she said they were going out to thriftshops. Although why they'd do that on a day like today, God knows."

"Is she going to be there tonight?" Since the disastrous party at the Wongs a few weeks before Juan had been plagued by every sort of suspicion. He was ashamed of being jealous of his wife, ashamed even more to show it, but there it was. It was possible that his life hadn't been what he thought it was, and it seemed only reasonable that he should check up on it. (But his mind slid off the prospect of a life spent in checking up.)

"Oh, Juan, for goodness' sake. Of *course* she is. You're just in a funk because you have to work, and we get to stay home and have all these magnificent good times like doing the laundry."

With a heavy Chinese dinner ahead Juan wasn't particularly ready to eat. He and his friends each had three margaritas—with much joking about Juan's authority and good taste in the matter of tequila. Ramirez ran stumbling, tripping in these conversations, but he managed.

"This afternoon it's back to *work*. Do you think you can make it?"

"Well, what do I do at work? I mean, are there projects I start on right now, this afternoon?"

"We have to have a talk. It's a question of what you're interested in. After all, we hired *you*. You get to do your number, not ours. It's a question of fitting the project to the mind, not the mind to the project. We'll talk about it, kick it around. But not this afternoon. There's plenty of time. In a day or so, maybe tomorrow, next week, when it cools off."

"Christ, it's hot," one of the others said, "even in here." Juan sweated heavily. When the waitress came he ordered barbecued ribs and another, fourth, margarita. The four men ate glumly, grease on their hands and jaws.

"I don't know, I don't know. I don't know what they expect us to do on a day like this. The smog is even in the *halls*, did you see that?"

"Sears is having a sale on garden furniture, you want to go over and see it after lunch?"

"Christ, no."

They walked back in the hot sun, there was nothing to say. Juan looked forward, in a mild way, to being in his own office, with his own secretary. He had been there before with Jimmy; he had even brought Lorraine in (with her own badge, a mass of nervous giggles), and later she had picked up a couple of posters, and framed a drawing of her own for the walls. So his room was ready, decorated, with his graduate school notebooks, a bound copy of his newly finished dissertation, a new blotter. It seemed like it might be cooler there.

Once inside AXEL, the men separated, hardly able to manage a jocular good-bye. It's strange, Ramirez thought, I should stand the heat better than they do but I don't. That man had been right, there was smog in the halls.

Once inside his office Ramirez sat down, considered a minute and took off his shoes. Two months had given him the welcome habit of idleness, after five years of the hardest work, and he was in no hurry. He lay his head down on the desk—just for a minute—and flattened, obliquely, out of the corner of his eye, saw a rumpled sheet of children's note-book paper. CONGRATS, its message read, in big block print. DON'T FORGET YOU WORK FOR US TOO.

For the last three months on the first Tuesday of every month, Juan had made a trip down to the fifth basement level of the university library. In the musty half-dark (where in earlier days he had stood for hours waiting for girls; a hunter decked out with gun, shells, hat with ear flaps, decoys, and an erection as unwieldly as a five-corner suitcase), he hustled through the stacks, full of purpose but looking cool, and headed for the darkest possible cul-de-sac, where on three sides the municipal records of the major cities of Peru rose about him, all in crimson, all dusty—no one read these, no one opened these books, except once a month when Ramirez opened the volume marked 1926–27 and pulled out an envelope which contained a check made out to him for a hundred and twenty-five dollars from the United African Students of America. Once one of these checks had bounced, but his bank put it through again and it was OK. Ramirez usually waited until the last ten days of the month to deposit it, since even with his new job he and Lorraine never had any money, and this extra check simply tided them over. Ramirez knew it was pitifully low, but (they had explained to him) their country was short on money, and he wasn't doing anything to earn his check anyway. When he was cleared the check would go to two hundred automatically, and raises would come as his work increased. He was four hundred dollars into them. They had paid, essentially, for having his dissertation typed and bound.

For a full hour Ramirez lay with his head on the desk, looking at the note, past it, into it. Then he sat up, found some scissors, cut it in strips, went out in the hall where every ten feet or so slots in the wall which looked like mail drops were labeled CLASSIFIED WASTEBASKET. Secret papers were thrown in here, then shunted to a large machine somewhere in the building which made excelsior out of them, then taken away and burned. Since the handful of paper in his hand was already in scraps Ramirez had trouble getting it into the slot. He had just started, bending over, jamming the scraps in one at a time, when Jimmy Joyce walked past him toward another wing of the building. "I wouldn't do that," he said. "They check out everything in those wastebaskets. They like disorderly passions, any little note from anyone they save."

Ramirez went back to the office; his phone was ringing. When he picked it up there was silence, then a high, queer voice remarked, "No one gets money for nothing."

"Look," Ramirez said. "Look, I don't know about this stuff. I don't know what I'm supposed to do. . . ."

"Watch it. . . ."

"For *anyone*. How can I help if I don't even know what I'm doing here?"

"We are, you think, a cheap outfit. You may find out differently if you decide to leave our employ. Death has no price, Ramirez. It is the cheapest thing in the world."

"Look, *please*, I'm just trying to tell you . . ." But the phone was dead.

Once again when Ramirez went home there was no one there. At least twice a week lately Lorraine had been gone through the whole day, at the dentist, or with her mother, or at the nursery school cooperative. Or so she said. He poured himself a drink—only since he'd finished his dissertation had he allowed himself the luxury of hard liquor in the house—and thought about his life, his wife. The little room was clean, dustless; the children gone—next door, he supposed. How many times he'd come home in the past five years, terrified from an exam, or some professor's bad talk in a seminar, or in a fit about his cheap clothes, or his raw bones, or a lapse of time lost with his anonymous women;

and Lorraine had cured him, cheered him. Those years he had been in terror by habit (it is terrible if they make fun of your seminar papers), but now he was in trouble, bona fide trouble, and there was no one, not one person in the world he could talk to. He finished his drink, made another one. Then he called Edith. "Where's Lorraine, do you know?"

"Gee, the kids are over here, and Walter's downtown making the last arrangements, helping, do you know he was a third cook one summer? The third cook cuts up everything. I hate the thought of tonight. I guess Lorraine's mother is taking care of all the kids, yours and ours. Do you think she'll come here first or over there? Can you stand to talk to her? That women is too tough, I can't deal with her."

Ramirez hated the woman on this phone; simple, imperfect, the roughest, most primitive imitation of his wife. (But so was he.) "Don't you know where Lorraine is?"

"Isn't she at the dentist?"

"She told me she was *finished* with the dentist."

"Well, I don't know, Juan. All she told me was she'd be gone for the afternoon, and if she didn't get back in time for the dinner to go on without her and for us to deal with her mother, and she'd get down there later."

A terrible thought took hold of Ramirez. It came from the real world, the world they told you all the time was out there waiting. He heard that voice again, that high, queer voice.

"Edith, *was there anything wrong*? Did you notice anything wrong?"

"Just a minute, the kids are into something." When she came back, her voice was loud; he heard it in ghastly stereo through the phone and through the wall of their apartment. "What was it you said?"

"Just, was there anything . . . wrong? Did she sound funny or anything? Did she look funny?"

"What are you getting at?"

"Look, are the kids there with you?"

"Juan, I already *told* you."

"I'm coming to get them right now."

"No! No, they're in the bathtub, they're somewhere back there. Look, Juan, we're all getting ready to go. You have to take me down there. And the kids are all staying here at this house, and Lorraine's mother is taking care of them, and Lorraine said she'd meet us later.''

''She *said* she wouldn't be home?''

''Look! If you want to know about Lorraine, ask Lorraine, *I* don't know.''

Ramirez moved, the phone in his hand, to his front windows, and looked out. Some few children were playing in the dust under stunted trees. There was the lavender beauty of the Los Angeles sunset. Everything looked the same. His little garden needed watering.

''Did she, did she say how she planned on getting down there?''

Edith's voice was sullen.

''She said she'd be down, is all I know. And you have to drive me, and her mother will be here pretty soon. I have to get the kids out of the tub. I don't think you have to shave or anything, but we better be ready to leave in about twenty minutes.'' She hung up without saying good-bye.

What I want to know, Ramirez thought, is, is it anything? Is it? Would they do anything? Would that do that?

By the time he and Edith drove downtown it was dark. She had sat sullenly beside him, declining to talk, but in her presence he had felt less fear. It couldn't happen, not with her living right next door, not with her sitting next to him now. ''Where's Chinatown from the freeway?'' he said at length. ''I don't know where to get off.''

''It isn't new Chinatown, it's the old business center down on Ord Street. You take the Union Station off-ramp.''

The central part of the city they drove through was continually in a process of violent change. Just in front of him the old Spanish plaza had survived maybe a hundred years, its hedges cut amateurishly into the shapes of animals—that whole effort would stay for another hundred; it had made it on seniority and cuteness. Across the street the Old Plaza Church was still in business; Juan had gone to mass there a few times. But three blocks away the heart of the old city had been torn up thirty years before to make room for the Union Station. Now there were no more passenger trains and soon it would be torn down in turn. And all around them were the beginnings of minimal, tentative high-rise buildings, the twenty-storied structures that were all builders could trust to the shifting, quaking soil beneath. This downtown, just north of the gray stone business buildings which echoed the drabness of the East, would never be crowded, had never been so. There were always vacant lots, empty spaces; people could never decide what they liked best. Two blocks to the south and twenty-five years before Little Tokyo had been dismantled for the duration of the war. Now the Japanese were back with banks and banners. Up here the Mexicans and Chinese lived in a mutual disorder of frame houses and cheap restaurants; they could never raise the money to do anything serious.

Juan turned off the freeway. This area was as strange to him as it was to Edith; he had lived ten miles east of here, she'd lived five miles west. "Walter grew up right where the station is when he was a boy," she told him. "Did you know that? They lived in a basement, and up on the sidewalk they had two big stone lions to guard the door. They had a lot of rats. His mother used to chase them with a broom. And right around here is where they had the plague epidemic—in 1926, I think. They were all Chinese in here, and the policemen held hands all around in a human cordon and locked them up. That's what Walter says."

"How many people were killed?" Those germs, he thought, are supposed to live for twenty, fifty years. Bubonic plague is endemic in southern California. He'd studied the epidemic she talked about and knew it was only luck that it had stopped at all; knew about the rats that they catch downtown, and tag, and let go, and the tagged rat turns up three months later in some movie star's beach-house basement.

"Twenty-six, I think, or maybe twelve, not too many."

They turned into a narrow street of Chinese stores that could have been a movie set. Oriental music blared from a ratty record shop, and they passed a butcher's establishment which boasted a life-sized gold pig as sign and decoration.

"Park here, we'll walk the rest of the way." It was like Edith that while she looked sad enough to die, and while it was quite true that she hated the race she'd married into, she took a solid, square-footed academic interest in all this, a sort of tourist-guide pride. "That butcher shop," she said to him, "is quite good, really. I often come here to buy *lop chung* or *cha siu*.'' Even in his other pain Juan winced, was able to feel sorry for her.

Then they went into the restaurant and back twenty, forty, sixty years in time. They were both hugged, embraced, yelled at, shown to a table. He realized that the hosts were— as a kind of malicious joke—treating them as a couple; that they'd kidnaped Walter back to the Chinese for one night and liked the idea.

Ramirez and Edith were alone in a sea of a hundred or so Chinese. They sat down at a long table near the back of the restaurant, reached for the bottles of whiskey and buckets of ice which were strung like centerpieces down the middle of each banquet table. ''I complain a lot sometimes,'' Edith whispered to him. ''I admit it. But I had one of these on my wedding night. It can't help but mark a person.''

The restaurant, which ordinarily served Chinese families and a few knowledgeable tourists, was rigged tonight for a banquet. Tables had been pushed together, covered with good white cloths and a thousand little bowls and contrivances; soy containers, chopstick rests, wineglasses, whiskey glasses, teacups, teapots, dishes of nuts, salted plums, an infinity of paraphernalia. The dishes themselves were good figured porcelain; ''smuggled out of Red China,'' Edith said. ''They can't stand anything from Formosa. If it's there in Red China somewhere, they've got to get it over here.'' The windows and doors of the restaurant were shut to the summer night; everyone smoked. The walls, which were covered in exotic gold brocade wallpaper out of a World War II movie, began to fade out, disappear, in the thick air. ''Don't worry about talking,'' Edith said. ''I never talk to anyone. You know, down here is the only time I can understand why Walter drinks.''

Ramirez nodded.

''But you know, the thing about Walter is that really, *really*, he likes this stuff and hates the rest of his life. He's big down here. A college man. He knows things. They *like* him, you know?''

Through the smoke, Ramirez saw that Walter, at a distant table, could look completely Chinese when he wanted to, and was doing it now. He was charming, from a distance, a smiling, handsome, lecherous god of drunkenness. ''You know," Edith said, "tonight I don't have to worry about him. They'll put him in the car, and what he does before that, he'll do over *there*. It won't be my worry. Is it bad of me to say that? Or is it bad for them to do it? Are they *trying* to make him drunk? Do they know what it does to him?"

"I don't know," Ramirez said.

"The food will be neat," she said. He saw her in a dream, her features smoother, untroubled, detached. "They only serve this little bit of rice because they have all these other dishes they've been working on for days, all these show-pieces. You're not supposed to eat rice."

"Yes," he said.

"They're very sneaky, you know." She poured herself another drink. "This party is for Walter's cousin, sure, and for Walter partly, but it's also this secret celebration that everyone knows about and nobody says."

"What is that?"

"They always have a lot of trouble with their wives. In the old days they couldn't bring their women over because the country didn't want them *breeding* over here. Which is why there are so many half-breeds now. Walter's father *snatched* his mother out of a sweet high school in Pomona somewhere. And he was just a sinister Chinaman. Or you get these double families. A Chinese man would get a white woman—they couldn't even marry them in California until a few years ago, did you know that? Walter is illegitimate, at least that's what they say—but then when he could raise the money he'd bring in a Chinese girl with forged papers, or concealed in a box or something and then he'd marry *her*, and both women would be furious, but all the brothers and sisters would sort of grow up together someway."

"I wish I could say something," he said. "I'm getting drunk, I think. We're so inexperienced."

"We gave up everything just for one thing. We thought if we would learn everything we'd be all right."

"Yes, but, Edith,"—he laughed, he felt so strange— "you're *white*, you know that? Lorraine says you were born in Pasadena. You're not even Jewish. So what about that?"

"Irish white trash. My mother ate tea and toast three times a day when she grew up. They didn't even know enough to go out and buy a bunch of carrots. They didn't *know* anything.''

''What's the other party about?''

''*This party?* Oh. Well, they had a lot of trouble with their wives. China was our friend in the war. But now it's all Communist again, and it's like supply and demand, there still aren't nearly enough Chinese wives. You can't get them out. Especially the old guys never have anybody. And they're family men—well, look at all *this*! The Filipinos don't even seem to care, they've never been able to bring in their ladies, but they just buy their zoot suits and get a six-inch knife and some kind of whore with bleached-blond hair and they're OK.''

''But what about all this?''

''The thing the Chinese do now—they're such con men, excuse me, but they are—is they set up a marriage through a broker, in the old way, with a girl in Red China. Then they smuggle her out to Hong Kong or Macao. Then they get her some forged papers and bring her over here. And the thing is, everyone on the way knows she's a genuine Chinese girl, they all have gold teeth and wear rimless glasses, they just *look* like it. . . . ''

''The way cops can tell a wetback from a Mexican-American on the way up from San Diego.''

''Right! So everyone knows and they have to pay everyone off, it's a very elaborate chain of people, and these poor men, I mean, they don't make nearly enough money, end up paying thousands of dollars for a wife. Five thousand, Walter says now.''

''How does he know so much about it?''

''They *all* know about it. *I* know about it. They really do that stuff all the time. They're very sneaky, I have to say. Walter's grandfather built a fake *mermaid* back in the eighteen eighties. He put it in a cart with curtains and charged people money to see it. They paid him. They *paid* him!''

''Did someone bring over a wife?'' Ramirez looked around through the smoke. The din was appalling; he and Edith had been shouting at each other, but in nearly perfect privacy. All around them in groups, middle-aged men and women dressed in blue spoke to each other in raucous Chinese.

''Yes, Loy brought over his wife. It's really sad, he's in

his fifties and so is she, they got married when they were young in China and he came over to raise money to bring her over. And the price kept getting higher, and her kids— they're both dentists in Red China—wanted her to stay with the Communists, so she's a traitor, sort of, but Loy's been sending money for years . . . *I* don't know, he still hasn't paid everything off, there's been a fuss about that too, he still owes some money. . . . ''

"Where are they?"

"They're not sitting together, that would give it away. He's over there with his bachelor friends. You know, every Chinese house has about four extra men. They help with the dishes, they bring toys for the kids, they *look* so weird! I don't know where she is right now. Off with the ladies somewhere."

Edith waved her arm vaguely in the direction of a table which was exclusively occupied by Chinese women and a few children. The children were Americanized, sporty, clean; they laughed and made great lunges with their chopsticks across the table to where their favorite dishes were. Chinese children were loved, indulged; it seemed that way to Ramirez, who, for all the affection in his home, could never remember raising his voice or laughing when he ate. The women were different; foreigners. Their language— which listening hard, he could discern—was shrill, dissonant, their eyes blank and malicious, their teeth filled with gold. The gestures they used seemed random; not, somehow, to go with whatever it was they were saying. It was like looking at lunch in a school for the mentally retarded.

"She's over there somewhere," Edith said.

Ramirez was drunk. The noise of the banquet enveloped him, lay about him like a heavy overcoat. He worried, somewhere, about his wife, but he thought just now of the pressed duck, the lobster cantonese, the sweet heavy taste of everything they gave him to eat. The straight whiskey— not usually what you'd drink with food—was perfect with this meal, extreme, heavy, sweetish; he felt wonderful, he felt swell. A world of indulgence and unpunished pleasure opened in front of him, a world where meals like this turned up all the time.

"You have to just let them *do* it," he explained incoherently. "It's what they do well, and it doesn't hurt anybody."

She didn't say anything and it occurred to him that if she was used to anything it was drunken men. "I'm not drunk," he explained earnestly. "Honestly, I feel fine."

Edith looked sad but kept quiet. Then she said, "Look, they're bringing pompano wrapped in paper. It's one of the better things."

He stared at the little greasy sacks with concentration. It was as though he saw everything; the crowded restaurant, the people and their souls, the night outside (where a thin mist began to cool the summer night), the cars on the freeway on their way to the Music Center, the neon pagodas of New Chinatown beyond, the leaky troughs in back of the Sam Sing Butcher Shop stained with the blood of reluctant pigs.

A group of tourists strolled by the windows of the restaurant. Some put their foreheads up against the glass and stared curiously in, then beckoned to their friends to see the local celebration. There was a stir at the door, a little burst of applause, and Hollywood's most famous and only Chinese actress entered; old by now, and haggard, but still incredibly beautiful.

"Do you know who that woman is?" Edith said. "We have her mattress. She's . . ."

"I know," Ramirez said. Then he sat up straight, grabbed Edith's arm. "That man, by the window. Do you know him . . . ?"

"Is he somebody famous?"

"He's Jimmy Joyce, he's my boss."

"I know Jimmy Joyce, he went to my high school. He was one class behind me. He married a friend of mine, where is he?"

"Edith, where's Lorraine, where's Lorraine? Don't you know, can't you tell me?"

"Juan, you're very *suspicious*. I don't know, but if you'll forgive my saying so, I couldn't stand that. She . . . loves you, she's good to you." Edith's voice was loud, even for this place. A few Chinese women looked at her with disapproval. "She does everything you want, she puts up with you, you aren't exactly cheerful. . . ."

Ramirez grabbed her arm. "Tell me, tell me, what is it? You know something. You have to tell me." Behind his rage, his fear, the conventions of the soap opera ticked off; he talked in well-known phrases but they weren't his own.

"I don't know what you're talking about." She was in it with him, reciting a pastiche of all the movies they'd seen—sometimes together—on television.

"Look, this isn't a fake. I'm in trouble, real trouble."

"How do you mean?"

It was an automatic question with her, the would-be schoolteacher putting her everlasting *Be Specific* in the margin.

"But the other side of it is," Juan admitted, moving his head from side to side, peering at every corner of this big and smoky room, "maybe I'm not. Maybe they do that to everybody, maybe it's just a way they have."

"They do what to everybody?"

"I thought you might know something about it."

"Even if I did," and his guts tightened horribly when she said the words, "it wouldn't be right for me to say anything, because whatever it is is your business."

"I don't understand. I can't understand." And yet, in his anguish, his anxiety, he was taking morsels of pressed duck in plum sauce from an oblong dish which a considerate waiter had placed right by his plate. He was good with chopsticks because of his friendship with Walter, but not good enough to reach all the way across the table.

"I mean there's just that idea of not interfering with another person's life. We know each other so well because of how we live, that place. We have to be careful."

"Can I ask you, could you think of a reason why my boss might be down here?"

"Are you worried about *that*?"

"Yes."

"Well, this is Old Chinatown. It always gets tourists. And right next door is another restaurant where they do all the cooking in the front window. Oh God, look at Walter."

Walter Wong was extravagantly dancing a young Chinese girl up and down the narrow aisles. An old man at Edith's and Juan's table nudged Edith as if to say, There's life in Walter yet, even if you can't recognzie it. Edith's mouth pursed into a thin line, turned down at each corner.

"Edith, he's all right, he's having a good time."

"He did this on our wedding night. I was remembering that."

Juan looked once more around the room. How strange, he thought, that I am here. And the corollary of that was: How strange that this is here, in Los Angeles, in America, at the end of the fifties. He wanted to tell Edith that it was all right, that they were both on a trip, that this was just one minute of it. His fear, for the moment, was gone.

Then the noise which Walter and his dancing partner made with their bumpings against tables and their shrieks was superseded by a chorus of wails. Walter and the girl stopped, sat down suddenly, as if it were their dancing which caused it. In the far corner of the smoky room where old women sat to gossip about the rest of the party, a few people stood up.

The room became a theater, instantly silent, and in the instant, through the smoke, the guests saw a woman sitting up now, a waiter grasping her wet hair. Noodles clung to her head, slipped down her dress, poured from her nose. The pull on her hair kept her eyes open. After the instant of silence the din began again. One of the waiters moved the woman to the floor and began artificial respiration. Other old ladies with gold teeth shrieked out the story.

A Chinese man who sat across from Juan and Edith translated for them in perfect English. "They were watching your husband, your friend. He was so funny. The waiters had begun to bring around the noodles for the end of this part of the meal. But they didn't want to eat until everyone was served. Sum Oy got tired. She went to sleep. Maybe she drank too much. It is death by drowning. No one saw her. It is death by drowning."

"Who is it?" Edith asked.

"I know who it is," Juan said. "That man's wife."

"How do you know that?" the man asked him, and they all turned in their seats to find the husband. Loy, in a rigid pantomime of unknowingness, sat motionless in his chair, tears streaming down his face, his friends by his side, locking him in, waiting to find out if his wife was dead.

Some women got up and began to clear the tables, distractedly taking only one or two dishes at a time to the kitchen. Walter, not drunk now, was talking to some of the men who showed less grief and concern than a kind of immense business concentration.

"How'd you know it was his wife?" Edith asked Juan.

"He didn't pay." Juan got up, jostled through the aisles, was out the door and into the street. He ran to his car and looked in the back seat before he got in. He knew they watched him now and were planning something else; another ignominious, cruel joke. He drove ninety miles an hour on the freeway as he headed west to the beach, to reasonable civilization. She'll be there, you know, you're making a fool of yourself. They haven't asked me to do anything yet. I haven't let them down yet.

They wouldn't kill her but it was perfectly reasonable that they might take her away. The only way a cheap outfit might get important information they couldn't afford was to deal in atrocities, in terror. The size of the check, the shabbiness of his employers had fooled him. He thought of the high, queer voice: "Death is cheap."

"This is insane," Juan said out loud. His car passed the Mormon Temple, the Angel Moroni up on his tower, and beyond that somewhere the vast `comfortable buildings of UCLA. He turned off the freeway and was lost again in side streets. "This is crazy."

Ramirez pulled into his garage, ran across the dusty playing field, looked in the Wongs' window and saw his mother-in-law placidly reading. So he knew then Lorraine wasn't home. He went into his little house, brushed his teeth, got into his pajamas, and lay down in terror to wait for his wife.

VI

LET ME TELL YOU how I began to suspect Ramirez. Because I know it's silly, it's like delusions of grandeur. (And I admit I never suspected him that much, or I suspected and then forgot.) A rapist is a petty criminal and maybe I wanted to know a grand one. Or once you notice there's evil in the world you begin to look around for causes and effects. Or you could say I stopped looking at Ramirez as my friend's husband. Or that, in the same way that a baby looks at the whole world in terms of mommies and daddies and babies, I stopped looking at the whole world like everyone was a husband or a wife, or going to be one or just had been one.

Toward the end of November, Walter came home one night and said there was going to be a party given for the whole department of anthropology. I was pleased, naturally. I love parties and always have, and all my friends have; they're a microcosm of life, if you can stand that chat. It was also officially a nice thing, because Walter was always in a stew about being a failure in his work and I was generally terrified about being all by myself. We'd been in graduate school three years, and in the barracks two, but the closed, inscrutable nature of the university was such that we knew everyone where we lived and almost no one where we worked. This party might mean contacts for him, an elusive track to that success he fretted over (how do you get to be a successful anthropologist?) and maybe some new friends for me. It was not an exclusive party, far from it.

The whole world was invited but that made it better yet. It was planned for the day after Thanksgiving, and was meant to be a nostalgic throwback to summer vacation.

Lorraine and Juan were to come with us; that was hard. It had been a little over three months since she took her— God, her *lover*. Juan, even after the knife fight, could only do more of what he'd been doing. That is, he hit Lorraine, he prayed over her, he made a novena to keep her chaste, to *make* her chaste; he even cooked dinner a few times (pic-adillo which would have raised the dead, and Lorraine only said thank you). He did everything in short that he could do, and it wasn't nearly anything. Lorraine made up excuses, she borrowed our car or anyone else's, she'd leave on any pretext, and come home flowing with that sexual health which is so sweet to see if you've induced it yourself, so agonizing if you haven't.

All this, as you can imagine, made Ramirez very strange to be around. He was literally in a fight with himself then— I guess he wanted so much to kick her out and couldn't—or to make her do right to him and couldn't do that either— that instead of hitting her he took to hitting himself. He wore long-sleeved shirts to hide the bruises and nail marks on his arms (his nails, not hers), and he came to dinner one night with his hand balled up in bandages—he'd broken three fingers hitting the wall. An outsider would have thought he was having a genuine nervous breakdown, but Lorraine said it was a mark of his increasing sociability (for which she took the credit) that Juan had walked all the way across to the library, and taken the elevator down to the fifth base-ment to hit his hand against a sturdy cement bulkhead in-stead of doing it at home, which would have destroyed their house and ours, and maybe the whole building. She laughed when she said it, and went on to tell an outrageous anecdote about Steve, and you know, I laughed too.

Of course, Lorraine's laughing was a lot hysteria, she really *was* burning the candle at both ends, if you'll forgive the cliché. Her stomach might have been a pool of hot wax— and then the mind constructs a tedious but apt metaphor about wick-dipping and all the rest. To finish out the figure of speech, Ramirez and Steve weren't dumping the stuff of life into her, or losing days off their life for every orgasm like those Elizabethan folk. On the contrary, they built themselves up at her expense, they took—literally—her energy, her time, her love, her lust. It's quite possible to think of a medium-sized, unimaginative, untalented prick cheering up a great deal, bending and bowing at the ladies, slickening and fattening up after a few trips into Lorraine. And to think that after a while, Lorraine might lose a little of that unregenerate sense of life with which she was so generous.

You see the digressions it's taken before I even get to this party. Lorraine and Juan were going with us. It wasn't the ideal double date but it was OK.

The party was to be held about ten miles west of our house, by the beach at the end of Topanga Canyon. There was a little slough or gulch at the mouth of the canyon which was surrounded on three sides by trees and hills and vegetation, and the Pacific Ocean on the other. Topanga Canyon is a very old, steep, isolated firetrap which slits through the Santa Monica Mountains, providing a natural road from San Fernando Valley suburbia to the sea. It opens to the ocean just at Malibu; north you have movie-star houses and brothels with mirrors on the ceilings and call girls and call boys (generally exchange students who live in and screw for room and board). To the south is a whole beach culture of Hollywood hangers-on who by and large don't work much, but live with precarious charm. Inland from the gulch are all the hard-nosed, brush-clearing, rattlesnake-crazy, possum-hunting people of the canyon itself—men and women who live fifteen minutes from the city and pump their own water and shear their own sheep and pluck their own chickens just for style. So the people in the gulch are surrounded on three sides by people worth knowing (there are few places in Los Angeles where that can be said) and shored up on the fourth by the Pacific, which in spite of the tons of sewer filth poured into it each day, is clean, clean, and neat, and the fish swim there and you can catch them every time.

To get to where the party was we had to drive inland from the sea about an eighth of a mile downhill, over a rutted, unpaved road. Then we were enclosed by hills. It was maybe four-thirty when we got there, the autumn sun was still up and would be for an hour or two more. Everything was pink and filled with that neat, glowing sunset light.

About fifty cars were already parked in every conceivable

place it seemed, though twice as many would finally end up
in that geographical sink, and maybe a hundred or more
parked along the coast. A friend of mine once went to a
nightclub in the Sonoran Desert which he said was really
one solid city block of nightclubs out in the sand, and the
innards of the city block were a hundred or so cribs where
little Mexican whores, their mouths full of gold teeth,
worked their way through grade school. The party had the
same map, as it were—a dozen or so houses circling the
dusty yard, wide vacant lots, and little sinks and swamps
separating the houses themselves, but still the houses form-
ing a circle which made up the one big party. It was the
neatest party we'd ever been to, an apotheosis of everything
we thought was good: dancing, drinking, laughs. You could
tell beforehand it would be the best because it had been set
up that way—in its magnitude of conception it rivaled those
three-day pig-killing orgies in New Zealand. (You think, I
know, another housewife aggrandizing her little life, but
that party would turn out to have international significance,
and double-spaced accounts of it still rest in the out-of-date
files of several organizations in several countries. It pleased
me later to think that what were some of the most important
hours of my life got that kind of official attention.)

Most of the activity centered in one house and we headed
there, passing through giant bushes of geraniums and almost
impassable thickets of wild anise. Little branches and twigs
tore off and clung to our sweaters. We smelled like an herb
garden or a Mexican grocery store.

"Watch out for the snakes," Walter said.

"Oh, they don't have *snakes* here. . . ."

"They do," he said. "They had one in the driveway a
week ago. They have possums too. And a frog came in last
summer and electrocuted itself on a faulty wire while Marina Bokleman was studying." We looked at the ground but
found only that we were slogging through vast beds of nasturtiums, moist and aromatic; crushing flowers and leaves
into the swampy ground. A horse stood by the house we
wanted, and the front yard was one incredible morning-
glory vine, the walls covered, the electric wires leading to
the house all twined in blue blossoms. An abandoned car
out front, its tires flat, was covered with morning glories;
the fenders, bumpers, doors, windshield all bright, bright

blue, with an occasional demented orange nasturtium. And on the steering wheel, more morning glories.

About a hundred Blacks were already there at the party, many more men than women, all parasites of their social scientist betters, all grinning wolfishly and on the make. And a million anthropologists, I recognized some of them as Walter's friends. And I overheard a civil rights lawyer telling someone about a case. (I think lawyers are the dumbest people we meet in modern life, their cases are their little houses, right?—and their little activities as boring as hanging out the wash.) Lorraine was already peering forward and around in her nearsighted way and jumping up and down.

This was the first party since the knife fight and all that, and I knew she was hoping for Steve to show up, though Ramirez had threatened to kill him, naturally. We passed a group of scholar-musicians playing *sones* from Veracruz, passably done, the insane tempo slowed down enough so that each risqué word could be clearly sung by the group.

"What's your name?" Walter asked.

The leader smiled. "Los Tigres de la Sierra Madre." He was white, fat, Caucasian as they all were; faggish and anxious, eager to please.

"Crazy," Walter said. As we went on, they broke into the strains of "Cascabel" or the Rattlesnake.

"They stink," Ramirez said. "They shouldn't do what they're not good at."

Lorraine just looked at him, but I will say, she was the *kindest* cruel person I've ever known, and she didn't say a thing.

Then, as the boys went on talking and went into the house to get a drink, she clutched my arm, and pointed. A heavy, buxom girl was climbing with some agility up onto the roof of the house. She pulled at wires, she slipped, she crushed a lot of flowers into slime, but then she was on the roof and standing up and smiling. A little clutch of friends stood on each other's shoulders to hand her up a sandwich and a drink.

"She says she's staying there the whole party," someone said.

"How long will that be?"

But no one knew. The girl looked down, she smiled, she

waved, she opened her blouse. Her friends yelled at her to take it off, but she buttoned up again, and settled down to eat.

How can I tell you what it was all like? Some parties have to be nursed along and then explode into brief, feverish life. Some never make it, some make you want to die. Some are formal and you have to mind your manners. At most you talk and talk and all the time look for someone else to take you away and provide you with something nice, the something stupendous which is why you came in the first place, and never hardly ever find. And yet it's in our myths; we were kids when they sang "Some Enchanted Evening," and our mothers or fathers believed it all before us.

This party was a honeypot, so big and sweet, and mostly all outdoors. The four of us separated right away—Walter went off gleefully to get drunk—even I couldn't say anything at a function like this. Ramirez stood with his arms folded listening grimly again to Los Tigres de la Sierra Madre, his glasses reflecting the last rays of the sun. Lorraine ran off looking for Steve, but flirting every step of the way—I watched her for a while, literally batting her eyes, bending her thin bones into a perfect crescent bent *toward* whoever she was talking to, offering them thin breasts, thin pelvic bones, thin little depraved snatch, and then as they lurched forward, conversationally or otherwise, she straightened up, waving her hand at them straight from a bony shoulder, patting their clean-shaven cheeks, and cutting out.

Watching her I felt bad, at a hundred and twenty-five pounds there was no fun in the world for me, but then someone asked me to dance, a simple boy in a clean white shirt, and we went behind the house to a green meadow where a pretty good rock group played, and danced and danced. The grass—just like with those Kipling elephants—turned from slime to threads to dust, I moved from partner to partner and hardly had to talk at all.

I remember calling my mother twice that night, once to say we'd be late, and then to say she'd have to spend the night with the baby and plan on the next day too. But other than that our little group drank, we went out for hamburgers, we walked up once to the ocean but didn't like the way it looked, and came back. As we walked back in the dark through the flowers, the dust, the cars, we glanced sideways into a no-man's-land, yet another damp and pulpy meadow, where in the night the mist rose and white arms and legs flailed in the swampy grass like the souls (or bodies) of the damned. Five or six couples making it in that vacant lot. It was astounding to me, I stared and stumbled on the rutted road, and the boy in the white shirt (his name was Mike) took my arm and placed himself between me and that sight. You can see I had fallen in with good companions.

In the middle of the second day, the girl on the roof stripped to the waist and stood twirling in the sun, but by that time no one had the energy to look at her; she was no more than the mechanical man or cowboy on stilts that department stores hire at Christmas as a come-on. But this early that Mike chivalrously blocked my view of those flesh-pots, and I suppose I wish I could have hired him later, *worn* him the way some people wear patriotism or mother-hood to keep on blocking my view.

Late the first night it was too cold to dance outside, so we went to another house, decorated in straw mats and packing cases and African masks, the home of a Black athlete married to an Australian girl. Walter was there, his shirt gone, his body streaming sweat, his arms around some Black trying to dance with him. The Black was patient. "Oh, man," he kept saying, "oh, *man*." Walter danced around him for a while and then said that if no one would dance with him, he would show everyone and be a doormat. He went to lie across the entrance to the house, moaning. As he passed me he hugged me, by which is meant he laid his whole life, his whole weight, across my shoulders, and sagged. I looked at him politely and I believe he didn't recognize me. Then I went on dancing. Actually it was a pretty good evening. A couple of carloads of Okies (the ladies with heads full of tight pin curls which they never combed out) came in from the Venice slums, but the crowd had a lot of relative elegance. As I said, there were many of the people then in civil rights, not to speak of those dull explorers who would one day write up their field trips like a long postcard to Mom. Now it seems like every month I read a review of some book I'd hate to read about the natives of here or there, or someone else's kinship system or sexual mores, and there on the back covers are those simple-faced boys I danced with, all named Bill or Bob or Joe or Mike;

they've put in their time getting malaria in North Africa, peeing into prickly pear cactus, going down the Amazon and getting their testicles stung with those silly ants, all that, and now they're back to their classrooms, their reputations secure, their health intact if precarious. It's nice to make it.

I saw Lorraine in a corner with several men. If she hadn't been laughing, it would have looked like a pornographic movie. She was trying to sing along with the music, but one man kept stopping her mouth with kisses, another leaned over to kiss her stomach, and another tried to put his hand up her skirt, which was difficult, since her legs were keeping spirited time to the music. It was the kind of scene that could get her in trouble if not killed. (Ramirez threatened murder so often then that we didn't believe him, like those suicide people you ignore and ignore and then they're dead.) Mike and I went to look for Juan, to decoy him, if possible, to the farthest periphery of the party, but that's where he was anyway, talking to a balding French professor.

We danced until the sun came up, and I remember it was one of the best nights of my life, although there wasn't any flirtation for me and only small talk, but that's what I liked the best. About five in the morning people began to flake out; there was no question of anyone going home. We kicked at Walter a little where he lay stretched across the door and he got up, unbelievably, gummy-eyed and amenable. Lorraine was asleep in the corner with her admirers, all their mouths engagingly open, their faces innocent, their hands all over each other like a Chinese puzzle. We let them lay and trudged out, about fifteen of us, dead beat, to get something to eat. We passed Juan watching some Blacks play the bongos.

"Come with us, Juan," Walter said, but Ramirez said, in an almost parody Mexican accent, "I have to watch over my wife," and gestured with his head to the house. It would have been sad except that he looked so dopey in his glasses and his little pursey lips. "God, that guy is a drag," Walter said to Mike and the others, and we let him alone, drove up the coast for hamburgers in the morning, played tag in the cold sand against the wall of cold sea, then slept. I woke up to see Walter trying to skip stones in the surf, and wanted to tell him I loved him, but it certainly wasn't the time, and

I went back to sleep. How nice it was—if you're the lonely type, you know—to sleep with people on each side of you and some at the bottom and at the top, all snuggled together in the rolling sand, with the sun to keep you warm, and though we woke up feeling like shit, our heads filled with sand, our underwear gritty, each bone in our body aching, still it was the best sleep, the best sleep.

We went for more hamburgers and I called Mother.

"Can you do it another night?"

"For heaven's sake, you aren't coming *home*?"

But we got her to stay another night and said we'd be home the next morning.

Back at the party, the girl on the roof was swirling and waving, naked to the waist. We went in the house. It was kind of a gloomy scene, dark, most people still asleep, some talking, resting on the floor. There was a sour smell of cigarettes. Ramirez had stretched out on the floor along the baseboards. He looked cold.

That second day I saw in a haze of alcohol. (Don't get tired, there is no third day in this account.) People were stiff and sullen and gloomy, but there was more food and lots of liquor, and so many had stashed so much away that all you had to do was stroll fifty feet into the bushes to find a bottle or some pot. There was a lot of dancing, but of the dirty dance variety; the couples lolled against each other, drew apart, crashed together, frequently fell down.

The sun was hot that day. There were more cars, less flowers. The air was full of the sweetish, sickening smell of dead flowers. I found Juan again and tried to talk to him. "You know," I said, really thinking that he'd believe me, he *could* believe me if he would, "it's not that she doesn't love you. Why, Lorraine *loves* you. She never says a word against you. She's with you. She *is* with you." I still think there's some truth in all that shit, but he didn't. He could only be prissy. "You wouldn't understand," he kept saying, pursing his lips, and if I give sketchy dialogue, it's because, remembering, it makes me sad, and ashamed to write it down. He made me mad finally, I couldn't figure out why Lorraine did love him, if she did, and why she ever married him. I got up to leave, and the room tilted slightly. I remember it clearly because I saw Juan look at me sardonically. I danced a couple of times, but it made me a little sick and I went to look for Walter outside. It was very hot, and the scene had increased to a kind of bedlam, an intensity it never had the night before. I guess it was about three in the afternoon, say twenty-two hours after we had come. Things were turning pink again, but it was hot, hot. I looked out back, I looked by those fake Mexican musicians, I looked in all the bedrooms of three or four houses and scared some people, and then I went back to the first house.

I found Walter standing in a bower of morning glories, between the flowered car and the house. The blue of all those flowers reflected on his face, and so did the pink sun. He faced me, his eyes wide open, and I thought he recognized me when he saw me, but went on. He was doing it standing up to some little girl. Outside, and in the sun.

"You. You." And it was like a nightmare when you try to scream and can't. He listened to me, preoccupied, and didn't miss a stroke. "You're not even that drunk," I said, and it seemed to me that he slightly nodded.

What I did then was go out back beyond the flowers and the meadows to where a brackish creek flowed, and went to sleep. I couldn't think. I couldn't think. Because what I haven't made clear here is that I loved Walter Wong so much. And I loved him and I loved him. I slept a long time and woke up sick. I felt like something awful had happened and then I remembered. My life and marriage was gone; that whole perspective of mommies and daddies, husbands and wives was gone. Each person was lonely, evil, just waiting to do in his friend, his spouse. Because if I've talked about Walter's eccentric ways, his profanity and lust, that's because they make the better story. Walter took his turn every other morning to get up and get breakfast when we went to school, which is more than I can say of any man I knew before or since. He helped me fold the laundry, and there were afternoons; one time when we were driving, when I put my knees up on the dashboard and he said I was OK, and another time at home where we curled up on the bed and watched Gerald Heard, on our old six-inch television, tell us that it took two thousand muscles to move the tongue. I fixed some scrambled eggs. We loafed around the whole day. Walter was my *husband*, you know?

After I woke up everything looked very strange to me. All those bushes at once flattened out and became transpar-

ent green curtains, thin scrims I pushed through. I heard
the music coming in waves, first loud, then receding, though
I was walking straight back to the party. Maybe he doesn't
even know her, I thought. Why, he couldn't know her or
else they'd be more cool. But maybe he knows her so well
he doesn't have to be cool, and at the thought my stomach
clutched, my knees almost buckled, I covered my face with
my hands. I'm suffering, I thought, I'm really suffering. You
have to remember this was before most of the sixties trash-
talking about the evils of exclusivity, jealousy and posses-
siveness. When we were married then most of us tried to
be faithful even if we weren't. Walter had gone and taken
everything else with him. Because if you believe a set of
things and one of them is fraudulent, then chances are they
all are. (A theological friend of ours who you may recognize
later said that if there is a God then it's all true, the hosts
of cherubim, the souls in hell, Mary's assumption by a cart-
load of angels, and the devil is a snake and every snake a
devil. He exaggerates, but the principle is correct.) I walked
back and everything looked dim and evil. The woman sitting now on the roof, bare-breasted, her elbows on her
knees, staring bleakly into space, oh, she was evil. Those
Blacks came only to make fun of us and plan. Lorraine,
Lorraine was an evil laughing woman. Because that was the
thing, they didn't care; life wasn't a family at all but a sustained infinite pratfall, and the cool thing was to pull the
chair, while those over a hundred and twenty pounds were
the ones who sat confidently down and then fell, panties
showing, legs up, suffering and ridiculous, while the rest
giggled, tittered, hooted.

In the last minutes of twilight whites looked black, Blacks
disappeared. People danced slowly now. A boy asked me
to dance, and then another and another, they were the same
ones as the night before but hateful now and ugly. Then I
danced with some Blacks. I saw what they had in their
minds; Fuck for Civil Rights. I wished them vaporized or
in the gas chamber. They were so proud of their athletic
bodies, their strong brown chests, their insistent, sexual
style. I kept thinking of Black wives at home with children,
working to put these twits through school, and them copping
feels from white girls with twice their IQs and manners too
good to tell them to stop. I saw Lorraine dancing and then

I saw Mr. Goodman; he'd made it to the party and was talking to my husband, who looked *just the same*. I asked my partner, some anonymous Black, if we could go outside and he agreed right away, radically; ah, he probably thought, this . . . is . . . it.

We went into a side yard under a grape arbor, crowded with sweating forms. We were, in fact, safer and more chaste outside, because bright bare bulbs were strung across just over our heads, and everyone saw everyone. They all seemed to be having a good time; that's what they seemed to be having, I promise you.

Mr. Ramirez passed through the dancers, he was after someone, on to something. I broke away and followed after him. I wanted to talk to Juan, to say OK, you poor schmuck, now I know, now we are wretched and unloved together, have your prissy laugh, because now I know. Ramirez headed toward a crowd of gabbling exchange students; Nigerians in bright, wild, Biblical clothes, all talking simultaneously in their dumb language.

In point of fact I don't know their nation, but they spoke one of those languages that the university linguists exploited and shook and sifted out and fed into their computers. Linguists loved the idea of transformational syntax in those days, and figured they could find it in every language, but cheated and picked on the easy ones first. Twee was one, I remember, and Tagalog, so that in every literature class I ever took at that place, not to mention education courses or linguistics, there was a gratuitous contingent of Filipinos with great national costumes and terrible pockmarked faces, or beautiful Africans who recited their clicks and grunts and glottal stops into a tape recorder for a couple of hours a day and had the rest of their lives to wander around in the American dream.

Juan went up to this group of Africans, he tapped one on the shoulder, and without a word they disappeared behind the house. I followed them, I didn't care, and there, against a pastoral background, a veritable wall of ivy, I saw Juan and this guy in close conversation, conspiring. The Black saw me, I saw *him*. It was Ino, no! It was Ibo, one of Lorraine's Paris screws, the one with the tribal markings. I remembered him perfectly. I remembered the North African wool bonnet he brought when the baby was born. He was here, five thousand miles away. I stared at Ibo and waited. Ibo. It didn't even seem strange. My first and only thought was that Juan wanted to keep Lorraine, to insure her by setting up contracts with all her former men, and that being an orderly person he was working in more or less chronological progression. The thing is, Ibo recognized me. He gestured out, I'd say he kicked Juan, but I don't know. Juan stopped talking and turned toward me, a wide loony grin on his face.

"Edith, what is it? Is something wrong?" His companion tried to smile.

"I wanted to say, I had to say to you, I thought you might be interested in knowing that I had something interesting happen. . . ."

"This is my friend, Ibo—"

"I know. We met years ago. Hello, Ibo."

"I don't know you." Ibo smiled and adjusted his hat, his smile a carbon of Juan's.

"Oh, Ibo, you bought my baby a bonnet."

They looked at each other uncomprehendingly.

"Ibo is a common name in my tribe."

"And didn't you have a cousin or a brother? Didn't he go out with Lorraine too?"

"What is it you had to say, Edith? You know, you look dead beat. Walter had better take you home."

It was much more strange that Juan was solicitous than that Ibo didn't know me. Juan had never said a sentence like that in his life, to my knowledge. Ibo leaned back and looked African and out of it. He'd just lost his English.

It was their business and I left, and as I left they continued talking animatedly, cheerfully, with wide expansive gestures. I found Walter sleeping alone on a bare mattress on a front porch and asked him to take me home. We drove home, and he drove home Mother, and not until the next day, Sunday noon, did I start to cry. I cried maybe six days, *straight*, didn't cook, clean, talk or deal with the baby. Walter wanted me to see a shrink, and even my mother when she found out, intimated I was being a little overdramatic, but it was my life, and it was supposed to have been good.

I remembered Ramirez and Ibo in a week or so and asked Lorraine if she knew Ibo was in town, and she said she was almost sure he wasn't. Ramirez from then on was sweet to me—what a word for the man he was then—but he'd come by after class and we'd have these agonizing chats: he'd talk and then I would and then him. God knows who it was worse for. Lorraine joked about his crush on me, and Walter and I had our terrible, boring scenes for a while, but every time I saw Juan talking to a Black I wondered; it was like clipping notices out of the newspaper, and he did it often, he did it a lot. How did someone who didn't talk at all start doing that? And then when those missing monographs turned up in the physics library, and the university bemusedly dealt with its first scandal which didn't have to do with sex or grades—that was only a couple of weeks later, I—an almost certified crazy, a jealousy-crazed housewife who didn't trust anyone—suspected Ramirez.

VII

*T*HE MONDAY AFTER the Thanksgiving party Juan Ramirez made it in to work about ten. He had been working full time now, in the six weeks since he'd been cleared, but at AXEL, full time was only a figure of speech. Confident-appearing he announced his name into the recorder, nodded to the guards, arose in the elevator, but only halfway, and strolled down the Chemical and Biological Warfare halls to his office. Through open doors (Security didn't like them closed) his colleagues waved hello. Their feet, up on unused desks, were encased in new shoes (but only desert boots), their chinos new or freshly pressed. These men weren't rich and didn't hope to be; their wealth (precious after ten years of the hardest concentration) was in this sweet leisure; morning hours spent as their wives spent time, gossiping, drinking coffee, planning parties or trips to the beach. Now, at the beginning of their thirties, all their values turned upside down: at AXEL, the less work you did the better. Not only did idleness bespeak genius and the thinking life within, but fewer people were apt to be killed in the following decade. So the boys blinked happily in the warm winter sun which shone through the tinted glass of their picture windows, thought about volleyball or jogging, phoned up ticket agencies to see about concerts and plays, gazed significantly at their young secretaries, and noted with satisfaction that Ramirez was beginning to square up, that is to say, simmer down, that is to say, stop trying so hard.

Ramirez—after a quick look at his blotter—sat down and eased back into his chair. His secretary peered around the corner of the open door.

"Hello, you want some coffee? Or I'll tell you what, there's a new machine they've got down there—hot chocolate made with real milk. And you can throw some coffee cream in after it's made, and Peggy just went out for some marshmallows."

"You could get me some of that, please."

"Sure."

"You know what else is good?" Ramirez shyly revealed. "The next time Peggy goes out, tell her to get some stick cinnamon. You put a stick in the cup while you drink it. And you can use the same stick over and over."

The girl trotted off, her heels clicking efficiently, and reappeared almost immediately with his steaming cup.

"You know what I did? I ran down to the snack bar and asked them if they had any cinnamon sticks, and they didn't, but they had the powdered kind, so I just sprinkled a tiny bit on top. I didn't know if you'd want it stirred up or not, so I brought you a spoon. And I put in two of Peggy's marshmallows. You know what she's doing? She's charging them to office supplies, I said *why not*? She's ordering a whole carton, I guess they're going to deliver them tomorrow. Do you want anything to eat with that? The snack bar has that great fruit salad with vanilla ice cream and chopped pineapple and sour cream. It really *goes* with chocolate, I brought some down for Larry and Jerome down in Slavic Studies. They say it's pretty good, and not very fattening, really, because it's got all that fresh fruit."

"I had breakfast before I left."

"Oh, Mr. Ramirez, you should never do that. Doesn't your wife have children? She has enough to do. Besides, the snack bar is better, excuse me, but I'm sure, I just *know* it is. They all say so. Their eggs and hash browns aren't so good, they're just like everyone else's, but they fix the best *brunches*! And you can order things ahead, if you really like something, steak and kidney pie, or kippers, or every two weeks they have kedgeree!"

The girl stopped, put her hand to her hair. "I don't mean to sound so silly. But there are all sorts of good things. That's all I meant to say."

Juan smiled. "From now on I'll eat breakfast here and I'll let you surprise me. You can bring me anything you want."

"Oh, that's *wonderful*! I'm so glad."

"But I think I'd like to work now if that's all right."

"Of course. I'll bring you some more papers I think you'll like. Not too many, and not the long ones, the morning's too beautiful. Just a few, all right? And I want to say, I think it's wonderful that you have the discipline to work so hard."

She returned with a thin stack of monographs.

"Remember, don't leave these on your desk or even in a drawer. Give them back to me and I'll lock them in the safe. They're *very* important. Would you like another cup of chocolate?"

"Yes," said Ramirez, "please."

When she returned he was already reading.

"I forgot to tell you," she said softly, placing the chocolate at his elbow, "you have two messages. One from Mr. Goodman from the department of English at UCLA, he'd like to meet you for lunch, he has a class now and will call back at eleven-thirty; the other is from your wife, she called before you even got here this morning to say she misses you." The girl smiled at him with her whole body and soul, proud, she seemed to say, to work for a genius who had friends and a wife to call him up, and who consented to take brunch in the mornings.

Ramirez tacitly agreed with her. Thinking over his situation, he had gradually moved to a position—as the newscasters like to say—of cautious optimism. Lorraine had betrayed him this summer, that was true, but she assured him it was over. Since that Saturday morning he hadn't seen Rader once or even heard his name. (In fact, Lorraine had told him after Rader left that he'd only wanted to fight because of his rage at being rejected by her.) And the second job which Ramirez had spent so much worry on had so far been limited to a series of simple oral reports. He had relayed AXEL's floor plan and room-numbering system to a series of likable Africans who he met at various places on the UCLA campus. It was taking a long time and Ramirez hoped he might stretch out this simple assignment for a few more months. And the Chinese woman had died by accident. A freak accident.

The secretary went away and Ramirez began again to read. If his stomach and his well-being had been coddled and made happy before, now his starlike brain, his other soul, could feast upon a Sunday brunch of formulas and color illustrations, delicate little drawings of desiccated nerves.

The main work in CBW was of course in the horrendous diseases, the special effects. They had thought up a nerve gas that killed you in minutes; a tasteless, odorless gas that penetrated the ordinary mask—and the victim after a single sniff began to retch and soon drowned in his own vomit. If he were unlucky enough to be able to rip off his mask, death took maybe a half hour longer; he threw up until his guts came out his mouth.

But there were a hundred gentler alternatives, and Ramirez chose to read about those. They seemed to him—given that he was working for the government and all that—to serve the same purpose, and with no real harm done. One paper projected an entire weapons theory based upon the childhood diseases. An entire army down with the mumps would cuddle up in foxholes with woolen scarves wound from their stomachs to their knees for a month or so, especially if the invading germs were accompanied by a judicious sprinkling of propaganda leaflets. Or what about a new strain of whooping cough? The principle of guerrilla warfare would certainly suffer if the enemy army coughed a lot on night patrols.

Ramirez read with delight a monograph which happily combined germ warfare and whatever they called its psychological counterpart. "One thing you'll find out about AXEL," Jimmy Joyce had told him, "is that they encourage interdisciplinary work. If a political scientist has an idea about epidemics, they'll let him think it over and write a paper. If a mathematician wants to take a turn at traffic problems, why not? Of course, if a sociologist wants to work on rocket ships, ha ha, that's a little different. But even then, even *then*, why, we have people in the humanities who take our computer classes at night, although they . . . never . . . ah . . ."

The paper envisioned a psychological disorientation which

might only be accomplished if a basic law of nature (or biology) had been successfully violated. "I once asked a physician," the writer of the monograph confided, "what was the most horrible, the most disgusting, sight he had encountered in his years of practice in the medical profession. His answer was immediate and unequivocal. The teratoma, a benign tumor found within the womb, usually covered with a spray of weedy hair, and which, through one of nature's inexplicable quirks, takes the shape of one or another of the victim's appendages; a finger, perhaps, or a nose, an ear. These are perfectly recognizable as such, and perfectly thrilling in the implicit insult which they offer to the carrier; a distorted mirror which makes fun of its host, its mother-image, in the most effective possible way."

The technological trick, the author admitted, would be to find the virus which caused the teratoma, isolate it, control it, and render a woman's disease somehow "catchable" by men. But tricks were easy. It was the author's theory that a hairy little hand growing out of fighting men's stomachs (together with the secret, blood-knowledge that this was a woman's disease) would so demoralize the "self," that an entire army might be rendered useless, incapable of fighting. A finger, sore, sensitive, covered with wet, kelplike hair, pointing out of one's armpit, one's knee, could not for long be kept a secret. Stories would be told, retold, embroidered, in brothels, hospitals, around the hearth. And not a single life would be lost, except perhaps by suicide. "In a country preoccupied by face . . ." the writer concluded, and Ramirez reached for another publication.

Perhaps twenty papers a month came out of AXEL. Some were for in-house reading only, but the last one was cleared to leave the building, to be sent to Washington, to be read, perhaps, by the very highest Pentagon executives. Grants might be forthcoming, a score of graduate students in an eastern university put to work with little pots and dishes, thousands of slides, shelves within shelves in vast wall refrigerators—and someday, God forbid, of course, in some remote country, Africa would be best, of course, but the author was right in what he said about Orientals—and not a life lost.

The phone rang. Ramirez answered it, chocolate milk and marshmallow foam on his upper lip.

"Take this number down," a friendly voice advised him. "Number 3-D-A16-571. That first three is a roman numeral, III. OK. Deliver it on payday. Good-bye."

"What number?" cried Ramirez, who couldn't find a pencil. "What was that?"

"III-D-A16-571. Good-bye."

"Wait, I've got one now. . . ."

"III-D-A16-571. You are not very quick, Ramirez."

"Wait a minute. Who is this? How do I deliver a number? What payday?"

"You do not know the numbering systems of your own documents there? If it were not in our interests to keep you there, we would see you fired, Ramirez. In fact, even if you do *no* work for us, I would suppose that it is in our own interest to keep you there. They say you are a genius, did you know that? I very much like the phrase 'Did you know that?' when properly delivered. I have learned much of your language from the now old poetry and jazz records. We ordered them by mistake, but we learned to like them very much. There was one . . . 'Did you know that?/And Isolena's flaxen hair is the color of the mud at the bottom of Rathbegan Creek./Her teeth are crooked and yellow now and more like an old sickly dog's than a woman's/ . . .' ''

They were disconnected.

The phone rang again immediately and Ramirez picked up the phone.

"If you do not do as we ask," the voice continued, "we cannot get our money back. We have only one way to protect our reputation. You cannot laugh at our country or some others I might mention. We will take your wife and kill her. First we will shave her head and cut her up and also perform unspeakable acts. She will talk to you on the phone, as we have often seen on television. But we will not take any half hour with her, you can bet your boots on that. We will leave you the children to take care of."

"Didn't I talk to you before? How could you think of that, when you know Lorraine? She's not just my wife . . ."

"We have never talked. You insult me to imply that mine is an African accent. In fact I have absolutely *no* accent. I have checked it out on Johnnie, the first—and some say the best—AXEL computer. Once it said, 'Eh?' The next time it said I have no accent at all, none. You take the document, you bring it to the place. You leave it by your check, of course.''

"But I can't take *threes* out of the building!"

"Quite right, Ramirez. But that—as they say—is why they pay you. Why we pay you.''

"Why do you call on the phone? Isn't that dangerous?''

"A genius. So they say. Did you know that? This is not your phone, *cabrón*! This is not your wire. We are not your switchboard, *estúpido*. Do you think we sit in the lobby? Someday, after several small wars, our country will have money and know-how. We will not have to rely on second-class fools. We will have the best that money will buy. But maybe by that time, you also will be better, and maybe you will be the best that money can buy. I do not wish to be unkind, Ramirez.''

This time, when Ramirez hung up, there was no insistent answering ring. Payday was today. And he'd looked forward to the money. When he realized he'd thought of the check first and then his wife, he simply sighed. What the priests said was true. One bad act leads to another. In fact, the first bad act was the one that counted, since it put you out of the state of grace. After that everything was tainted; you became, for all intents and purposes, a swine.

The phone rang again and Ramirez answered, his voice trembling over the first hello.

"Ramirez, is that you? Goodman here. I'm out here in Santa Monica at the library, and I thought we might have lunch.''

"I've got a lot of papers to go through.''

"You've got to have lunch no matter how busy you are. And I want to talk to you.''

"Is anything wrong?''

"No! No, it's just, I haven't seen you for a while, and you've got to eat anyway.''

Goodman didn't sound right. The thought crossed Ramirez's mind that maybe the phone was on its other, sinister, wire.

"Where are you phoning from anyway?''

"What?''

"Where are you phoning from!''

"From the pay phone in the basement of the Santa Monica library next to the rare book room. They have a couple of eighteenth-century pamphlets that even the Clark and Huntington don't have. So they sent me over to get them Xeroxed. They should have them on microfilm at our place but they don't. They even gave me money, so I wouldn't have to spend my own. But not enough, so we'll have to eat cheap.''

Ramirez's mind, used to language which only described things and otherwise kept its place, groped through what was being said. Was this what they meant when they said they didn't mean to be unkind? Xerox, photostating, microfilm. Microdots? Perhaps that was the way. He could never get a bulky III document out of the building. Or if he did it would be missed during the security check at night. What about a tiny camera? Would they notice that? How did people *do* these things? Ramirez had heard that there were two-way mirrors throughout the building, that guards amused themselves by watching the late-night embraces of the thinkers and their youthful assistants, before they hustled across the street to the Surf Rider for refreshments and a room. There was talk that the bar and bedrooms of the Surf Rider itself were mirrored and bugged. You could get a camera in, but they'd see you taking a picture. How did people do these things?

"Ramirez," Goodman said, "I have something to ask you."

"What?"

"Where are *you* phoning from?"

Ramirez and Goodman sat across from each other on hard seats of a local Mexican restaurant, drinking watery beer.

"You said you wanted to talk to me."

Goodman's eyes, always so excited and happy when he spun his learned yarns or made charts about the Renaissance or finally thought he glimpsed—just for a minute—the real reason for the decline of eighteenth-century drama (though it always turned out to be a false alarm), seemed dull and edgy.

"I *am* talking to you. You haven't said a thing since we got here. Tell me, Ramirez, do you feel better since you got the degree? The famous degree? Did it change your life? Will it change your life? I console myself that it hasn't, that it won't. I don't see how it can. You're a family man already, you've got your wife, your little cozy ways, your kids. Nothing's going to change that. Even with a brand-new wife, even if you did that whole thing they do when they get a degree, you'd still have the same kids. You're a Family Man, right? And you want to take care of it. I meant that whole thing you've got.''

I knew, Ramirez thought, I knew it all along. But how long has he been in on it? Was it Goodman who thought up getting to me through Lorraine? Did he put them on to me in the first place? It was him on the phone too. I should have recognized those sentences.

''I'm not a family man, and you know what? I think I may never be. I'll tell you the truth, I like *it* but I don't like them. The dumb ones drive you nuts—when Sarah was out here making her move for me she'd do anything, I'd screw her in any position, in any way, shape or form. She'd do it, she'd do anything. But she'd make those awful cheesecakes. You'd have to eat them. That was a worse perversion than anything *I* could think up, even after reading Clelland and the Earl of Rochester. Then she'd say she loved me, and *wait*, with those reproachful goiterish eyes fixed upon me even in my sleep. I couldn't eat, I couldn't sleep. She'd leave her underwear around. It was always a little dirty even when she'd just washed it. Debby was a little better but at the time I couldn't think so. Maybe I still don't think so. An IQ so high they couldn't chart it, a lifetime membership in Mensa Society. She wanted to share my life, you know? She wanted to share my interest in the eighteenth century. Couldn't she see I *hated* the eighteenth century? And what if she found out about the drama before I did? She was, I admit it, a passionate woman. A very passionate woman. She put brains to what she was doing. And she cooked better. But she'd bring those cookies around to the office—offhand, right?''

Goodman looked out of the window, his eyes watering a little from the chilies he'd been eating without bothering to take out the seeds. ''The thing is, Ramirez, they're all a little bit dirty. They don't wash or something. They're all a little bit dirty.''

''What is it you're telling me? What is it you want me to say? What is it you want me to know?''

''Do you like my shirt? This is a sublime shirt. The eighteenth century would have been better off, I often think, without the concept of the sublime. One of my students brought me this, an elderly number, she's somewhere in her late thirties. The thing I like best about the eighteenth century is their idea about marriage, that it's only for the clods who can't avoid it, that to be trapped in marriage is to be a fool before you start. But that it isn't a tragic matter.'' Goodman's gray eyes shyly searched Ramirez's face. ''They always laughed about it. You see that in all the comedies. To be married was to know beforehand that you'd be a . . . cuckold, that to be married was to be an animal, to affirm your animal nature, to give in to it, and since you'd done that, your troubles didn't deserve to be tragedy, just comedy, Ramirez. You know?''

''I don't see it that way. People like you see it that way, or you wouldn't be what you are. Lorraine and I have had some trouble but it's over now. My family, my wife, means everything to me.'' Ramirez began to breathe heavily, his long legs, feeling numb to him, began to move uncontrollably under the table. He pressed them together.

''It's all a question of values. In the eighteenth century friendship was the highest value. You were loyal to your friends. They stayed with you for a lifetime. They didn't think about marriage. There's a poem that King carried around with him all the time, and in this poem the guy says if he has to have women around he'd like one as a companion in later years, somebody to *visit*. So even women became friends. And . . . since they were friends you could trust them. You were right to trust them.''

Adults, Ramirez thought. We're in the adult world right now. Goodman's owlish pedantic face had more to do with comic books, with long afternoons spent in some gray, neglected bedroom bent over on the edge of the bed reading comic books. He knew that even if Goodman were the veritable head of whatever organization he worked for, that he (Ramirez) could stop this genteel terror simply by asking him how his dissertation was coming. Some things were more important to Goodman than treason, death.

''I never knew you very well, Goodman. In fact, now that I think about it, I hardly know you at all. People think when they go to the same parties, they know each other.''

''I think,'' Goodman said fearfully, ''I like to think, that our stations in life, our common interests, entitle us to be friends.''

"What common interests?" Ramirez reached for his pocket, and only later knew that he reached for the knife of his youth; a knife, in fact, that he had never carried in his youth, trying as he had to be American, but which, in spite of that, he carried now and knew how to use (with minimum practice, with *no* practice).

"It's true I'm in the humanities and you are a scientist, that I'm a Jew with the prerequisite overprotective mother and you are Mexican, with, I imagine, an overprotective— what I mean to say is, don't you think we're in school to learn? Look around you, Ramirez. Don't you see we finally have school the way we want it? High school, ooh, ooh? In grammar school I moved around a lot. Nobody talked to me. I had glasses too. Now you know what I have? Cronies. My time in the office is time redeemed. But it's redeemed through books. To learn something is to be free. This is my best life, Ramirez. And maybe it was for you too. The Mexican boy marries the prom queen. You couldn't have done that without school."

"I'll kill you," Ramirez muttered, but Goodman went on.

"The thing is, how do we know what's best for us?"

"You're not my friend."

"I am," Goodman said, trembling. "I like to think I am your friend. That's why I'm here."

"You son of a bitch."

"Listen. If it's one thing I notice it's cars. Actually that's not true. I notice all those things. It was the one normal thing I could talk about when I was young. Like what awful things they put in hamburger, you know? Or how old the cottage cheese already is when you buy it? I *notice* cars, Ramirez, I can't help it. Maybe you don't?" Goodman pulled at the collar of his shirt. "I have to say this. I feel like I have to, someone has to . . ."

"Ramirez jumped to his feet. Their rickety table fell over. Shredded lettuce caught in spilled beer foamed audibly, then was silent.

"Say it."

"I only meant, like when that car careened around the corner between the dorms and Vets Housing last week and almost killed the kid . . ."

Ramirez pulled Goodman to his feet. Goodman still had

to tilt his head back to see Ramirez, "Well, I couldn't help but notice . . ."

Ramirez's arm flashed clumsily out, clipped Goodman at the side of the eye. Then he let his friend go, and was gone.

Goodman, childishly covering his eyes, began to cry with embarrassment and pain by himself in the restaurant. "A nineteen fifty-three bright green Chevy convertible, top up. Who do you think that *is*? Don't you see anything?"

When Ramirez got back to the office the phone was ringing. He picked it up and heard electric mocking silence.

"It's no good trying to threaten me," Ramirez told whoever it was. "You can send anyone you want. I can tell you what happens. I just get angry, then I don't care what happens."

"I only remind you that payday is tonight. You must bring out the publication and get it to the library by midnight. You bring it out of the building tonight, you take it back tomorrow morning."

"How do I do it?"

"Simply take it out!"

The light on Ramirez's phone began to flash. "They know about us! A light's flashing here."

"Put me on hold, son of a sheep."

"Hold?" Ramirez said, bewildered. "Hold what?"

His secretary appeared at the door. "I hope you don't mind, sir, I answered your other line. It's your wife. Shall I have her call back?"

"No." He cleared his throat, looked down into his phone. "I have to hang up now, good-bye."

"Listen," his wife said, "I want to know, what is that syrupy-voiced sweety like?"

He wondered if his secretary was still on the line.

"She's very nice," he said. "Where are you now?"

"I'm at Edith's. She's crying around over here. That's why I'm calling. It seems we have Walter in a squalid still life out on the couch. His hand is *trailing*, palm up along the—I must include this, Edith dear—the disgracefully dusty living room floor. Juan, he's drunk and he has an exam tomorrow at eight. His German. He says he's willing to sober up if only he can have some tea. He says coffee makes him sick and he won't drink it. So Edith, she's crying right here, says can you possibly bring out some of that tea they have down there?''

"Why don't they, why doesn't . . . she . . . go to the store?" I'm going mad, he thought. He looked around his office filled with all his possessions, his books, his own blotter, a picture of his mother in a double frame, and on the other side, his laughing wife and handsome kids. Outside, the ocean sparkled with wholesome familiarity, but it had nothing to do with him.

"But you said the others take tea bags and things all the time! They don't have any *money* over here, what do you think? I told Edith, well, I told her before, in fact I *gave* her all the tea we had a couple of weeks ago, so you can bring some for us too."

"Can . . . you lend . . . her . . . a dollar?"

Lorraine's voice became impatient. "My dear. If we had it, I'd lend it. But you don't get paid until Thursday. I have two dollars and thirty-seven cents. I don't begrudge my friends, but what about my babies? In fact, I was going to ask you to smuggle out some cream, but Edith, here, is in hysterics . . ."

Surely, dully, he could hear genuine hysterics. He saw Lorraine taking the receiver from her ear, holding it over her supine, sodden neighbor, to transmit the authentic sound.

"Juan, Edith says they can't go on like this forever. She says she'll leave him if he doesn't get a degree sometime and go out and get a job like other people."

"What does he say?"

"He says she's a whiner, that she's never had it so good, that he's never asked her to go out and work."

"What does she say to that?"

"She says, she's never asked him to work either, but he's going to have to do something pretty quick. That's why they need these tea bags, see? You could do a good turn for a friend."

He wondered, for an instant, just how funny Lorraine thought this was, and then, to top off his overloaded grid of emotions, felt not just distaste for his heartless wife, and fear for her welfare, but that nagging admiration for her threadbare ability to turn dross into gold. His success, his danger, notwithstanding—she still spent her afternoons within cardboard walls with a drunk and a domestic martyr as her closest associates.

"Walter says he'll really try and sober up?"

"He swears it, and Edith says there's no wine in the house anywhere—he drank it all before he offered to stop—and that he really knows his German. So. If you could bring the tea."

"All right. All right."

"A lot of it. And one lemon."

"All right."

"He says he'll do it, Edith. So that's *one* thing, right? 'If Winter comes, can Spring be far behind?' " Lorraine giggled and Ramirez gently replaced the receiver without saying good-bye.

He went into the outer office. "I think I'm going to the library for a while. Can you just say I'm gone? Not say where I am?"

"Sure. There's a lot of magazines down at the library, did you know that? They take everything. People can read whatever they want. There's *The Realist* and the *Minority of One* if you hold those political views, or those things by H. L. Hunt if you hold the other kind, there's all the magazines on fashion for the girls, and adventure magazines for the men, and science, *of course*, and all the learned journals, but nobody reads those, and magazines on surfing and skiing and motorboating and skin diving . . ."

"Well, I think I'll go down there for a while."

"And, Mr. Ramirez, you never seem to take advantage of our recreational facilities. There's bowling, there's organized tennis on the weekend, a free film once a week—you could bring your wife to that, there's, oh my gosh, running on the beach, a lot of the boys have won trophies, and they have uniforms, and a lot of the kids just work out in the summer to keep in shape, they all run on the beach, I even do that. The Surf Rider rents us lockers or you can use the pool there. . . ."

Ramirez rushed out as her voice followed after: "Oh, just everything!"

Once outside in the hall he paused. His mental state recalled his old days in the deepest stacks; his face flushed dark vermilion, his large hands trembled. He decided to go to his car to see once again just how much the guards noticed as one passed through the lobby on the way out. He walked purposefully down the one flight of stairs, poised, frightened, like an enormous bird, then opened the unmarked door. The lobby by now seemed to him the most ordinary place imaginable. He tried to look at it with the eyes of a spy. It was a sunny enclosed space about twenty feet square; a corner room, glassed in on two sides. Enormous potted trees stood along one wall, and on the wall to the left the police sat behind their counter. Three men were generally on duty; one at the door to the inner building with a tape recorder, one to type up employees' voices and names, one to answer the phone in case the switchboard had an emergency call. All three men were armed. Right now the lobby was full of visitors, labeled and noisy, who had just returned from lunch and were waiting for their in-office escort to take them inside. After pronouncing his name for the guards Juan slowed his steps to a comic shuffle and made his way across the lobby as slowly as possible. Behind him he heard another voice snap out a name, then watched as some one of his go-getter colleagues moved adroitly in front of him, through the collected visitors and out the door. He wore a suit and carried a briefcase. A briefcase! The obvious occurred to Ramirez but he rejected it. They couldn't just let you carry a briefcase in and out. "I feel kind of dizzy all of a sudden," he mumbled to the guard at the phone. "I'm just going to sit down for a while."

"Sure you're OK, Mr. Ramirez? Want me to get you some water or something?"

"No, I'll just rest a minute." He heavily sat on one of the vinyl couches opposite the police counter and through half-shut eyes watched the unmarked door into the building. The visitors were taken in and he waited in conspicuous silence, the guards constrained in their own conversations because of his foreign presence, Ramirez in fear that they would know something was up, or phone Jimmy Joyce, or pay even more special attention to him tonight. The guards finally disregarded him and began somewhat amateurishly to string a wire across the floor (in answer to his timorous question, explaining that they wanted to hook up a camera in the corner to photograph each employee as he left, and that each photo would in turn be matched up or synchronized with the taped name—or voice print as they insisted on calling it—of the person who had just passed through the door). The telephone and typewriter guards were down on their knees now, affable enough, glad to explain their own research project. The tape recorder guard remained at his post.

"We've had a lot of trouble the last six months or so," the telephone guard explained from his hands and knees. "Not a *lot*, but two or three guys, you know? Well, we petitioned the Air Force for closed-circuit television to cover the lobby at all times. But they didn't want to spend the money, and thinking it over we were just as glad, because then they might not need us any more. I mean a couple of hired guns, *maybe*, but not good professional police protection. So then we thought of a movie camera, and they sprang for a used one, just as a trial procedure. We rented one, but it took another guard to work the thing, and the men inside didn't like it. So now Jack here thought up the idea of a camera. The guy on the door presses the tape recorder button and the camera lever by remote control at the same time."

"Don't you think they'll mind the flashbulbs?" Ramirez asked.

"What flashbulbs?"

"Well, I don't know much about photography, but don't you need a flashbulb to take a picture indoors?"

The guards looked at each other.

"We can't use flashbulbs," the man at the door said.

"We'll just use the other kind," the typewriter guard said.

"I don't think it will work," Ramirez said from the couch. "It will be underexposed. You don't have enough light in here."

The telephone guard looked ready to cry. "Isn't there a special kind of film you can buy? Infrared or something?"

"That's for night photography, this is daytime in here. It has to be dark for infrared to work, I think."

Ramirez realized that the three of them were looking at him with hatred. "Of course," he said hastily, "you have to try everything out. Why, ordinary film might work in here just fine. That's how you find out things anyway, isn't it? I mean, that's the whole spirit of scientific research. . . ."

As the guards stared silently at him the door swung open,

a sport-shirted employee carrying an attaché case muttered his name into the machine, slouched carelessly through the lobby and was gone.

"I guess I'm bothering you fellows," Ramirez said with difficulty. "I'll let you get on with your work." Against their silence he got up and almost ran to the door outside. He had seen what he came for. Perhaps because of the camera check upstairs, they let you leave the building with a briefcase.

Ramirez stopped at the pay phone in the parking lot and phoned the Wongs. "Tell my wife," he said to Edith, in what he conceived to be a joking style, "that if I'm going to perform this big heist I'll have to be a little late. In fact, I'll eat dinner here in town."

"What big heist?" Edith asked.

Ramirez hesitated. "The tea bags?" he said.

"Oh, that. OK, I'll tell her." She hung up.

Ramirez thumbed through the phone book to find the address of a nearby leather store. It struck him that he was extremely pleased to have an excuse to be buying a new briefcase, in the way that a new widow might, through her sorrow, be glad of the chance to buy a new black dress. There was a luggage shop only three blocks away, and because of his AXEL card he would be able to get a discount. He chose an enormous briefcase in a soft dark brown, the best leather. It would be the nicest thing he owned.

"You can go out of town with that," the salesman said.

"Yes," Ramirez promptly answered, though he wasn't too sure what the man meant.

Years later, when the seams on the briefcase were torn through, the leather flattened, dampened, and used as a part of a bed for starting seeds, Ramirez would remember and tell his friends how it was. "That afternoon, walking back after I bought the case, I was happy. I wasn't *very* happy, but until that year I had never been happy at all. It was an unaccustomed feeling. I couldn't recognize it. I thought I was afraid, my heart was pounding and I was out of breath. Instead of going right back into the building I walked past AXEL and down on the Santa Monica Pier. I ordered a drink to calm my nerves in a little bar at the end of the pier and watched the sun set on the ocean. I had the idea I might be killed, but I wasn't watching the end of the day on purpose. It was the first time in years that I'd looked around me. The world was so beautiful. I noticed that while I should have been scared to death I was smiling. On the way back I remember just breathing the cool air. No, the things that happened during that time weren't bad at all.''

It took every bit of discipline Ramirez had learned in East Side parochial schools to walk from the pier across Ocean Avenue and back into the AXEL building. But as he walked, he hugged his briefcase to his chest and reached inside the paper bag to feel the leather.

In the lobby he stopped at the counter and smiled at the guards. ''I'm going to be working a little late tonight,'' he said. Two of them didn't look up from their work, but the man bent over the typewriter sourly nodded. Ramirez didn't have to worry about working late; AXEL kept its doors open twenty-four hours a day (except for Christmas) against the possibility of sudden inspiration of one of its geniuses. The parking lot was almost as full by night as by day, since many thinkers preferred as a matter of course to work without the sounds of secretaries and typewriters, as well as taking advantage of the added luxury of spending their nights away from their wives and children. ''It generally happens,'' Jimmy Joyce had told Ramirez, ''that a guy screws his secretary or an assistant until his brains fall out. He buys her lunches and little presents, he gets her a raise—but it can only be a small one—and they run up a hell of a bill at the Surf Rider. So to save money—and also by the time he's banged her a couple of times on the desk or she's talked about an abortion on the company phone, he's afraid he's going to be fired—they get married. He buys a big house maybe in the Valley but probably in a good neighborhood like the Palisades or Malibu. He thinks he's going to save money. His wife quits work and has a kid who cries all the time, so he can't stand to go home. Besides, he can only think around young pretty girls. He bangs his new assistant, he starts running up another big bill at the Surf Rider. His wife divorces him, he marries his new assistant, and so on. The head of the Astro-Dynamics Department went through four of those in little less than ten years.''

Whatever the reasons, the building wasn't lonely when Ramirez returned to his office. He saw several people he recognized, either from school or from his earlier Preclearance work. He nodded to them, they nodded back.

Once in his office he went through the rest of the publications which his secretary had brought for him this morning and took copious notes. They were far along here at AXEL, he could see they did good work, but Jimmy Joyce had been right; they had been keeping secrets from him that he already knew, and in many cases he knew more than they did. The evening passed pleasantly. Ramirez, who had been too nervous to eat dinner, was able to drink two more large cups of hot chocolate made the way his secretary had shown him earlier that morning. He saw a cozy future with many nights like this, like the university only better, better.

During graduate school, night classes had run from seven to ten, and Ramirez, walking home almost a mile across the enormous campus, had made it a point (even allowing for an occasional peep into another apartment) to always be home by eleven. Accordingly, at ten o'clock he took his briefcase into the Chemical and Biological Warfare coffee room, his heart pounding suddenly, irregularly, as he began, again, to hustle. The room—a tiny cubicle perhaps five feet square—was deserted. He reached with nerveless clumsy hands into packages of tea bags, dropping one handful, then two, into the depths of his case. They made a thin noise like insects. He hesitated, then took two more packages and emptied the entire contents in with the rest. That should make two hundred or so bags, enough, he thought, for a dozen of Walter's drunks and some left over for himself and his wife. He picked up a handful of sugar envelopes and threw them in too. He jerked open the tiny refrigerator, found two uncut lemons and threw them in, also two envelopes of instant hot chocolate; through his panic he thought he might want to have some when he got home. He turned to go, then remembered that Lorraine wanted some cream. He cursed in Spanish; his neck and upper lip began to sweat, but it seemed preferable to be caught by armed AXEL guards than to see Lorraine's face become detached, exasperated. He looked around the room, focused on the cream dispenser. It was a stainless steel cylindrical device the size of a large pumpkin, suspended by a thick stem. If someone wanted cream he held his cup underneath the cylinder, tapped a lever, and a dollop of cream dropped from underneath into the cup. It was the kind of machine that ordinarily pleased Ramirez because it was associated with restaurants, bright lights, clean waitresses, American bustle, a whole other life. Tonight he looked at it and groaned. In haste he put his huge brown hands on either side of it and lifted, but it was securely screwed to the counter. Then he frantically tapped the lever. Cream splashed on the counter, over on his suit, and spattered his glasses. He frantically daubed at them and his field of vision from then on was washed in cream, he saw the rest of his project through a fog. Ramirez paused for a minute, breathing heavily, and considered leaving with what he had. Then he remembered and once again opened up the tiny refrigerator. Two pints of cream, still tightly closed, remained from the day. He grabbed them both and jammed them in on top of the various miniature envelopes, shut his case and hurried back to his office.

Once there he began to grin, not from relief but for the benefit of hidden cameras. Earlier in the day he had removed the document he was supposed to steal from the security file and placed it among the papers his secretary had given him, then locked the whole stack into his own desk. This had been a (perhaps futile) attempt to elude the cameras, since more people were at work, and Ramirez's theory had been that they wouldn't take pictures of a man going through his own files during the day. The night was something else. They might be bored, or curious, or simply want to chart employee interest for a graph which would be sent to Washington to gather dust (until somebody, somewhere realized that this particular document was missing now, and here was a picture of the greasy stealer himself).

Ramirez walked, slightly bent over, across to his desk and sat down, his briefcase beside him. He shuffled through his stack of documents, found the one he was supposed to take and picked it up, covering it from the outside with the work on childhood diseases. For some moments, still grinning, he hunched over, pretending to read. If they had a camera placed just behind his back—which would be an ideal place, certainly—well, too bad. He leaned further over, and in a schoolboy gesture, half-covered the top of the page with his curved fingers. So he grinned, and pretended to read. Time passed, and he should be home by eleven. Ramirez took off his watch, laid it on the edge of his desk, then awkwardly knocked it off. He grabbed the documents and fell to his knees under the desk. "Where is that watch?" he said loudly to himself, "It's my father's. I'll be in trouble if I lose it." He knocked the watch a little further under the desk, then pulled the briefcase in underneath with him. OK, hurry up, he thought. Doubled up between drawers and the typewriter compartment he pulled out handfuls of tea bags, tried laying the document flat against the bottom of the case, discovered that that way it would be bent when he brought it back in the morning, and so stood it straight up and stacked all his little envelopes on either side of it. The pints of cream he set in opposite corners. Then he closed the case, pushed it back out to its position by the chair, picked up his watch. "Ah, there it is," he said. He clambered out, sat down for an instant, reached underneath, picked up the other document, laid it on the desk in front of him. "I guess I'd better be getting home," he said aloud, and then realized that AXEL might not be too happy about hiring someone who compulsively talked to himself. He grabbed his brief-case and left.

At the door to the lobby he paused, said his name into the taping machine, looked around. The same guards were on duty, looking sour and drawn, waiting for their graveyard shift relief. "Did you ever get the camera hooked up?" Ramirez asked, but no one answered him. He walked pur-posefully toward the outside, tripped halfway across the room on the wire and fell heavily. The clasp on his case snapped; teabags and papers spilled over the floor. For a stunned moment the company police regarded him, then they began to laugh. They giggled, they howled, they struck their thighs, they leaned weakly against the wall.

"He's so *smart*," one of them began.

"He knows all that stuff," the man on the tape machine said. "Think what they pay him!"

"Infrared!" the telephone man remarked, and tears ran down his cheeks.

Ramirez sat on the floor, his head in his hands.

"Here, buddy," one of them said, "I'll help you up. I knew you guys *took* things," he staggered with mirth, "but this is ridiculous! He's got *cream* in there, you guys!"

The telephone man could laugh no more. He gave a long quivering sigh and laid his head on his machine.

Ramirez watched while the guard crammed everything back in the case, everything.

"I couldn't remember, I don't think they told me in the security briefing," he said, his voice quavering. "Is it all right to take III's out of the building?"

"Overnight, sure. If you take them out over twenty-four hours you have to sign for them. But you've got a clearance."

"They clear them, all right," the guard on the tape machine said. "But do they clear them for kleptomania?"

Weak-kneed, Ramirez left. Maybe it was a test, he thought. Or maybe they just didn't know that about the documents! If that were true, his job, his life, would be so easy! He dropped off the document at the rendezvous and was home by five minutes after eleven. Lorraine was over at the Wongs'. The three of them lay across the bed, propped up on pillows watching the news. Walter was drunk but not extravagantly so.

"I brought you everything," Ramirez said, "but I got caught. My new briefcase fell open in the lobby and everything came out."

"I got caught taking some cream cheese from a supermarket when I was an undergraduate," Edith said. "They wouldn't let me come back."

"I got caught in Paris with a bunch of books," Lorraine said. "I cried a lot and they said they wouldn't turn me in. I had a whole other book under my blouse they never found."

"I got caught stealing a dashboard from a city dump," Walter muttered.

"A *dashboard*!" Lorraine breathed.

"Yeah."

Ramirez stood and watched them, his briefcase still in his hand. "Come on, you guys," Edith said, "move over." She patted the empty slot on the bed and he scrounched down among them to watch the news.

VIII

AFTER THANKSGIVING I knew for the first time what everyone else meant when they talked about their domestic troubles. Walter complained about his eggs, he complained about the messiness of the house (what pretensions for a cardboard slip), he complained that my studies took up too much time, and that I was spoiling and/or neglecting the kid. Up to my neck in culturally approved indignation, I officially announced that I would never screw him again (he was only using me as a whore, right?). If he complained about the house I ostentatiously cleaned it from top to bottom, taking care to leave a runny dab of Jell-O on his chair, or a long hair by his toothbrush. I smiled at him in front of company, kept my voice carefully down in our nightly arguments, so that to the neighbors they sounded like the monologues of a madman. I cried and cried, and couldn't think, as they say, of a way out. The truth was, of course, that after as little as six days of this, Walter became measurably more amiable, even brought me presents—packets of yellow notebook paper—and took to reading stories again at night to little China. We were in yet another stage of comic-book living; the Profligate Chinese Dagwood, and his cold and vicious Anglo-Saxon wife.

Walter stayed late at school, coming home at a quarter of seven at night instead of spending gamey drunken recriminating afternoons with me. He retreated into his studies, and at eleven-fifteen at night, when, before, he had looked up from his language cards with surprise, noticed me in the room after three hours, and cheerfully said hello, how are you, how was the kid today, how's school—all this small talk his inscrutable idea of erotic foreplay—well, now I was left without this daily fifteen minutes of conversation, this weekly hour and forty-five minutes which, after all, was the social cement of our marriage. Now he got up, stretched, lumbered over to look out the window, maybe opened the door and sniffed the fresh damp air, then said, "Coming to bed?" I'd go shower and get ready and he'd be asleep. I hated him now, but in the approved way of a lady who's been done wrong; I was prepared to be violated, nightly, and hate him for it, and he deprived me even of that.

And I who knew nothing about pleasure, who had never wanted anyone in my life, began immediately to be tormented by the flesh. I dreamed of my professors, fusty old men who in my dreams took off my blouse in the Student Union, or exposed themselves beside their podiums. For ten days I dreamed of television personalities, of the man who sat in front of me in my Renaissance class, of a fat public defender I'd always detested—and at that last I rebelled, or revolted, told Walter about my dreams, and said as long as we were going to stay married, which seemed to be the consensus of his relatives, of mine, and even of ourselves, that he might screw me every once in a while, even though I hated it; it was too depressing all around if he didn't. Well, he actually said he was too old to be doing it all the time, and that he was having trouble narrowing down his dissertation topic. (Which he was, trying to trace vowel changes in a language which wasn't even written down, and where all the vowels sounded like grunts anyway, and the transcriptions depended on the vagaries of anthropological maniacs. Walter spent hours staring at photographs of some brand of native who lived their lives in trees, painted white, gazing into the scientific camera. What did they say? What were their vowels? How did they say *tree bark*? How did the natives just up the way say *tree bark*?) He said it made him impotent just to think about it, and in other circumstances I might have believed him, but remembering that wall of morning glories, and that odor which couldn't be called flowery *at all*, well, I didn't. Walter was more depressed than I; let me say I think he might not have remembered what he did, and only been made conscious of it later by my recriminations, the congratulations of his friends, the coy looks of the lady (she was, it turned out, interested in city planning; a pale redhead who wore glasses), and a tough lecture on being a Chinese *mensch* by his father. Walter tended to black out when he drank.

Whatever our situation, there was no question that Walter was in it too, and our misery increased. After ten days of chastity we went through an evening of amazing sexual gymnastics, but doing it to a lady whose face is spongy with weeping isn't much fun. Afterwards, crying, I asked him, well, was it as good as with that woman? He said, no, not by a long shot. For two solid weeks I fed him awful dinners and wouldn't leave the house; he went out alone and when he returned I'd ask him if he'd had a nice time, to which he'd say yes, or no, depending on either how he felt toward me, or, I guess, if he'd had one. He drank less, studied more, and, as I said, went as long as he could without carrying on.

Why didn't I leave, or why didn't he? Because we were a misfortune, organically part of it; it was what was to be expected. It would have been like asking a leukemia victim to drain out all his old blood and find some new. We were married forever and life was a piece of shit. That our marriage had taken this wrong turn was just a particularly ugly detour on a road that no one had thought was very scenic anyway.

On days I didn't go to school I spent my mornings cleaning up, making phone calls, then gave China a frugal lunch, put her out to play, and lay down on the bed to cry until Walter came home. He spent his days in the library studying. All day in the Graduate Reading Room close to the roof, he studied; he had his own cubicle and leaned nose first into it like a horse in his stall. At the end of the day, sweating, hot, he'd pack up his little cards with the speckled probable vowel changes, cram them into a paper bag and head for home. He'd open the door into darkness, the baby at this hour in a corner six inches away from our six-inch TV, ruining her eyes, and I, a supine, tear-swollen heap on the bed. When Walter came in, I'd get up wordless and go to the kitchen to fix him a plain and tasteless dinner; wordless he'd eat it. Not a word about his work, my tears, the weather, the kid. A nap for Walter while I did the dishes, then he'd unpack his cards on the kitchen table for another few hours of fruitless work while I lay down again to watch television or to sob.

The days I went to school were different.

Events, when they occurred in our lives, were sharp, close together. The trouble is, they hardly ever occurred. We weren't used to measuring time by events—years passed before the Ramirez marriage went under, ours went under. In fact, the real events which marked off our lives came every five months or so when semesters began and ended. Now, in the seventies, I can't imagine any student caring for the little rituals of scholastic life. I can't imagine that they care about running for classes (which as supercilious graduate students we supervised), or the quiet fiendish pleasure when for the first time as a reader you sit down after dinner with a bright overhead light and a stack of hopeful papers and you grade instead of—as in all your life—being graded. No one cares now about being a teaching assistant and looking at your first class and loving them so much, wanting to tell them *everything*, not just the structure of a poem, but to wake up! Look at the world, we told them, and in the established tradition of teachers and parents everywhere, don't do as we do, do as we'd like.

"I don't know what it was about those days," Jorge Alphonse told me when he blew in recently from his job teaching medievalism to kids in the Midwest. "We were all desperate in one way or another, but I look back on those days with such nostalgia. I'm *happier* now, I know that. . . ."

At about this same time (that is, in this semester), it dawned on me and my soulmate in studies, Mr. Goodman, that our couple of years of hard work and heavy reading in the English department (work at once random and terribly difficult) were going, maybe, to pay off. Professors said hello to us in the halls; we'd been complimented on a couple of papers. The girls in the office knew our names. Next year we would take the PhD qualifying exams which would decide our future for us. Goodman had doubts about the academic life. (Me, never. For me it was first a desperate tunnel dug out of rock with fingers and broken knives in hopeful preparation for a prison break which might never come, and later a homey Garden of Eden where I rested on the grass all day and drank coffee with friends.) But whatever it was, there it was, opening up.

Just after Thanksgiving we had midterms as usual. I was taking two graduate classes and did well in them, but the real politics and stress had to do with undergraduate classes Mr. Goodman and I were reading for, that is, correcting other people's endless midterms. If we did well, ingratiated ourselves with whatever professor we worked for, got in our grades promptly (being sure they followed a reasonable curve), didn't precipitate a rash of complaints, we stood, within another semester, to become teaching assistants with an office to sit in, and a measurably better chance at finally getting the PhD—if we wanted it.

I read midterms for one large class—American Literature, the second half—and noticed that Ottoline Joyce was in there. Her blue book wasn't bad so I gave her an A; I'd known her since Thomas Starr King Junior High and it was the least I could do, I would have expected the same from her. I came to class the day they gave the blue books back, my swollen eyes hidden behind dark glasses. (One of my small consolations was that I'd been paid a little over the minimum wage for my hours of crying in the past few days.)

The professors generally liked to have the reader right there in class when they gave back exams as a kind of ritual scapegoat to throw to irate students in case there had been a real fuck-up. To my profound relief the mutters and rustlings never even came near the danger point as three hundred students came face to face with an infinitesimal part of their destiny. (Let me say we managed to hardly ever flunk a young man, thus doing our part to keep them out of the draft. In those days that was the practical extent of our political commitment. But enough of us felt that way to probably save some lives.) OK. Ottoline came up afterward giggling insanely. She hadn't even studied that much, she said. Jimmy would be pleased, or at least mollified; he was always after her to quit school and stay home and take care of their big house and be a grown-up hostess.

As I said, I'd known Ot for years, and Jimmy was a year behind me all through high school. In fact I think I went out with him then a couple of times, and Lorraine says she did too, but she says that about everybody. I do remember wearing his club jacket for two consecutive Wednesdays. Ot never knew him except to say hi to until her first year in college; she quit right away to marry him. At least I think that's how it was. Everyone I know continually loses track of old infant acquaintances and finds them again, loses them, and so on. Except for glimpses and chance encounters, I hadn't seen either one of them for maybe five years. (On the other hand, Mr. Goodman, who shouldn't have known either one of them, had taken an extension course in photography with Jimmy, and was currently taking out a friend of Ot's little sister.)

Jimmy had taken what we'd all considered to be a wrong turn in college—majored in business administration and right afterwards gone over to AXEL without a single skill except how to run things. As a result the Joyces had a big house out in the cliffs above Malibu, he made forty thousand a year to our four, and Ottoline was wearing real pearls over her cashmere sweater. But such is the strength of those goofy values of the mind that I felt a little sorry for her; she had no *purpose* to her life. Ot and I had lunch; she obliged me by saying she had no purpose to her life and felt all at loose ends. (The subject of ladies being useful to their kids never came up, naturally.) We had lunch the following Monday and Wednesday and fell into being school friends again. She talked of parties at her house but didn't invite me; people often hesitated because of Walter. I mean, without being disloyal, if you wanted one kind of party you invited Walter, and if you didn't, then you didn't. But Jimmy and Juan worked at the same place, and there was a general feeling we'd all get together soon. Ot had known Lorraine since junior high or maybe grade school and was a little put off by her; again, if you like that style (I do) you like it, but a lot of people think it's a pain in the neck.

I mentioned to Ot one day that I'd seen Jimmy down in Chinatown around the beginning of the semester and she became profoundly agitated. She knew he couldn't be down there by himself, they went everywhere together. But if it really was him, was he there with anybody? After seven years of marriage, she was convinced he was in love with his secretary, she didn't know what to do, she was crazy about him. She *knew* he really couldn't be unfaithful to her. He worked late maybe two or three nights a week but she called him every hour and a half. Actually, that wasn't quite it, he hated for her to call him at work, and had given word to the night switchboard to not relay any calls to his office.

But he called *her* two or three times a night. Meanwhile she had a sixty-five-thousand-dollar house with the ocean down there at the bottom of the cliff someplace, and a Mexican maid and two kids. And she told me she really liked Jimmy's mouth. "Even after all those years," she said, "I really like to look at his lower lip. Isn't that something?"

Mr. Goodman came down to the house to visit one morning right after the anthro party carrying sacks of doughnuts from the hut and paper cups of coffee. He wanted to talk to me privately, he said, so we left the house and walked to the far end of a dusty playing field which the vets used sometimes for a seedy Saturday morning of football. Goodman was in a funk.

He'd taken his mother, he said, out to dinner for her birthday. (Mrs. Goodman figured strongly in many of our myths. She washed oranges and apples in soap and water, besides a golden host of other eccentricities.) We always knew each other's childhood histories, polished, the way they get, by repeated telling; in fact, as I've already said, we all got to be enormous symbols for something; selected collections of exaggerated behavior. But the strange thing is, people in our world consistently lived up to their cardboard projections instead of refuting them. Later, when Mr. Goodman had his degree and was going to marry a nice girl, his mother advised him to wait seven years, the way Jacob did in the Bible. And another colleague of ours, a specialist in the American Romantics and famed for his sweet tooth—in his case it was a veritable bridge, a denture—saw to it (when he finally became a Doctor of Philosophy and married for the second time) that the bride's parents included a chocolate layer in the wedding cake, just for him.

Anyway, Mr. Goodman had taken his dear old mother out to dinner for her birthday. They'd gone to some kind of Polynesian establishment, very expensive. He estimated that it had cost him four, maybe five days' salary. The dinner had gone all right—except his mother hadn't eaten anything, not knowing whether it had been properly washed—and as they left, winding their way through dark anterooms where tropical fishes sported in lighted tanks and like that, Mr. Goodman had felt a distinct sense of well-being.

"Then I saw Steve Rader," Goodman said. "He had his arm around this girl. I couldn't see her, she was looking at the fish.

Mother recognized him and went up to say hello. Then I saw he had this girl's skirt up in back. They were doing it right there in Trader Vic's! I grabbed Mother away. I know she saw them, but she didn't believe the evidence of her senses, like in Book I of *The Faerie Queene*, you know? I looked back at them and it was Juan's wife he had there with him.''

I told him I knew all about it, but Mr. Goodman was upset. "You *know* it and nobody's doing anything? I mean a party is one thing, but this is really . . . a disgrace. We're all responsible."

"Why not tell him?" I dully said. I wondered if he knew about Walter and me.

"Doesn't he know already? He certainly saw them that night at the party."

"People can know," I said bitterly, "and not know. Come on, Mr. Goodman, why don't you tell him?"

Mr. Goodman came back a couple of days later with a cut forehead and a sore arm. "You know?" he said, as we walked down to Campbell's Bookstore with the baby to get some paperbacks, "I think he knows. But you know? I'm glad I did it. I'll probably never have a chance at that kind of experience again. You know, Edith, I really wasn't afraid, and I can see now a little more about the nature of violence, and why the eighteenth century feared it, along with love. Wit really is a stable, social quality. Even its hostility is tightly controlled, put to a social use. Poets who engaged in a battle of wits considered themselves equals. When they really wanted to insult someone in the eighteenth century, they hired ruffians to beat him up. He was beneath the dignity of any kind of duel, you know? Violence and lust are right up there together, aren't they? But the only way to know it is to find it out yourself." He lectured for twelve blocks or so, huffing toward the end because he had to carry the baby on the way back. I nodded dumbly, you could embroider it any way you wanted to; all I knew was that it hurt.

We had been having an amazing winter of good weather, and all around us people appeared to be enjoying themselves; their skin tightened up as it tanned, even the badly nourished women in our little covens began to glow with ersatz health. Two weeks after that awful party Walter glumly drove the baby and me (and, naturally, Lorraine's kids) to the beach; we took little Davey's crib and carried it across what seemed like miles of endless sand. Walter, thanks to his race, always had a tan, but I was in agony about my white, soft, tapioca-like skin. And we were in poor bathing suits, and poor Davey was a sort of evil-smelling, wistful, piggy thing who didn't own a bathing suit at all. Deeply tanned teenagers glanced at us and looked away—how did they *do* it, how did they know without trying what we were years trying to learn? It does no good to say that Virginia Woolf had trouble with clothes all her life— that's exactly what I mean. Look how she died. It didn't matter that those brown kids didn't know any theory of Australian language, that they never read any eighteenth-century novels. Looking at old photographs I can't as readily see the difference between us and our mindless neighbors on the beach, but at the time it was there. Davey wore his diaper into the water, waddled back waterlogged, then sat in the sand, then shit in his wet sandy diaper; I had more diapers but had forgot a bag for the dirty ones. And as I changed him, beet red from the embarrassment you feel that no one's looking at you because they simply can't bear to look at you, and had no place then to put the old diaper, too out of it even then to let him go nude, so put on another diaper so that he could follow the same cycle, well, it seemed to me once again that there was no fun in life for us, that the clear patchwork of ocean was there all right but not for us, that other people lay on the glittery sand but that it only got in *our* bathing suits. I lay on my stomach, miserable and self-conscious, watching China boss Jennifer around while Davey dozed filthy and content in his heavy crib. Walter swam far out for hours, and later coming home gritty in the car, I discovered I had the worst sunburn of my life, from the back of my neck to the soles of my feet. In my current martyrish style I'd oiled up the kids and forgotten myself. Well, what else.

It's an ill wind that blows no good. Walter and I were supposed to go to Chinatown for dinner with his family, and for once I didn't have to go. I put old China, fresh-washed and as rosy as a persimmon, to bed, showered with pain, allowed Walter to douse my back with vinegar and take my temperature. It was a hundred and two. Oh, I knew how I looked! Hangdog and two-toned, it was more than I could bear. He reluctantly offered to stay home with me; I vivaciously urged him to go. For that day we'd both heroically done more than enough. He couldn't tough out any more, and after some civil amenities, he left.

I watched him drive away, bearded and red-eyed, hunched balefully over the wheel of that old Chrysler. My husband. I left the door open; the air for once was soft and neutral, a caress on the skin, but also pretty enough to see, with that antique California clearness you might associate with clear white wine, or more prosaic and even better, a clear glass of greenish, warm, Mexican beer, soft, boy, and pleasant. For the first time in two whole weeks, deceived woman and all, I felt pretty good without even knowing why. In fact, the moment it crossed my mind I was shocked, in a way, and left the door open where I'd been leaning, and walked over to the couch and lay down to cry. I'd forgotten about my sunburn and jumped up in a hurry. I went into the kitchen for a beer—all in this beautiful, warm-winter half-light—looked in at my little girl, thought she really wasn't too bad, she looked good, she looked like those beach kids I'd seen that afternoon. I went out to our little living room again, Walter's Chinese silk kimono brushing not too unpleasantly against my blistering shoulders and thighs. No, I wasn't going to cry, I felt all right. I lay down on the bed, carefully this time, on my stomach, and watched television for about two hours. Then the machine, as it always did, overheated and went out. We had a semijoking agreement with the Ramirezes next door that if a program stopped on our set within fifteen minutes of its end we could watch the end on their set, and I considered if it were worthwhile going over; my back by this time was stiff and unbearably inflamed. When I got up everything went black and I waited in some anticipation to faint. I never had, but the prospect looked good. More to keep my precarious sense of well-being than anything else, I decided to go over, the habit of crying whenever I found myself alone was strong by now.

The Ramirez house most of the time was much like ours, that is, I tell about the fights and all those scandals, which along with ours and all the others in the barracks added up to something splendid and cacophonous. But five out of seven nights they did as we all did, Lorraine set up her paints on the kitchen table, turned on the same terrible overhead light that Walter used to illuminate his language cards, and worked, a nice Jewish intellectual lady, her glasses sliding down her narrow, aristocratic nose, her tongue bruised between her teeth. In the living room Juan sat in an occasional chair, a kind of lantern rigged up right by his head, either a heavy book in his lap or a pad of yellow paper where in his spidery beautiful handwriting, he worked out (correctly) one abstruse formula after another. Now that he'd gotten his degree he read (mostly out of the liturgy of the mass, or the early mystics), but the principle of quiet hard work was the same. So you see, when I go on about scandals and fights, "hosing and fucking" (as Lorraine herself once called it, describing her endless adventures with the foreigners of the world), I leave out the most important. We're probably more the result of those monastic, fanatic hours than our drunken highlights.

I went next door in my bathrobe and knocked. Juan answered. I hadn't thought of the possibility Lorraine wouldn't be home, although she never was any more. But it wasn't so bad, Juan and I were friends and more, almost relatives by now. "Turn on your television," I said, "quick." He did and we stood in front of it for the last five minutes of Perry Mason. When it was over Juan asked me to sit down and have a beer. "I can't," I said, "I can never sit or lie down again," and with the characteristic lack of modesty of a sunburn victim lifted my kimono in back. "My God," he said.

"And wait until you see this!" I showed him my violet shoulder blade. "Oh, Edith," he said. "Is there something I can do?" It struck me funny, I don't know why, two grotesque losers in such a position, such a conversation. I couldn't stop laughing, and I got him laughing too. I let him wet me down with cold vinegar, and I should be able to work up some erotic description about folds beneath the buttocks or something, but the truth is as he dabbed me with cold cotton from the back of my neck and the soles of my feet, I couldn't stop laughing, while he groaned and told me how awful I looked.

When he was finished, he asked if he could get me some tea.

"It would be nice."

"Where is Walter?"

"He's with his family, it's our night down there."

"They're nice people."

I couldn't say yes to that in good faith. High style, yes; nice, not necessarily. But I couldn't say where's Lorraine, either.

"Where's Lorraine?"

"She's out. With her family."

Well, a lie.

He was standing in his little kitchen, about eight feet away from me, waiting for the water to boil. He took two ceramic goblets out of the cupboard, and put some Constant Comment tea in the bottom of each. Then he put back the tea. I watched him. It was quiet, qui—et. Something began to fold up and around me; a big black crescent cloud, who I was and what; a black magic, but I could see it. With my sunburn and all, that fluggy misery of the past two weeks and all my life had been gone. I was scrubbed, rubbed clean, but when it showed signs of coming back, oh . . .

Juan knew I watched him, and in the yellow overhead light turned around. The circles under his eyes were damp and blue, the black crescent was there for him too, palpable, *rotating*, planetary; inevitable for him too. Behind his glasses I saw his eyes, maybe looked at Juan for the first time, kind eyes, not staring, focused on *me*. He didn't move, or talk or jitter around. He let me see how he felt, and the dumb animal misery was gone, for me, and I'd guess, for him, replaced in theatrical Grauman's Chinese fashion by four-star pain, a pain for ourselves and for the whole world, but there we were, and fixing tea. Tears began to roll out of my eyes, I couldn't talk. He said, looking at me, and past me to the darkened living room decorated by his wife, and behind him to where his own two children lay asleep, and not to blame, "It's all right Edith, it's all right."

"It's *not*. It's just, it's just . . ." I sat down to weep in earnest, and hurt my sunburn. "Oh my *God*," I said. He watched, not moving, and I jumped up to leave.

"I have some sherry," he said. "If you'd rather have that."

"OK."

"And there's some cake."

"Yeah."

Now when I try to remember what we said, I can't. We sat in yellow light gobbling up sweet cake, when that ran out we found some canned *baba au rhum*, and drank a whole bottle of sherry, then finished with more tea. We talked carefully. My mind was drunk, feverish, I was conscious of speaking in parallel sentences, and felt that he did the same, heard it. We talked of love, the nature of love, the battle that love is, the peace that it should be.

"Some people," he said, "think that it is like a rainstorm or an earthquake, or an act of God," and high and feverish as I was I thought of that rape, "but I think we will find that it is like an artichoke, that only by diligent effort can we get to the—"

"—the heart of the matter," I finished.

"Yes," he said, "and then it is gone." Again we sat, like stones on a collector's shelf, and smiled at each other mindlessly, endlessly.

"I have to go home."

He got right up, staring still, breathing high in his chest. When I try to think what he looked like then I can't remember, his old face had melted off like wax, but his new one wasn't there yet; he had a shifty look, dishonest, opaque, and yet his eyes were *there*, not flinching or sliding away at all. I suppose you can guess.

He walked me to the door.

"Thank you," I said.

"It was nice to have a cordial glass."

He *never* talked like that. "The cake was great."

He nodded.

"And the tea."

He stood facing three quarters away from me, looking partly over his shoulder, as though posing for his picture.

"Good-bye." Then, like a fool, I ran back over to him and was crushed. (You may have wondered how I described those other scenes.) "Oh my God," I said, and it wasn't profound emotion, "Oh, Juan, my back." He hugged me until my backbone cracked, then he picked me up to kiss (with Juan, lovemaking must have been forever associated with weight lifting), and the skin scraped from my back altogether. "Call me," I gasped. "Call me tomorrow."

Back in my house, I turned on the television and waited for Walter. I wasn't in love certainly, but while I watched an old and late show my mind clicked on, and how good it felt; *how interesting, how interesting, how interesting.*

IX

Howᴇᴠᴇʀ ɴɪᴄᴇ and full of childish anticipation it was the night before it didn't seem so great the next. Rather it wasn't *great* and *not great*, but one way one time, one way the next. How's that? That is, I woke up anxious and miserable, guilty and depressed, or rather, those words don't do either. Where I'd gone to sleep literally feeling as light as air, a feverish dirigible, kindled and sent sailing both by Juan Ramirez and the fire in my back, I woke up cold and nauseated, and the guilt I felt took on these physical characteristics.

In the following days I found my symptoms were less to be defined in terms of romantic love than by headaches, dizziness, nausea. I could never persuade myself I felt bad over Juan Ramirez—that was insane to begin with. I'd expected to feel *bad* about Walter, and for a while I did, cried ever so much, and been sad enough—betrayed—sad enough to die. So when a scant three weeks later I'd have a cryptic, useless, cold conversation with my next-door neighbor and have to lie down with an antacid tablet—do you see what I mean? It was a matter less of tears than the digestion.

Here I was with, I guess, a potential lover. A very exciting situation as anyone who has ever read *Madame Bovary* or *Anna Karenina* will know. I waited for him to call the next day and he didn't. I lay in bed on my stomach, watching television, and when it went off, reading. Lorraine took the baby. I was sick. Once, when I got up to go to the bathroom I fainted, but in the most inglorious way. I woke up sitting on the floor, having fallen just to a sitting position and now the end of my backbone as well as my whole back was in some fancy pain. Through the morning I dreaded his call, the afternoon I waited for it; by evening the phone had become—we ladies know it, don't we—this semianimate spiteful crouching thing and I was too sick to eat dinner. Shit! I didn't even *like* him, and I hadn't forgotten what he looked like, what he *did* for Christ's sake.

And yet those insane days had their advantages even then, because that night when Walter came home I'd been up long enough to fix him a decent dinner. I was too preoccupied to be anything but OK. I'd wrapped Walter up in some kind of metaphysical Saran Wrap; he was laminated in plastic, I couldn't notice him. He was quieter than usual, and looked over at me a couple of times, once as I cleared the table he even put an arm around me and I jumped and pulled the thin silk from my back so that he could see the blisters. But, you know, I hadn't even cried all day and hadn't even thought about it, and I guess Walter thought it was good news for him or us. That night we didn't study and watched some more television (what's monotonous for you was such a treat for us), and I willed the program to go off in the middle so we could go next door, but of course it stayed on until the last commercial.

The next day I waited inside the house all day long and he never called. Juan I mean, and how interesting, how interesting, that one entire English pronoun was usurped by dumb Juan Ramirez, so that if in my mind I thought, why he never, or he always does, or why doesn't he, it never was my husband; it was like learning (as they always say) not just to speak a foreign language but think in it.

The next day was Wednesday. Lorraine had a morning class and went to it. If I phoned she wouldn't be there to hear me through the walls. I waited around, how hard not to be able to go outdoors—and with about twenty minutes left until she was due back, I'm ashamed to admit it, I called him up at work. Feeling lousy by now, out of control, yes, but through it all, the relief that this was the third day I hadn't cried.

Ah, adultery, or what passes for it. I could hardly say hello. And, I believe, neither could he, although my nervous or physical disorder might have passed by that time to my ears. And what a conversation:

"Hello."

"Hello."

"Oh, hello." (With great feeling.)

I am stirred in spite of myself, in spite of history.

"I shouldn't be calling you. . . ."

"No, I was just meaning to call you."

"Oh, well . . ." A pause, but he won't say anything. "I just guess it's brazen or something, ha ha."

"Brazen?" He laughs appreciatively, conveying that I could no more be brazen than Shirley Temple.

"Well, I have your kids over here, they've all been playing very well together, sometimes they all seem to get in these terrible moods at once and other times they're just so neat. . . ."

"How is your back?"

"Oh, it's fine." I blush, embarrassed for my red and bulky body. "It's fine now," and then quake, because if he does ask me to—my God—then I certainly can't lie on my back, but no fear of that.

"You were up pretty late last night."

"Yes, Walter has this paper . . . so were you."

With greater smugness and as though I weren't there to see their lights and hear their conversations every night anyway, he announces, "I stay up reading almost every night until three o'clock or so."

Big deal, who doesn't, I want to say, but am dissuaded by this clench in my lungs, the bile in my stomach, the sweat on my palms. It's too ridiculous. I giggle instead. We talk on like this until from my window I see Lorraine, thin and elegant, approaching the barracks. At the last minute I say, "Well, I think I'll have to let you go now," and I barely have a chance to squeeze in good-bye before he hangs up.

Not the next day but the day after, when Lorraine had her class again, he called me minutes after she'd gone and we talked for two and a half hours. That Saturday night the Ramirezes were supposed to come over for dinner, but I sent word that my back was too sore for company and Lorraine said that was all right; Juan had an ear infection.

Monday he didn't call; I didn't leave the house once except to hang out the clothes and then I left the phone off the hook. In eight days I'd lost four pounds and I cursed the phone, myself, my life, and especially Walter (who I figured was responsible for getting my life into such a mess). But I didn't cry, and although in the following days we took up screwing again with what was close to our former frequency and with unusual ingenuity because of the sunburn, I hadn't for eight days bestowed a serious thought on Walter, or felt a flicker of pain. Once I thought, Is this how one whole marriage goes down the drain? In a day? Because of a lunatic you don't even *like*? But that seemed overly dramatic and beside the point; and I could only concentrate on that dumb phone, or on that *wall*, which like the phone became malicious and animate, a slidey slippy creature whose molecules made noises when I tried to hear.

Wednesday he called and said, "I thought I'd hear from you on Monday."

I said, well, no, I'd thought that I'd probably hear from him. Then he said that was funny, there we had been waiting for each other to call. Laughter. How was the kid? Fine, how were his kids? Then I asked him why he was calling up and got, I guess, the first of those oracular rejection-slip answers, answers you had to read twice to figure out what was being said, and even then, after every possible interpretation, the answer came up: on the one hand yes, on the other hand no; on the one hand hello, on the other hand good-bye.

I took a deep breath and stepped out into chaos. "We need each other, don't you think that's possible? Juan? Don't you think we might somehow go on with this?"

"I think that such a step, considering what we've . . . *both* been through (incredible, weightless silence) might perhaps be ill-advised."

"Why do you say that?" I ask him, nervously hanging icicles on our small tree with one hand, desperately clutching the phone.

"Oh, I think that . . ." and in a couple of short exchanges I found myself, by the same depressing cold-war dynamics that continually put the United States, the South Vietnamese and Latin American aristocrats at such profound disadvantage, coming out strong for lust and coming on strong to Juan Ramirez. He defended chastity and like the Communists, had, of course, all the good arguments.

We talked guardedly, hostilely, and finally, five minutes before Lorraine was due home, I hung up, saying huffily I had the wrong idea; that it wasn't the first time I'd been put on, been made a fool of by some man.

When Lorraine asked that afternoon if I'd watch Davey and Jennifer so that she could meet Steve, I said irritably, "Let *him* take a day off and take care of the kids," jerking my head at the wall, and Lorraine looked puzzled and said, "I just thought it'd be nice if they could all play together." But on Friday he called again, and we talked for two hours, and that afternoon while Lorraine met Steve, he did come home early and we collaborated and took care of the three kids together. Another afternoon we took them to see Santa Claus.

It had been almost two weeks since I'd given Walter a first thought. I took to sleeping on the inside, near the wall, so that I could hear Juan Ramirez breathe in his sleep; when Walter and I carried on it didn't dismay or embarrass me at all; it was a kind of advertisement for myself.

In the morning I woke up to think, Is he breathing over there? And the rest of the day was taken up with my obsession. I'd think, Yes, this is kind of dumb, I don't like him, he's bats, he's undesirable (and, remember, on another whole level those exchange students glimmered around in my mind). I'd wonder, offhand, what was going to happen in my life, my marriage, even my work. Each day I did all the stuff, read two hundred pages a day, did the ironing, talked on the phone to ordinary people; my whole life was suffused with wondering what, exactly, my next-door neighbor in Veterans Housing was doing as he worked, went to lunch, and would he call me up.

To hurry up a situation which in a period of less than two weeks became scholastic, theological, oracular, labyrinthian (crammed with muted conversations, symbolic excursions, ethical cutting and filling *and* total chastity), let me recall the last Thursday, I think the day after Christmas. Lorraine had been out for the afternoon with Steve and phoned me to say that she was at her mother's and would be late, her mother calling up just after and asking to speak to her daughter (it was Lorraine's style and sacred obligation to get caught even by me), and Walter, my sainted Chinese Walter, strolled in about eight with lipstick on his shirt and drunk as a lizard. He called me a cunt, naturally, and frigid bitch, and worst of all a lard-ass. Amazed at myself and rather cheerful, I began to scream, I who, I'd flattered myself, more than all the rest, cared about the proprieties of our barracks, and then, as Walter stood foolishly grinning and amused, I grabbed my coat, ran to another neighbor's (her husband was a paraplegic) and said she had to watch the kid because I was leaving, and she came down, freckled and scared, and sat gingerly on the bed, Walter, asleep now, on the floor like a bundle of old rags for the Salvation Army. Not content, I ran next door, and when Juan Ramirez answered, found as usual that expression of sympathetic anguish on his face which enraged me since it seemed to promise so much *something*, and delivered, I thought, nothing at all. I yelled and said, "Martha will watch yours too," and without a word he picked up his kids, awake and screaming under each arm, threw them—more or less—in my door, where in the half-dark Martha sat scared, and we drove away in Juan Ramirez's car.

We drove on the freeway; down the Santa Monica freeway to the San Diego freeway, where we drove all around in a circle to try out the interchange, then back on the Santa Monica to the Harbor freeway, then through town to the Pasadena freeway, out on the Arroyo Seco, skimming across all those little houses and lights, driving a hundred miles through the city, then all the way back to the beach. We talked about our families—our parents. He tried to explain Catholicism, his big defense for chastity, but when I asked him if that was what stood in his way, he said no, it wasn't that. Once in the warm car I said, "How do you reconcile all that with what you did to Lorraine?" And he said, nervously, "When?" and I, aware it wasn't exactly tactful, said, "When you, you know . . . in that building . . ." and he said, "You don't understand at all, that's not the kind of thing that they pay that much attention to."

"Oh," I said.

That night I yelled at him, I pleaded, I told him that we had to do it, that even if he didn't want me, he *had* to because I needed compensation, I'd been wronged, I'd been robbed and someone had to make amends.

He said, "I swear to you, it's not as if I don't admire you. It's not as if I wouldn't *want* to" (looking out the car window, clasping his hands against the steering wheel). "It's a question of *time*. It would be . . . like planting seeds in autumn. Each of us only has so much *time*." Then I started to cry and asked him to take me home. It was no use, no one wanted me. He put an arm around me and croaked, as though it were his own death sentence, "I'll try and think about it."

"OK," I said, cheerful as could be, "just as long as you really try." And how the ace frigid woman came to be saying that to the legendary rapist and bizarre screw of her own time (not to mention her best friend's husband), I leave you to decide, because the more reasons I think up for it, the more the issue is obscured.

Two nights later, the amateurs, armed with every sort of trumped-up excuse, met. Oh my, I was clean for my first adultery, the inside of my ears glowed, the cuticle on my toenails was pushed back and softened. I'd washed my hair which lay, still faintly damp, down along my shoulders instead of pinned back scholar-style. I was scared to death.

Mr. Ramirez, a great lover of classical music, had his car radio tuned to KFAC. We talked, depressingly enough, about school. I nodded my head a lot to whatever he said and laughed appreciatively, my hands cold with sweat.

Even then it wasn't easy. Because he wouldn't stop the car to perform that simple act. From the beginning, Juan had been looking covertly at his watch, then slowing down or, inexplicably, speeding up. We had driven across Los Angeles and out to the beach, when he stopped the car and went into a liquor store. He came back with a bottle of champagne and two cigars. I braced myself for our upcoming night of crime, vice, love. But he hopped back in the car and drove at least thirty more miles up the coast. Then, in a fit of conscience, he turned back, changed his mind again, and stopped at a little motel which, though on the ocean side of the highway, was out of sight of the sea. The hills on either side of where we parked were covered with geraniums, daisies, or those little white flowers that look like weeds, and some purple ones I don't know the name of but they used to grow all over California when I was a kid—before all the land filled up with housing projects.

If I seem to digress, that's how my mind was then: I sniffed the air which was dusty rather than damp, and picked out the flowers from my girlhood while Juan Ramirez signed the register. And then in great haste he drove to the door, and while I got out, shivering, he reached a long arm back into the back seat, grabbing not only the champagne but armloads of junk. You would have thought we were moving in.

There we were. And there we were and there we were. For all that talk of hippie love in the sixties or that beat style of the fifties, which I guess we had some of, or even the Lost Generation, I think I'm the voice of conservatism saying that making love to someone you don't know very well is always going to be difficult. I don't care how strict we all are or how giddy. My father lost his virginity—it makes a good story—by driving out on a horse or in a flivver at the beginning of the century to a home for wayward girls. Under cottonwood trees he parked and howled up at the bare frame house. "Ho," he yelled, "you wayward girls, come out!" And at a curtainless window a thin wayward face appeared, a bare little thirteen-year-old arm hung out and beckoned him up, and somehow he got up there, and they did it in the dormitory gloom, with sleeping girls, watching girls, and that one wayward girl, recipient of my father's innocent virility, muttering, "I bet a hundred this knocks me up, I bet a hundred this knocks me up." The story ends there, always, but did my father say thank you, or pleased to meet you? Or did they meet again? Do I have an elderly brother or sister? Screwing is like parties, a lot of fun, they *say*, but when you get there—or *to* get there—you must giggle, or flirt, or swear, or punch someone in the nose and fall down in the flower bed, or get drunk and pass out. We're always free from those public morals, if I may make a tedious observation, we're always just ourselves under those trees, standing swathed in mosquito netting; it's never what people say, and I bet the coolest hippie in the world meeting the second coolest hippie, in a roomful of incense where they're about to screw for the first time, has a moment of chagrin, a flush of irrelevant good manners.

I went over to the dressing table and put down my purse. I hung up my coat in the closet. There was silence, by God, amazing silence. I turned on the panel heater. "I guess you know I'm pretty frightened," I remarked conversationally. He didn't answer. I began to think of what time it was. It was already late and what would we say when we came home? How would I get home? Would I get home? *Would* I get home?

We went out on the balcony for a few minutes but all too soon we were back inside and there in the corner Juan stood rapidly but sadly peeling off his clothes. He didn't look so good, to tell the truth. There were blemishes on his back, a few, and a little pot of a stomach. His legs were beautiful and well formed, pretty as a woman's but muscular. They were big, very big, but I feel I must say that his middle leg, as it were, was—where? Not immediately apparent. He looked like a great, sterile angel, one of God's own *castrati*. There's a melancholy in this world, when we're embarked on an erotic adventure, but we just want that ferryboat to go home. The trouble is I had nowhere to look; if I looked at his face, I couldn't believe it, if I looked at his body, I just got so sad. I couldn't believe it.

"They're having a fight next door," Ramirez said. He gave me a wide, empty smile and pressed his ear to the wall, him in jockey shorts—that silly air-conditioned kind—me dressed in nothing but a coat. (My hair had gotten wet again.) I began to walk over to him but he shook his head.

"Get into bed," he said.

Juan crouched over by the wall holding—I couldn't believe it—some kind of tape recorder. He fastened two little plugs to the wall, and gave me that wide, delirious smile again. "This way, even if we don't listen, we can hear everything that goes on," he said. "It all goes in there." And he pointed to the aluminum box. I guess I nodded brightly. I won't deny I thought of our own wall, and Walter and I plugged into that metal box, but Lorraine wouldn't put up with that in silence; I knew I would have heard her bright, interested laughter, her consuming interest in that machine. It came over very clearly to me that I was locked up in a motel room with a certified rapist, and that I should have known better made me sadder than ever. If I had to commit adultery, why with a maniac who was even sadder and weirder than myself? Well, because that was our life. And *that* made me so sad I can't tell you. A whole future of dingy curtains and ill-fitting blouses and maniacs lay there in front of me as I sat nervously nude in the crisp, new-made bed and watched my new friend, ridiculous in those shorts, and a behind just a shade too big for his back and shoulders, finish adjusting his plugs and knobs.

Then he turned off the light and slid into bed beside me. It was by far the worst of its kind I can remember, an English tea party, a nightmare, a misery, a symphony of embarrassment, an agony. Once he looked down at me and said politely, desperately, a man waiting to put down a grand piano, and said, "Have you come yet?" Clearly he wasn't in the same bed I was. To say it was the worst ever doesn't say it; he moving shoulders and legs and us not moving anything else (what Lorraine said was right). Then he was momentarily beyond politeness and stopped moving at all; he was in pain, and came.

Beyond my fear and regret and distaste and longing for my own home and bed, I saw, I think, for the flicker of a shutter, the man. Which may explain why, immediately afterwards, when I knew I could breathe easier knowing it was over, I began at once to plan how I might see him again. My God, I didn't know him at all.

"They're still going on over there," he said. Lying together, we began haltingly, distrustfully, to talk. He made me very nervous and I didn't learn very much about him. What he wanted with that tape I didn't much feel like asking.

X

In the three months or so since his clearance, in spite or because of all his public and private troubles, Juan Ramirez had tentatively settled upon an AXEL project. The life at AXEL was too full of unaccustomed pleasure to let him get much done, but most of his evenings at home were spent alone now, and by old habit he filled them up with work. His project should have pleased the Air Force, since deployment of this strategic weapon could (theoretically at least) demoralize entire populations, but he'd had trouble getting it approved because the effects were neither dramatic nor demonstrable. The Air Force wanted swollen guts, vomit and blood. It would settle for an ear growing out of a stomach because that could be photographed in color and sent around to Congressmen. Ramirez's project was low on selling power.

He envisioned a nerve gas—or perhaps a powerful virus—which would ever so slightly knock out a person's sense of reality. The trick, the part that pleased him, would be its inconsistency (as well as its harmlessness). A soldier might return from a patrol, sit down to his frugal dinner, talk quietly with his friends (or better, his wife, his tired kids), and at the point where he felt more relaxed, would reach to pick up his teacup and scratch himself instead. Or reach to scratch himself and put his hand into the tea. Or lowering himself to sit on a tatami mat would sit just to the side of it. And his wife would look (and his children look). Next

142

time he would carefully, *carefully* manage to sit square on the mat, but his wife would still look, or so ostentatiously (by that time) *not* look, that he would be more sure than ever that something was wrong. This virus (or whatever he decided) should ideally be timed to last for at least a year, but in never increasing intensity. After a few months, each man knowing his own disability, looking secretly for it in others, even finally talking about it, comparing notes, would wait for more symptoms, would *want* more, so that the infirmity could be once and for all recognized, identified. But a week might go by, ten days, and the soldier in question would be fine, begin to breathe easy, and as he sat down again another night, beginning cautiously to relax, he would see his wife slowly, with some beauty, turn every color of the rainbow. He would watch this panoply with mingled horror and delight (because it would look so nice in spite of all); his wife would notice, speak to him sharply, and he would notice that under her pale luminous violet (or lemon yellow or the palest blue) that she would be *looking* at him again (and the children looking, and looking quickly away).

They'd let him go ahead with it at AXEL; it was no crazier than a hundred other things they were doing and had the advantage of relating to other projects they were doing on drugs and domestic riot control. But certain colonels in the Washington office had sent memos saying that they couldn't see how any of this would necessarily impair the efficiency of the fighting man (especially if he had been trained up in the highly dedicated, terrifically disciplined, brainwashing background of the average Communist cadre, etc., etc.). Juan knew it would work, knew it more than he would have liked, because without the benefit of tasteless vapors or fine powders or any virus he doubted his senses more every day.

He had seen a woman killed and no one else had noticed, he'd entertained his wife's lover and the evening had been no worse than many others. People over on the East Side generally could say with some assurance whether they loved their wives or hated them—his own mind changed about that not daily or hourly but (as he said to himself) minutely.

He was engaged in serious work, deadly serious work. He was, by certificate and vocation, one of the country's elite. It was conceivable that generals, statesmen, even the

President might one day read a monograph of his and make a decision which might change the world, but Lorraine was right, he couldn't keep gas in the car.

Ramirez (as he drove to and from work, watering his tiny garden from his front porch, doing the Saturday shopping, reading a magazine across the living room from his wife, drinking chocolate under the watchful eyes of his secretary) was obsessed by the feeling that people were looking at him, that people knew. He *knew* they knew, but what did they know and how much did it matter? He was fairly certain that he was the butt of a joke, but what joke, and why?

By the hour he tried to calculate in his mind how long his wife and her lover had known each other. It must have been long before the party where he had first discovered them. That terrible chase had been part of a joke. And everyone had known. Even now he blushed to think of it. He'd pleaded with Lorraine to tell him when she was leaving him, *if* she was leaving him, but it pleased her to say there was no lover; that was also part of the joke. After that party he had been fairly certain she hadn't seen much of Rader, she always had dinner ready for him (Ramirez), she always wanted to make love, she kept the house, she had seemed so happy that Juan simply couldn't believe he was deceived. And he couldn't believe that she would choose a man who had a dirty neck and wore a dirty shirt, who had already left one wife, who drank at parties almost as much as Walter Wong. And then he had found the letter. Juan, sitting alone in his living room, shrank. He shook his head, he covered his eyes in all the trite manifestations of disbelief. He still couldn't believe it. It seemed likely that Rader was part of the monstrous joke, that the morning with the steak knives was one more prank, something along the line of the note which had first sent him, shy and everybody's sucker, down into the basement of the music building. He had heard that Rader's father had had money, that he had lived in Shanghai during World War II, that he had afterwards sold cars to both the Nationalists and Communists until both sides had gotten mad enough to chase him (and his wife and seedy son) out. Now he had a fleet of pickup trucks in Australia. Ramirez had spent one whole afternoon considering whether the phone calls and modest checks from his employers in espionage were not really from Steve Rader, whether the exchange students were not in fact hired by Rader (wearing, for God's sake, bedspreads). One way to immobilize a husband is to hire him out to a false organization, to keep him busy on nonexistent projects, to send him, laughing (how he and Lorraine must laugh together), to his knees.

Everyone was looking at him. Everyone looked at him, or carefully looked away. After he had taken the first publication from AXEL, he had found it the following morning between the same pages of the municipal records of Lima. He was almost sure that it had not been touched. Twice more the disembodied voice (or voices) had demanded publications which he had jammed down into his briefcase among the growing collection of his own legitimate writings and research (sprinkled from above with the ubiquitous tea bags which went to quench Walter Wong's endless thirst, a thirst stronger even than his one for Red Mountain Burgundy).

Ramirez had tried once to trap his employers. One evening when, along with Lorraine, he had lain stretched out with the Wongs watching television, he'd spied a long hair of Edith's not eight inches from his nose in the dust by the bed. He'd picked it up, secreted it in his pocket, and stretched it across the title page of the next publication he put in volume 1927: *Lima: Municipal Records*. When he'd picked up the publication, the hair was still there. He'd felt momentary triumph, then terror. He'd caught them, right? But if he wasn't spying for someone, then what was he doing? Was Rader really keeping Lorraine by proxy? Buying her goodies and presents, using her own loutish husband as agent? He couldn't think of anyone else who would want to take the time and trouble to do all this to him. She must be seeing him, he thought in a rush of truth—and looking up from his chair, the living room was suddenly in focus—she was never home when he called. And Edith always had the children. But, really, Lorraine was always *home*, she was, she had dinner ready for him, she wanted to make love, she kept the house, she had seemed so happy—and so on, and so on.

Juan had gotten used to his own tortured thoughts the way people learn to live with a bad back or chronic headache. He no longer tried to manage them, but tried instead just for detachment; tried, in a sense, to keep his mind off what his mind was doing. Also, what would agents of another power be doing looking at the title page? They ostensibly knew what they wanted (or else how could they even know what publication to ask for?). There must be other people inside the AXEL building who were using him, as the most recently hired, the least trustworthy, the stupidest, simply to take the publication out of the building so that it could be photographed. The actual taking out of the publications could be traced to him in case AXEL noticed a security leak, so that would be where the most risk would lie. He would be fired from both agencies, put in jail. There would be a divorce. (Could that be part of Rader's master plan?)

Ramirez's Catholic mind put divorce somewhere on a par with murder although he knew other people didn't feel that way. He knew Lorraine took pills to keep from having more babies; he'd tried to tell her what the Church thought about that, what *he* thought about that: "Why not wait until it's born?" he'd asked her once, in one of the only real arguments they'd had since their marriage, "and *then* take its life?" using the by-now unaccustomed diction and rhetoric of his Jesuit high school teachers, and she'd smiled fondly at him and gone on with her (he recognized that most people didn't feel that way but he couldn't see why not) systematic murder. But Lorraine was a lost soul. Lorraine was a lost soul. And the next time he'd taken a document down to the basement he'd noticed that there was all over the library, on every level, a good supply of single, long hairs; on the floor, on steps, in cubicles, on top of books. Girls had taken to wearing their hair long. It might have been another hair he'd seen. Or he might have been mistaken altogether and the hair might not have been there when he opened up the title page—the color of Edith's hair was absolutely neutral; he simply might have perceived something that was not there. Was not there.

At first Juan had made a distinction between his misery now and his misery when he was younger; there should be a distinction between the anxieties of the graduate student, who—even if he is fifty—is an adolescent to the world, still preparing for the riddles which he doesn't care to confront without additional information, and the troubles which happened in the real world. This trouble was *real*, whatever it was. Real money was involved, real time, real war, real life.

But his new business friends—Lorraine and he had been invited out to dinner by them a few times, like real married couples—had the same prints on their walls, the same books, the same varieties of plants, all the cheap anodynes of life that passed for real life here in Vets Housing. And he had felt—in exactly the same way if not to the same degree—that people were looking at him.

More specifically, disorientation of the senses had been a ground rule in graduate school. Since—as in a military fitness report—everyone was given excellent grades, the question of whether you were doing well; whether, in fact, they liked you, saw you as a potential future microbiologist, a credit to their elitist race, was purely metaphysical. A person who thought he had done fine for three years might find himself, upon taking his PhD qualifying exams, in possession of a terminal master's degree; from then on a deportee from the world of learning, doomed to high school teaching or the civil service. Students stared at themselves in mirrors and windows, trying, forever unsuccessfully, to get at the rules of the game, to find some law, some consistency, which would—by the scientific method they believed in—stamp their perceptions as accurate or not.

Ramirez remembered having collaborated on a paper for a seminar with another student—like him, with a wife and child or two—a sallow fellow, intensely fearful, whose shirts dripped with sweat if he were called to the front of any class to speak at length on anything. The day that he and Ramirez were to present their paper they had met early to mark out a succession of formulas on the blackboard. The other student (already with preliminary aging wrinkles around his eyes and at the corners of his mouth) had complained about his health. "I have trouble raising my arm," he said. "Last spring when I picked up the baby to put her in the crib something happened to my back. I was in bed, flat on my back, for three days. The doctor said it was acute fatigue. My back is better now but I still have trouble raising my arms. I have trouble with my liver. When I raise my arms it gets me right in the liver." He'd pounded the skin just below his collarbone. "Right here."

"Your liver?" Ramirez idiotically had asked. "I thought . . . it was a little further down."

The student had moved over and stood directly beside

Ramirez, watching now as he wrote the finishing numbers of the first half of the progression on the board. Ramirez, for no apparent reason, had begun to tremble. "The liver," the student said, "is the largest organ in the body." He had laid his bony hand against his upper chest, rubbing the offending part, and stared at Ramirez.

"Yes," Ramirez answered, and they stood together in the cold and silent room, while anger, hatred, certainty, suspicion, and finally awful doubt, passed through their souls and bodies like an electric current, only more slowly, more like rainbows.

Lorraine was out tonight. The children were spending the night with her parents, who had recently moved out of their house and into a spacious modern apartment with a pool. This December it was still warm enough to swim and the kids could take advantage of the unseasonable warmth. It was nice that they had two sets of grandparents to be able to visit. And it cut down the work for Lorraine.

Last Sunday, Ramirez had taken the children down to Long Beach Harbor to watch the ships come in. Lorraine stayed home, her hair tied back, and cooked an excellent dinner. His folks had come over in the evening and everything had gone well. I am a father taking his children for an excursion, Ramirez had thought in the warm sun. It's nice to be able to do that. Somehow he had managed to fake his way into the adult community. It was nice to be able to do that. But he envisioned statesmen, dignified and portentous, thinking, I am on the brink of declaring war (or peace); it's nice to be able to do that. Was there an adult community? Did everybody carry fake credentials?

Someone was knocking, must have been knocking for some time. He clumsily got up and answered the door. Edith stood in the doorway. He blinked. She was red, red as blood. He stood stupidly, the sense of unreality around him, in him. Like an overcoat. Like a suitcase. Like a sandwich. Like a rock.

"My television went off," she said, and shivered even in the warmth of the night. Her teeth caught the light from his lamp and flashed like sparklers. "Can I come in just for ten minutes to see the end?"

The ground under his feet began to turn sedately.

"Yes," he said. "Yes. Come in." He crossed carefully to the television set and turned it on.

She wore an iridescent white wrapper, with—as far as he could see without appearing indecently to stare—nothing on underneath. In fact, she had nothing on underneath.

From a no-man's-land of feeling, Ramirez felt a rush of wild, irrational delight. A woman sat on the edge of his bed bright red with glittery teeth, and white! A white wrapper, and underneath that serious familiar head, a regular woman's body. He felt not a particle of lust—what if you saw a woman's body with a lollypop on top of it, or a cactus or a sandwich? Only delight.

"I was reading in the *Daily Bruin* yesterday—you know, I haven't been out much recently, but I went over to the humanities library today and picked up a paper—that there's some stuff missing from the physics department. I mean at first they thought it was just kids checking things out and not bringing them back—like Marina works in the reserve book room and she says they have a thirty percent rebuy policy, they don't get new books, or hardly ever, but they keep having to buy old ones because kids keep checking out and never returning them. There's about a hundred million dollars due in uncollected fines, Marina says. Do you know Marina?"

"You're *sunburned*," Ramirez said with delight (and a little disappointment). Edith stood up, turned her back to him and lifted her wrapper; rolls of red and white flesh waved sedately. He gasped. The girl, the woman, the mother, turned and regarded him with grave eyes. Her breasts looked at him with wry intelligence; her cunt kept its mouth shut—just to keep from laughing. It was a pioneer. It talked in salty dialogue like Walter Brennan. It rode along with the straight man of her head and talked along in pithy sayings, it talked behind her back.

"I've never been so sunburned in my whole life," her proper mouth said. Her crotch muttered, "I'll say!" and her breasts winked silently and his little room swung around stately, magnificent, remote.

"I'll get something to put on that," he told her and walked the few feet into the kitchen. He poured clear water and vinegar together—oh brown, but with light all through it! He found a Kleenex, put it in the cup, and saw it suspended, translucent. I'm going mad, he thought with some clarity, but then dismissed the thought. It wasn't a real problem any more than there were real spies or real anything. He took the cup back to the living room and sat down by the girl. She turned her back to him—sitting on the edge of the low bed, her plump knees came within inches of her shoulders, her belly pushed a little to the side and became her hips. Self-conscious now, she lowered her wrapper so that all her bright red back was exposed, but still with careful hands she covered her white breasts. He tried to be as gentle as possible. She shivered as the water ran over her shoulders and back.

"So they thought that it was only that kids wanted to cram for exams and never returned the pamphlets or monographs or whatever, but then somebody went to check up on one of the students to send him a notice—you know, in those private libraries around school they hardly ever check up, they have their own system, like in the English department that bitch in the English reading room has a set of three-by-five cards and she notes down your mannerisms—Paul worked there for a while and he says she puts down things like whether you're Jewish, can you imagine? Or whether you smoke. But you know, they don't send out notices, and they don't keep very good track of their books. So they *knew* a lot of stuff was being taken but they didn't pay much attention until a government agent came by, he was just checking up he said, but he said there was a security leak somewhere. But all along they'd thought they only had things without security limits, you know, just textbooks, and new monographs as they came out—we have the same thing in English with that new crazy linguist who thought up transformational syntax—if something's two weeks old it's of historical interest only. Isn't that great? Historical interest only. So you have to read these crazy monographs that keep changing all the time. When are you going to get your tree? Walter usually waits until Christmas Eve."

"So what happened?" Ramirez said. He crouched and began to pat cold water and vinegar on her bright red legs.

"Well, in one way they were secret and in another way they weren't. Because they were just working along in theoretical physics or whatever they call it, just fooling around, but they're smarter than they should be, because they shouldn't be doing that stuff and just leaving it around to be read.''

"Didn't they realize that might happen?"

"Oh, yes, that's why all that stuff is in the physics library instead of the regular one, and they thought they knew all the physics students. Another thing, they took a lot of stuff that isn't very secret, like how to make airplanes. So they just can't figure it out. And they're going to fire all the ladies in the physics library.''

"Do you happen to know where Lorraine is?" Ramirez asked.

"Over at her mother's?"

"That's right.''

"It was the biggest headline they ever had in the *Bruin*. They say it's the biggest one.''

"Edith," Ramirez said, "I'm in the middle of my life, almost, and everything I've worked for is nothing. Oh, I have everything I want, my PhD, my parents are proud of me, all my family is proud of me, I have two beautiful children, and Lorraine. . . .''

"And a new briefcase," Edith ventured. He looked at her, she smiled, and sparks came again from her teeth and fell to her wrapper where they disappeared.

"I'm very unhappy, but I don't seem to feel it."

"Yes.''

"Would you like some sherry?"

"Yes.''

They talked far into the night. He liked the idea of talking far into the night. It was one of the advantages of being an adult. As the hours passed he calmed himself; the company of that poor serious woman had its sedative effect. When she left, he looked a last time at her, and in some kindly apparition, the matron—his wife's close friend and therefore someone not to be liked—merged with the red and white Catherine wheel he'd been entertaining (and entertained by) earlier in the evening. A regular woman, friendly and kind, highly sunburned, stood saying good-bye to him.

"Thank you for coming to visit me, Edith. It was a pleasant evening. It really was.''

She silently smiled and nodded and he gave her a grateful hug.

It wasn't until a couple of days later that he realized incredulously, with more than disbelief, that she had developed what he had to recognize as a crush on him. Lorraine had told him that Edith and Walter were quarreling but he hadn't paid much attention. Now, daily, he got phone calls which he either paid attention to or not. Edith's breathy voice asked him tremulous questions, he answered with awkward politeness or remnants of the delight he'd felt that night. Sometimes he called her. He kept her on the phone for hours, talking about the Pope, the garbage pickup at the barracks, their respective children, anything to keep his phone busy and his poor soul and brain from his tormenting other callers.

Edith had been right, or rather, he'd guessed right about what Edith had told him. He was almost sure his colleagues were real. And being stupid, they'd been found out if not caught; the strain told in their voices on the phone. They gave orders to take out a document then countermanded the same order an hour or so later; they once had ordered him out of the office to a pay phone and even there had been reluctant to tell him what to take from the building. One night in the stacks, putting a routine delivery in the dusty volumes, he had found a message explaining their new code, and stamped over and over with the dire warning. *Burn this Burn this Burn this.* He'd dutifully burned it in his bathroom at home, although it had made a mess and Lorraine had sniffed suspiciously when she'd taken a shower. Now he talked to the voices about bubble gum and elephants, and when he'd mildly suggested that this kind of talk might arouse more suspicion than the other kind they'd hung up on him.

For Ramirez each day was an interesting dream. He spoke civilly to his wife, to his tremulous neighbor, to his voices, and did his work, which required another part of his mind altogether, and which remained peaceful and unchanged through everything. He saw what was happening, at least he thought he did; his marriage was spinning off and away, there were genuine people spying on the people he worked for, he was in danger. He knew—after seeing that medusa head pulled from its soggy bed of Chinese noodles—that they would be only too happy to kill his wife, indeed as disgruntled ex-boyfriends might look forward to it with relish. He understood the thought. He couldn't go to the police. How could he look at those sullen moon faces capped by plastic crash helmets, and say, "You know, it just looks like UCLA over at AXEL, they have those lights and all, and you get sandwiches out of machines if you want, and everyone went to UCLA or still does, *you* know. . . ." They'd put him in the *really* real world soon enough, a branch of it that some of his uncles and cousins knew well enough and had told him enough about. No, he chose—for as long as he could manage it—this bright unreality. And, after years in graduate school and the interminable length of the shortest three-hour seminar, he found himself enjoying this snip of time, the acute sense of the shortness of whatever time he had left in his falling-down life.

Ramirez sat at his desk at work talking to Edith. He'd been on the phone for an hour or so, his secretary had brought him three cups of hot chocolate which he'd consumed with enjoyment, absently answering his new friend's rhetorical questions. The night before he had seen her again and it had been a disaster (though he was beginning to like the idea of being idolized by somebody somewhere). He had to go to the bathroom, finally, and told Edith he was going to hang up.

"I know," she said furiously, "you're not even thinking about it, all you care about is yourself."

"Don't say that."

"You make my life worthwhile. There's nothing left in my life but you. . . ."

That she should have no one but me, Ramirez thought wryly. We both know how bad off she is.

"I like you more than I can say," Ramirez said. "That's why I don't think I can do it. It's a sin, Edith. It would hurt us both, and it would hurt the people we're married to."

"Are you *kidding*?" Edith wailed, but Ramirez continued.

"I'm sorry," he said, "I really am," and hung up.

His secretary came in, knocking softly as she passed the doorjamb, carrying a fourth cup of chocolate. She set it carefully on his desk. Three marshmallows spread into sticky foam.

"You know," he said, "this is quite a lot, even for me."

A tear fell on his blotter.

"What's wrong?" he asked. "I certainly didn't mean

anything. I mean, is it something in the office? Do you feel sick? Do you want to go home?''

"It's little enough," the girl sobbed. "It's little enough I can do . . . a few stuffed dates, a handful of cookies, chocolate from a machine! I want to give you everything, and I can only give you marshmallows.''

"It's very good," Ramirez said. "It's just that I've had four cups, or this *is* my fourth cup, I guess. . . .''

He took a big sip of chocolate which left a foamy coat on his upper lip. Then the girl was in his lap, covering his face with kisses.

"So sweet," she said earnestly to him, "you're so *sweet.*"

"Elaine, Elaine, I'm a married man.''

"That's not your wife on the phone every day.''

"She's just a friend. Honestly, she's just a friend.''

The girl sat back on his lap and steadily regarded him.

Again, for no reason at all—except, perhaps, the obvious—he was overwhelmed with delight. He licked his lips. It might be a good thing for him to grow a mustache. Is this how most people in the world feel when they're doing things? he thought. But he didn't think so. Perhaps because they hadn't been so sad, they didn't have the chance to be so happy. He looked at the girl on his lap. His hands caressed her skin still fresh from her morning's shower. There was an innocence, underneath her nylon blouse, which was to him utterly invulnerable, no matter how many AXEL bachelors for whom she was the dessert after a ritual, expensive dinner—or, for that matter, no matter how many previous, married, feeling-old employers she'd fed her machine-made (but lovingly poured) hot chocolate.

"Is it that you already have someone else?''

"My life is falling apart. I can't explain it to you. I'm in terrible trouble.''

She just looked at him. She was so fresh, so beautiful, so utterly expectant that he kissed her. Her mouth tasted like clover.

She shifted her weight on his lap and he was able to see that Jimmy Joyce was standing in the doorway. "Don't bother," he said, while Elaine said, "Oh!" and slid off his lap and trotted over to the filing cabinet. "It can wait.''

Joyce left and Ramirez stared from the doorway to the girl,

delight clicking on and off against his normal anxiety like a light, an electric light, clicked on, off, on, off, by a kid who loves the light, just loves it.

His secretary was crying, however.

"My dear," he said, and was about to get up and go over to her, when the phone rang.

"Is it that *girl*?" his secretary spitefully said, and one of his voices said, "Now, Ramirez, listen carefully, we have not much time."

"Wait a minute," Ramirez said into the phone, and looked at the tearful girl. She didn't budge.

"I have to ask you to leave," Ramirez told her.

"Stupid clod, we have not much time," the voice hissed and crackled, adding a few words in a language he didn't understand. His secretary said feelingly, "You heartless, selfish . . ." and went back to her typing, while the voice went on.

"Listen, I better get off, you call me back," Ramirez said. "It's quite important. I think I might have aroused some suspicion."

"We have reason to believe that we are being betrayed from within."

"That's one thing I didn't do, come *on*!" Ramirez protested. He was beginning to talk louder since he'd left school; situations seemed more to call for it.

"Idiot, to whom would you betray us? We know your life from the moment you wake in the morning. Now listen. We give you an assignment now—no code—just listen. If you succeed, we triple your pay, but just for this month. Saturday night, this Saturday, you must go to the Starlight Motel in Malibu after the hour of nine-thirty. To be safe, inconspicuously find a blue 1958 Pontiac parked outside whatever door. Then check into a room, the room next door. In the yellow trash can in the cubicle next to the checkpoint where you find your check you will find a machine whose directions you should understand. There is an ear, there is a drill. What the machine records, you will return to us. I recommend you do not play the tape. We will know if it has been tampered with and we will kill you."

"What's my excuse for going to the motel? I'm a married man. I'm not that close to my wife any more, but you've got the wrong man. I'm not that kind of a person. I mean, you're in trouble now anyway . . . why don't you wait for a while? Find somebody else. I can't do that kind of thing.''

"Trouble?" The voice said quiet, controlled. "Why do you say trouble, Ramirez? What makes you say that?"

"My next-door neighbor read something in the *Daily Bruin*. I just think it was you, that's all."

"Do you want your wife to be ravished, killed?"

"You know," Ramirez said, "half the time any more I don't seem to care, I'd sort of like for her to be dead. I mean, I wouldn't want to kill her or anything, but I'd sort of like for her to be dead. I never thought I'd feel that way, much less say it." If Elaine is listening, he thought, she'll think I'm talking to my girl friend, isn't that something? "I just don't seem to care," he repeated.

"Ramirez," the voice coldly said, "we'll kill your kids, we'll kill you." The voice stopped, the line buzzed. Ramirez replaced the receiver; the phone immediately rang again and before it had made more than the puniest noise, he had it to his ear. "A person you know will soon die," the voice said.

"Never mind, I'll do it," Ramirez said.

"No matter. A person you know will soon die. And if you betray us, the rest will die, and you last of all. Were we wrong about you, Ramirez?" The phone clicked again.

Ramirez stood up; the room reeled. He rushed to the outside office, where his secretary sat, ankles crossed, at her typewriter. Over her shoulder he read: "Dear Mother, nothing much is happening around here, I have been writing letters all morning . . ." The girl stood up, frightened; he grabbed her wrist and pulled her into his office, slamming the door behind him.

"Nobody is supposed to shut their doors, Mr. Ramirez, that's a security regulation they're very strict about. They'll just come by and open it right up."

He had her in a corner against the wall. The filing cabinet hid them from view even if the door were opened, his own body closed off another side of her, but just to their other side the venetian blinds were open; there were people out there who could watch. He jammed the girl up against the blinds, mashing them shut. He locked his hand against the back of her neck. She was much taller than his wife, but still too short for him. He lifted her off her feet and planted her against the blinds. Who cares? he thought dimly. Who cares anyway? He kissed her neck. Now he had one enormous hand across her breasts, one underneath her behind, supporting her against him. He squeezed desperately on everything he felt. Sweat ran down his back, down his legs, down the back of his neck. "OK, sweetheart," he said, "it's fine with me. We'll go out—we'll go anywhere you want. . . ." He rubbed himself, insinuated himself, against the tops of her legs. "Anywhere. Ah, God, we'll do it, you *want* me to do it. . . ."

She grunted. Her hands were flat against his chest. He took one of them and pressed it further down. She grunted again. A button snapped from her blouse and rolled across the office floor.

The door opened and Jimmy Joyce peered in. "What's happening?" he mildly asked the air. "This door should never be shut." Ramirez heard him but didn't relax his hold. The tip of the girl's shoe caught him smartly on his shin. He grunted in his turn and let her go. The blinds clattered open. The girl staggered to the center of the room, bruises already appearing on her wrists and neck. "I want," she said, also to the air, "I, I . . ." Her blouse was ripped, her hair wet in places from Ramirez's unstructured kisses, "I want a transfer."

She went into the outer office and slumped over her desk.

Mr. Joyce looked obliquely at Ramirez. "You can't win them all," he diplomatically ventured. "Remember after this to keep the door open."

The phone rang on Ramirez's desk. He stared at it, then at the girl in the other room. There was a minute, he later realized, when she still might have been won over. But he answered the phone.

It was his wife. "Juan, my mother's sick. They took her to the hospital. Just *now*, I'm on my way there. Daddy just called. They don't even know what it is, it might be a stroke, but she's conscious. . . ."

"So how long are you going to be at the hospital?"

"Oh, *Juan*, she's sick, she's really sick! Won't you come with me? Couldn't you come there with me?"

"Can I meet you there later? Things are pretty busy around here."

"Juan, Juan. What are you saying? My mother is terribly

sick!" Her voice started neutrally and traveled to a shriek.
Juan heard what he heard in himself all the time; it was
strident, depressing, it was fear. It marred his wife, it made
her human.

"How sick is she?"

"She's . . . sick. They don't even know what she's got.
But she's awfully bad. Oh, Juan, *please*, I'll come by there
and we can go to the hospital."

"Can't Steve take you?"

In the silence that followed he marveled at his own au-
dacity and then thought that after all it must not have taken
much because here he was, not hating her, but certainly
untouched.

"Because, because, Lorraine, I'm not angry, and I'm
sorry about all this, but I just haven't got the time to be
fooling with all this now. What hospital is she in? You call
me from there later and I'll try to get away. And you call
me if things get any worse. But really, I don't see that there's
that much to worry about. How did it happen anyway?"

He spoke into echoing walls of silence. After a minute,
his wife's voice answered from far away. "Somebody . . .
rang the doorbell over there at the apartment, and Mother
went to the door, and there was a box on the doormat, and
she opened it—a little carved box—and she had this stroke
or whatever it is. She came back in the living room and fell
over. That's what Daddy says."

"But you know," Ramirez said, "I don't really think
she's going to die. I just don't think so."

"All right, Juan, all right. I guess I can't blame you. And
you have a right, I guess, I *know*. But I didn't think you'd
wait until a time like this. Because, after all, Juan, I don't
have times like this very often. You might have had to wait
a long time."

Lorraine hung up. Ramirez went into the outer office. As
long as they had to pick someone I'm glad it was her, he
thought. Then he bent over his secretary's desk and put his
hand on the back of her neck.

"I'm sorry I behaved so badly in there."

She froze for a second, the looked up and smiled.

"Oh, me too. I'm sorry I said that about being trans-
ferred. I really like it here, Mr. Ramirez. I hope I do my

work well, and I'm sorry if I was . . . bold this morning. I really didn't mean for it to seem as if I, as if I, was bold."

"Are you free Saturday night?" Ramirez asked. "My wife will be visiting her mother, and I thought we might see each other Saturday night."

"Oh, Mr. Ramirez, I'd love to, you know I'd love to, but gee, I'm going out that night. Gee, if I'd only known, but I already have a date."

"Break it," Ramirez said. "Can't you go with me instead?"

The girl bit her lip. "Gee, I'd love to, can't you see that? And I'm really sorry I acted the way I did this morning. Oh, Mr. Ramirez, *please* don't make me do it!"

"OK," Ramirez said. "OK." He went back to the office to check on his mother-in-law, remembered he didn't know the name of the hospital, phoned his home instead. There was no answer.

He replaced the receiver; the phone rang again. "You see?" one of the voices triumphantly said. "A person you know will die. We said it, we did it. You see?"

"Yeah, well," Ramirez said, and afterwards he would remember it as one of the turning points, one of the growing moments of his life, though there were some before and plenty afterwards. "You sure did it all right. That was pretty interesting," then he hung up. And though they phoned right back and hissed and threatened, and though he was maneuvered into assuring them that he would do—of course—as they asked, and though he was afraid later, more than ever; for eight or ten minutes he was tough and brave.

But he knew he had to do as they asked, so he called up the lady who lived next door.

"Oh, Juan, did you hear about Lorraine's mother? It's a terrible thing. . . ."

"She'll be all right," he said, and she seemed content to leave it at that. They were back in their long conversation.

"How is it over there in Veterans Housing?" He knew that, for his purposes, that wasn't the best possible question.

"Well, it's about the same as when you left."

"Yes, well, I . . ."

"The children are outside playing with their Christmas toys, and I'm about to have lunch. This is a nice time because all the housework's done and the kids won't eat until later. . . ."

"Did Lorraine take the kids to the hospital?"

"No, they're with me."

Then he asked if she could get away the following night, and apparently stunned, she said yes.

"All right, I'll meet you at the corner of Wilshire and Westwood . . . in front of that new tall building, you stand inside it, so no one will see us, there's a pay phone, you be making a phone call."

She said something unintelligible.

"What?"

"I said, how will I get out of the *house*?"

"You know what to say, don't you?" he said. "You've got to go to the dentist."

"On Saturday *night*?"

"Well, then, go to a . . . meeting on opening up the ghettos. Or isn't there a lecture up at school? Or a recital?"

"I know what," Edith said. "I'll get Lorraine to take care of all of them."

"Why not?" he said. "If she's home, why not?"

Ramirez was alone. His office was quiet. He looked out his window at the wide Pacific. Soon it would be time for lunch. He'd stopped going to the dark bars of his colleagues since that first night of crime and now walked along the pier eating french fries from a paper bag and crunching down on fried shrimp, eating them tails and all. He watched the children swimming, and sometimes, when the merry-go-round was open, stopped to watch and listen, his bones and cell structure rattling, vibrating with the music. In a few minutes he'd go over and look at it again. He regretted that he'd never asked his secretary to one of those windblown lunches.

One thing was clear. He had to find out who he was working for. It was time to get out and he couldn't get out unless he knew who he was getting away from. Outside of the danger there was the whole question of money to think of, the whole question of making good (it couldn't be that he'd spent those years of anxiety and deprivation for nothing, that he'd worked as hard as he could to get exactly where he didn't want to be). Around him were sundry alternatives; a brilliant scientific position with some reputable firm, probably this one—a heavily mustachioed Ramirez dancing in a tiny room lined with blinking computers (he touches first this one then that with his baton, they light up and out comes a pink slip with a neatly printed cure for cancer). Jail. Unemployment (magazines stacked around him in great pyramids, a stomach fat from the starches which would be all that Lorraine's tiny salary could buy). Exile (a trim austere shack in the Sonoran Desert, Ramirez stands outside his door alone, his only living, his only friends, a few thin sheep). Or there was a life of crime out there too.

If whoever he worked with was being double-crossed, it might be to his interest to work for the double-crossers as a first step in getting out entirely. Or if it were the government which was after them, he would place himself on the government's side. At least he would find out everything he could. He'd go to the motel, working not for them, but for himself. They think I'm stupid, Ramirez thought. Well, maybe I'm not.

Ramirez flung himself down the halls and out into the lovely clear air of Santa Monica. The weather was everything it should be. Flowers still bloomed—perhaps better than they did in the hottest months, and it was convention rather than necessity that kept crowds from the beach. A few children swam while pretty mothers sunned themselves. Walking now on the pier Ramirez crunched his hot french fries, and took deep breaths of the salt air. He was thinking of something else.

He was planning like a maniac.

He went back to the office, took the phone off the hook, found a notebook, made a list. He would need one of those tiny cameras. He'd need another tape recorder to take a tape from the first one. (He didn't believe they'd have a way of checking whether he played it, but he'd try to find out their particular brand and ask a dealer.) He could say he worked for industry, that he was an industrial spy—no, an industrial counterspy, that they were a small firm and suspected that they'd been betrayed from within. He would see if there was a phone somewhere that he could tap, he'd ask the phone company, no, they wouldn't do it, he'd have to ask a detective . . . he'd need a gun. A gun. He'd get one on the East Side in a pawnshop. They'd never ask questions of a Chicano buddy. He'd need a sweat shirt, he'd need bathing trunks, if Edith could spend the night they'd go to the beach the next day. Binoculars! If they took a walk he'd take binoculars, he'd look around, maybe in the windows of the place next door. He'd need a notebook, a ball-point pen (to write down the license number of the Pontiac). Could he put a bugging device on his phone here at the office? And, and, what else? Champagne (did they have glasses in motel rooms?). No, he'd buy some. Should he stop for it after he'd picked up Edith so it would look spontaneous? How could he stop the car, say to that serious face, "Wait a minute," go into a store, come back to the car—his teeth chattered but he remembered the lights spilling from her mouth to her silk kimono. OK, OK, he'd do it, he *could* do it.

He took the rest of the afternoon off, did errands and shopped until the back of his car was filled with parcels. In the late afternoon he pulled his car into a vacant lot on the East Side, jacked up his car, pulled off a tire, then squatted beside it in the soft wild rye weeds burned gold from last summer and carefully cleaned his gun. Then he removed everything he'd bought from the back seat and packed it carefully back. He made a parcel of the wrappings, walked a half-block to a trash can, shoved them in. A great sunset turned all the little stucco houses and tiny grocery stores, dirty gas stations and good little restaurants to a brilliant candy-box pink as he replaced his tire, hid the gun (wrapped in an oiled cloth) under the seat.

He spent the evening with his parents, returned late to find his wife not home and a note from Edith saying she had the kids next door. He lay awake feverishly planning and finally took a sleeping pill. The next day was Saturday. Late in the afternoon he went next door, offered to take the kids off Edith's hands (not looking at her), drove them to McDonald's Golden Arches where each child confided his order to a mechanical clown and was rewarded just across the asphalt parking lot by a thin hamburger and french fries. Ramirez ordered two chocolate milk shakes and drank them slowly. As the sun set again he took the kids to a park, and standing storklike, swung the three of them, clumsily pushed them on a tin merry-go-round which slanted into the sand, watched unblinking and intent as they slid over and over down the slide screaming *watch me watch me watch me*.

He took the kids back to the Wongs' apartment. Walter,

on the bed with his wine, asked him in. But Edith, just out of the shower, her hair wet and clinging to her neck, didn't say anything and Juan declined.

"It's OK," Walter said. "We're going out a little later and there's no point in getting settled."

Juan looked in alarm at Edith and she said in a voice so low he could hardly hear, "You don't have to worry about your kids. Walter's going to some anthro lecture and he'll be back early, and I have this meeting to go to but I got a girl from the dorms to come over. If you pay part of it we can afford her for once."

"Of course," Ramirez said. He handed her some money and felt a tremendous sexual complicity. She took it without looking at him once.

Ramirez stood awkwardly in the door. He wanted to kiss his children good-bye but was embarrassed. He went next door, took a long shower, checked his list, burned it (the second time he didn't feel silly), shaved, and after some consideration put on his black silk suit. He counted his money, walked the length of his house a couple of times, checked his watch and left.

By eight o'clock he was waiting at the corner of Wilshire and Westwood. There was no place to park so he went around the block. The second time Edith walked quickly from the door of the building, opened the door and climbed in.

XI

RAMIREZ AND EDITH drove in silence through the rush hour congestion of Wilshire Boulevard, past the baroque Victorian homes which for years had been a Veterans Hospital. (Sometimes students drove through the grounds as a restful shortcut, the grass and trees were pleasing and the traffic was light, but no time could be saved since the speed limit was eighteen miles an hour. Any faster and the doddering vets dragged themselves from their park benches to the curb and thence under the passing cars.) Ramirez decided that a crush of cars and bus smoke was better than that, and so they crept under tarnished tinfoil arches left over from Christmas, blinking into the harsh sun, out Wilshire to the sea.

Ramirez found himself talking about school. (Here I am, he thought wistfully, committing treason and adultery in one entire evening, I have gas, champagne, camera, tapes . . .) He told Edith—who wondered if she ought to take the PhD qualifying exams or settle simply for an MA—"I don't know. I found that learning to read in one foreign language wasn't so bad (they knew I spoke Spanish so they didn't let me use it), I did the French even though it was no use to me. The first language isn't so bad, but the German was *terrible*. When you've already gone to so much pains to learn the one language, it's terribly discouraging to go on to the next."

"Of course, they'd let me take Italian as a second language," Edith said. Her left hand was clasped in her lap, her right grasped the door handle.

"Well, they'd never let a person in the sciences do that, because so many important things are in German. That's the language of science."

"Do you ever use it now? I mean have you ever read anything in German except for your exam?"

"Well, I know that one book I read for the exam very well."

They both managed a laugh, until Ramirez remembered that with Edith he should have been learning another language entirely. He clenched the steering wheel and tried to change lanes without looking in the rearview mirror, then swerved back into his own lane as someone leaned on his horn and whizzed by them.

"I thought," the girl quavered beside him in a voice he could scarcely hear, "I would have thought that they'd let you take a math exam instead of a second language. I've heard that they do that."

"I don't need if for what I'm doing. I need a knowledge of computers and chemistry and statistics and maybe some physics, but not the straight math they would have wanted me to take."

"Gee," Edith said, "I guess if people aren't in English or anthropology, I expect them to know everything else, like astronomy and geography and everything."

It was true. Students he'd met outside his field were as ignorant of what he was doing as his parents, as *everyone's* parents. One third of the world he knew was made up of anxious, elderly folks who continually asked, "Just *what* is it you're doing now? I mean, when will you be *out*? And what is it this is going to teach you to do? And are there jobs open for a climatologist, astronomer, geologist, folklorist, art historian, sociologist, anthropologist, philosopher, oceanographer—for that matter, microbiologist? Two or three times a year, over Christmas turkeys or Easter hams or the sweet wines of the Seder, you tried to tell them, and they nodded with that rare combination of abstract awe and practical contempt which might someday separate not just one generation but one class from another (for after all, it was *their* birds, *their* ham, *their* gefültefish, which their precocious—sometimes balding—children ate as they explained). Yes, even departments didn't know what was going on across the next patch of university grass, and one grad-

uate student, in fact, was a stranger to his colleague down
the hall, each one locked in a private struggle with enzymes
or Sidney Lanier or the San Andreas fault.

"If you decide to go on, what would your dissertation
topic be?" he inquired politely. "Would you like something
to eat? Some Mexican food? Something Japanese? Or there's
that Indonesian place right on the beach."

"No. No, thank you. I don't know. I like American literature but there are so many of those American lit people
around that even the men can't get a job. I like seventeenth-
century poetry, but I can't stand the prose. And I guess I
should do something about women but I don't know what
to say, and I should find someone minor to work on so it
won't get out of hand, but I can't find any—"

"Do you really want to go on? I mean, do you want to
teach? What can you do with a PhD in English?"

"I don't know."

"Don't know about which, what?"

"I don't know about any of it."

"Well, then . . ."

"You know what I like? I like sitting in the arcade of the
art building and having lunch, or, *you know*, since I started
reading for those courses, they let me use an office sometimes. I like to sit in that office. I used to be so afraid I'd
keep the door closed. I'd do work and I'd hear people laughing on either side of me. They all knew each other, Juan.
But now, you know, really just since—that first party, I leave
the door open, and sometimes I go over to talk, and sometimes they come over."

They faced the beach. The sun was close to setting but
the sky remained a clear perfect blue, the ocean another
two perfect shades of blue—a little clutch of boats were
blowing and bowing inside the tiny breakwater by the Santa
Monica Pier. Ramirez glanced up toward his left where the
all-night lights of the AXEL Corporation were already
turned on, and then turned right, toward Topanga Canyon,
Malibu, the open beach, the little motel.

"You know what, Juan?" And as he looked at her politely, the old brown friend and his crazy rainbow almost
came together again, "what I love to think about is we all
know so *much*, you know? We don't have anything but pretty
soon we're bound to, and in a few years all the people we

meet in those offices, they'll be like in Wisconsin or Florida. They'll be all over. The Voltaires are in political science, he could be a politician. You'll invent a cure for something—you're not going to stay at that place forever, are you?—and Lorraine will be a famous artist, and Walter will *own* some set of natives, and I knew some musicians when I was an undergraduate, we could all be part of a gigantic cartel. You know, we could rule the world. Wouldn't you like to be part of a gigantic cartel. Juan?''

But he was thinking about something else. "Did you bring your bathing suit? We could spend the night. I was hoping we could spend the night. That way we could swim tomorrow morning. If you wanted to, of course"

Her face became strict and wide. "Oh no. Walter wouldn't know where I am."

"But isn't he out anyway? You could call the sitter . . ."

"No! I couldn't leave the kids alone *overnight.*"

"You've left them alone before."

She looked out the window on her side and again her hand grasped the door handle. He'd offended her. In one of his—now usual—shifts of perception he saw, just for a second, a glimpse of their situation through her eyes. She might feel—anything. Her feelings ran right along beside his and took up equal space.

He drove past the motel. In his intense wish to do everything right, he had quizzed Edith on every activity in her life, beginning with school right back through high school to her childhood, her infancy, her dreams—such as they were. After an hour or so of driving along the coast he knew more about her than he knew about any woman in the world, more than his mother, certainly more than he knew about his wife. Edith answered right up; he knew, finally, rather more about her than he wanted to know. The coast, free finally of the little shacks and clapboard homes of middle-class Malibu, became more beautiful. They were well on their way to Ventura when Edith stopped the steady drone of her informational voice and rapped out, "Don't you intend to stop? Are you going to drive the night away and then say, Oh well, it's just too late, and then go home?''

"No! There's this place I've seen, that's all, and it always looked so inviting that I thought it would be a nice place for us to go together."

"Do you do this kind of thing a lot?"

"Never in my life before," he said.

"Me either."

"Jesus," he sighed, "it ought to be around here some-place."

"Well, *Juan*," she complained wifishly, "we're almost to Oxnard. Maybe we ought to stop somewhere else."

"This place I want," he said abstractedly, "is just a little north of Zuma Beach. That's what they said."

"*Who* said?"

"Oh, just—did I say that?"

"Well, we're way beyond there now. So why don't we just stop somewhere else?"

He'd driven miles out of his way, lost valuable time, and succeeded in looking like a fool to a girl whose threshold in that area must be very high. He made a U turn in the high-way, his brakes screeching, the car—and project—skidding wildly as he began again, this time racing south. It was get-ting dark, Christ Jesus, and they weren't even there yet. He had to find the car—that would be difficult, maybe impossible in the dark. He had to rent the room next to where the car was—what if the car was parked away from the building, on the street, maybe, or down by the beach? What if the rooms on either side were *rented*? He increased his speed to eighty and Edith cringed in her seat and kept quiet.

The place he was looking for was there all right, on the side of a little hill between the highway and the ocean. The motel looked to have been someone's bad idea in the twen-ties. It was arbitrary even now; half-hidden from the high-way—too far north for the city's teen-age trade, too far south to be a rich man's whim, too close to LA for anyone to spend the night there on a bona fide coastal trip, too shabby for any big spender who wanted to show his girl of the evening a good time.

In fact, when Juan turned into the dirt driveway and un-derneath the decent but hardly spectacular sign which blinked sedately on a homemade hanging arch, he heard Edith give a tiny but unmistakable sigh. She wants something big, he thought. She's giving up her virtue for a six-dollar night.

"Remember I have that champagne," he said to her after his fifteen minutes of silent desperate driving. "More than we can possibly drink. They give it to you in a regular bucket of ice. It's made of cardboard and they give it to you with the ice. So that it looks like a real celebration.''

She didn't answer.

"I'll tell you what," he said. "Since it's . . . uh . . . your night, why don't we just sort of drive through, and then if you don't like it, if it doesn't seem right to you, we'll find someplace else.''

She nodded her head.

"But I have to tell you," he said, "that if you don't like it I'll kill you.'' It was the kind of thing Lorraine said, and she was Lorraine's closest friend. She doesn't want to be reminded of my wife, he thought furiously to himself. Ramirez! Now, for once in your life, do the right thing!

The motel was actually perhaps a dozen tiny apartments. Some of them were built together in clumps of two or three, some were separate, actually cottages. They hugged the hill's incline, out of sight from the highway, and still, by some geographical fluke, out of sight of the sea, although the only sound above Ramirez's silent motor was the extraordinary crashing of the waves somewhere at the bottom of the bluffs. Behind the cottages a bank of wild daisies swept up high and broad into the sky. To the south, in a miniature valley before the hill went up again, geranium, bougainvillea and passion flower grew wild. The grounds of the motel itself were neatly tended; each place had its own little balcony with potted succulents and slatted wooden furniture—dating back forty years—but even in this poor light, painted and clean.

If they're in a separate house, Ramirez thought, I'll just say I have to go out for a walk or for something to eat. I'll leave the recorder in the car, and then fasten it on from the outside. But the car was parked in front of a duplex. That meant he would have to unload his taping equipment and camera along with his champagne and bathing suit, then he would have to make love to this decent, uninteresting girl and put up the equipment before her unblinking eyes, that he would—still, somehow, have to find out who was next door, and with never a moment alone.

"How do you like it?" he said brutishly. "It's OK, isn't it?"

"Fine, it's fine."

He put the car in reverse, backed speedily toward the sound of highway traffic and stopped in front of the little house labeled *Manager*.

Edith took a deep breath.

"What is it?"

"It's just . . . that I've never done this before."

The manager of the motel sat in his darkening living room watching a program on wildlife, a beer by his hand. Ramirez rang the bell on the counter which stood as a divider between private life and office, and the man jumped up, skipped over, snapped on his desk light, all but stood at attention. When he saw Ramirez was a Mexican, his welcoming smile faded a little.

"Fine night, isn't it?"

"Yes."

"Your wife with you?"

"Yes."

"I guess I'll give you number twelve. That one's closest to the ocean if you want to go for a walk. There's a path right down to the beach, it starts from your balcony, but I wouldn't try it at night, it's pretty steep in some places. . . ."

"No!"

The manager looked up apprehensively.

"What I mean is, I don't think I want number twelve."

"Why *not*?"

"My wife is afraid of heights. Just a minute, I'll see which one she wants." Ramirez bolted from the room, slammed the door, raced past the car where Edith waited, and down the path. Once near the blue Pontiac he stopped and stepped clumsily behind a hedge. I could have brought the tape recorder now, he thought; but realized immediately that he was never going to reach that level of organization— at least not tonight. One thing, I'm here. I've done this much, he reassured himself, and squinted to see the number next door to the occupied apartment. It had to be seven. Ramirez remembered that warmth in the winter brought out snakes in these hills and the back of his neck began to tingle. Perhaps he should dash out into the road and check the registration on the Pontiac. But it was almost sure to be a cover name. If he could get across the road and look in the back windows of the occupied apartment—but the front blinds were tightly drawn and there was no reason why the back windows should be any more accessible. After all, they were spies; their business was privacy. If I can only use my camera, Ramirez thought intently, and was amazed at how quickly he'd lost his self-consciousness in the whole business, how natural it seemed, after all, to be creeping around in the bushes on a dark night, after someone he didn't even know. Then he remembered Edith and thought, If we can go out on the balcony to look at the moon or something then I can see the back windows. That way, they won't suspect anything.

He raced from behind the hedge back up the dirt road, grimaced at the girl in the car, slammed into the office.

"Seven," he said to the manager, and rubbed furiously at the back of his neck. "Seven will do fine."

"I couldn't help noticing you didn't ask your . . . wife."

"Oh, she gets nervous, *you* know. I know what she's most comfortable with."

"But that's next to number eight. That and number two are the only other occupied rooms we have so far."

"She likes the sound of voices near her. She's very afraid of heights *and* ocean. She wanted to stop inland somewhere but this seemed like such a pretty place . . ."

The manager still hesitated.

"It was the *trip*," Ramirez went on. "All the way from San Francisco. Highway One. Those cliffs. And the fog."

"Number seven it is. It's close to the road."

Finally they were there. Ramirez got out, pushed his own seat forward and rummaged about in the back seat. "There're just a few things here I want to bring in," he muttered. "Would you just take the champagne here?" He turned to look at Edith, who sat motionless staring at him. "Oh! Sorry." He untangled himself from the back seat and his parcels, and ran around the car to open the door.

Ramirez handed her the bucket of champagne and then stacked the tape recorder together with a coil of wire (in case he had to hook it up outside). The camera he shoved into his pocket. He'd had trouble getting the equipment he wanted; everything he had was larger than he'd expected. He left the gun under the seat.

He opened the door of their tiny room and Edith walked in in front of him and set the cardboard bucket on the table.

"This is a pretty place," she said. The bed and bureau were made of painted wood from the thirties; the chenille bedspread was spanking clean. There was extra furniture, an easy chair and an old-fashioned floor lamp. He turned on the lamp and the dark room turned rosy.

"Let's go out on the balcony," Ramirez said. He opened the door, and they stepped outside. This time Edith said, "The air is beautiful," and again it was, fragrant with jasmine which had been trained as a natural wall to divide number seven's balcony from its neighbor.

"I think I can see the ocean," Edith said. "Right down there where the two hills come together. See that little triangle?" He became aware that she had her arm around his waist. She was three or four inches taller than Lorraine, but still very short for him. Actually, she was about the size of his mother, and somehow, though she was certainly thinner than his mother, the same sort of feeling seemed to emanate from her; solidity, a great physical comfortableness. All of the glittering hallucinations he'd had about her were for the moment gone, but a good portion of the euphoria remained. She seemed *good* to him; and even she seemed less afraid now that they were here.

"You can smell all the flowers out here," she said to him. "Is that jasmine? I think my mother had a night-blooming jasmine once. She said she didn't like it, it was too strong."

Edith laid her head against his chest. Her hair smelled clean and natural, she wasn't wearing any perfume. He thought for an instant what Lorraine would bring to a night like this; the artifice, the slick fabrics, the heady scents, the wit, the hectic pleasures, but he couldn't feel bad about it, because he was right here. After years of organization and fear and activity, he'd—at least for the moment—come to a stop. She didn't move and neither did he, except to fold his long arms around her while she snuggled against him and made herself comfortable. Underneath the sound of the ocean he could hear both of them breathing.

"Your hair smells like flowers," he whispered to her, and she responded somehow, not by tightening her arms, but he could feel through her body that she'd heard him.

Right after Lorraine, Ramirez thought about mortal sin, and dismissed that too. He'd just have to deal with all that later, but not now, because here they were, and in the eye of all his personal pain and maybe real international problems, and the whole world scurrying around them, he and Edith were getting some rest.

They stood quietly together for perhaps five, fifteen minutes. Then she turned up her face to him; he bent down, but it was too difficult; he didn't feel that it should be difficult. He sank to his knees, not to be theatrical, and with no recollection that he did this every week and sometimes twice a week in church but just to get more easily to her face. They kissed, with languor.

The door to number eight opened. Two men came out and stood on their veranda no more than four feet from them. Ramirez and Edith froze. They spoke in a foreign tongue, perhaps Chinese, Japanese, Filipino, maybe some African dialect. Both voices seemed familiar, one much more than the other, achingly familiar. Edith said, rather clearly, "Please, you're hurting me."

The voices stopped, Juan scrambled to his feet, keeping his back to number eight, and bending over began to cover Edith's neck and shoulder with desperate kisses. "Please, please," she muttered, and scrambled about somewhere underneath him.

The men, after listening a minute, moved back inside, rather ostentatiously shutting their door.

"Let's go in," Ramirez said. "Listen, did you happen to see what they looked like?"

"No," Edith said, and her voice sounded queer and cold. "Why should I have?"

"No reason, no reason," he answered, and pushed her back in their room. Once there he began again his desperate hugging and kissing. If his huge hand chanced on any part of hers, elbow, breast, ear, knee, he grabbed it with fine impartiality, kneaded it. She stood impassive and let him do anything.

"You go take a shower," he told her, "I'll wait here for you."

"I already took a shower."

His hands clasped her shoulders until she flinched. "I . . . like my women to be completely fresh."

For a minute he thought she might simply walk out. I won't let her go, he thought, or maybe it would be better.

"Do you want to go home?" he asked hopefully. "Well, if you do, you'll have to go by yourself. You could hitchhike if you really wanted to. But *I'm* not taking you anywhere. If you want to go you'll have to go by yourself."

She went into the bathroom and shut the door.

Ramirez ripped off his shirt and pants, then he lunged toward the bed where he'd dumped his equipment. He opened the tape recorder, pulled out the bugging plugs, held them, thought. Did he have time to set up the plugs against the wall, attach the wires, place the main part of the device under the bed where Edith (pray God) wouldn't notice it? Or should he just go ahead and put the whole thing right against the wall? Detaching it wouldn't be a problem; he could come back after he'd taken Edith home. In fact, why hadn't he come alone in the first place? Because, he supposed, a couple attracted less attention at a place like this. It didn't matter; he'd jam it against the wall, she wouldn't notice because she wouldn't be looking.

Ramirez was better with plants than machines. There were two simple suction attachments which were meant to adhere to the wall, rather in the manner of tiny ears. He had only managed to get one of them to stick when Edith, solemn and quiet, came out of the shower, her coat on over her damp, naked body, and stood without a word beside him.

"I'm just . . ." he said, to her pointed silence, "I'm attaching these. Now, we'll hear what goes on next door, the way they heard us when we were out on the balcony. Sort of tit for tat, OK?"

She didn't answer. Both ears were in place now, and he set the tape going.

"It's like a . . . souvenir. So that we'll always remember tonight." Ramirez laboriously got up from his knees. "How about some champagne now? As a celebration. Or did I say that before?" He opened the champagne.

This is insane, he thought once again and with finality. I am going mad. This can't absolutely can't, can't be me. He was the same Juan Ramirez—though his life had lately rocked and shifted and distorted—who had eaten two fried eggs this morning, whose kids were home asleep. But (now he knew it) spies had breakfast, took out their laundry, had their cars lubed. And murderers and child molesters spoke kindly and naturally to tradesmen.

"Look, Juan," Edith said, shifting her weight from one foot to the other as though they were standing in line for pastrami sandwiches at school, "I think, if you don't mind, that I'll take you up on your offer. I *mean*," she continued,

as he started to object, "that just because Walter's done all
that to me, I don't have to do it to him. And after all, we're
neighbors and all, and all that. And what you said really is
true, I mean you bought the champagne, and drove all the
way out here, and you got your whole evening free when you
could have stayed home or been working, so what you said
is *right* and I think I'll just start on home now. And I'll see
you tomorrow, OK?" She started casually toward the door.

"What about your clothes?" Ramirez said thickly.

"Oh, *those*, well, you know, I'll just button my coat, and
you can—would you mind?—just bring them home in the
car, and I'll pick them up tomorrow."

"That's crazy! You're acting crazy!"

"Certainly not. I don't think so at all. And I don't want
you to think, Juan, that it has anything to do with you, it's
just that I don't want to stay here, I guess I must just feel a
little bit guilty, you see that, don't you?"

"You're worried about the machine. I can explain."

"Certainly not! I can even see how it would be interesting. And if I knew you a little bit better I'm not saying I
wouldn't like it. In fact, it's silly isn't it? We don't' even
need machines where we live, we hear everything all the
time."

She got to the door, tried to jerk it open, but Ramirez
had locked it when he came in. She was just able to get it
open before he pulled her hands from the knob, shut the
door and locked it again.

"Nobody's going anywhere," he told her, and reached
down and shelled off her coat.

It was like the old days, all days, for him. He was desperate, as usual, and went on from there. In the grip of
violence, as usual, overcome with his usual blind rage, he
attacked her; lifted her up to his face, then pushed her down
to his groin, trying to make the point that lust was all that
he'd come here for and convincing himself in short order.
Unlike Lorraine, she did nothing to please him, was not
oblique, was not active. She simply waited. He'd heard Walter Wong call his wife a cold bitch often enough through
their porous walls, but this didn't seem to be coldness; he'd
seen that, moved against that. Frigidity was a spur to lust.
This was waiting, and curiosity.

Was he a curiosity then?

After the first minutes he tried to make love as he never had before. At once detached and attentive he noticed what they did. He was afraid for a moment he wouldn't be able to do it at all, but he was all right, he seemed all right to himself. He went on for a while, felt no response, came, stopped, looked down at her still wide-open eyes.

"I'm sorry," he said. "I guess you didn't. Did you?"

"Actually it was very nice, Juan. Thank you very much."

He rolled off, stared at the ceiling. The tape recorder made a tiny whir.

"Listen. Edith."

She listened to him in the profoundest silence.

"Was it OK?"

She took a breath and he went on. "I mean. Am I all right?"

"Gee, Juan. I ought to say yes, but I don't know. I don't think I'm the right person to ask. I don't know anything about it at all. Nothing at all."

After a minute she spoke again. "What time is it? I've got to go home."

"I don't think it's more than eleven or so."

"It must be more than that because it got dark so late."

He lay there motionless until she prodded him again with her voice. "Juan?"

And he pulled his arm up to see the time. "It's twelve-fifteen," he said. "That's not so late. He knew you were going out."

She tossed around in the bed. She wasn't a feather like Lorraine, certainly.

"Do you feel—sad about what we did?"

"No. But you know? I feel sad being away from home. I feel homesick."

"Yes," Ramirez said after a pause. "You just want it to be so . . ."

"So everybody could have a home," Edith said passionately. "So all the kids would have mothers and daddies and all the grown-ups would have friends, and on the weekends get together to play cards or do some work together. . . ."

"The mothers would cook," Ramirez said. "The fathers would work on their cars or maybe have little gardens. My relatives lived that way in New Mexico. They'd get together, like that, after church on Sundays."

"I don't know about church, but I know one thing, there'd be no drinking and no screwing around. People would stay married forever. They wouldn't, they wouldn't . . ." She got up and went into the bathroom.

"Where are you going?" Ramirez nervously said. "I mean, are you really going somewhere? Do you really want to go now?"

"Oh, yes, Juan, I'm sorry." She came to the bathroom door with her underwear already on, zipping up her skirt.

"You can't go yet! I'm not ready to go."

"What do you mean?" She reached for her blouse.

"Well, we haven't found out yet what they're doing next door."

"My goodness. I don't even know what you're *doing*, can I go home or *not*? You wouldn't hurt me, I know that, you've been so kind to me, we *know* each other. Please, Juan, let me go home now."

"I know what it is," he said slowly. "You remember from Lorraine, I don't know why I didn't think of it. I must have remembered it every day of my life except right now. So why did you come here with me?" He sat up on the edge of the bed. "Or is that why you came here with me?"

"No! I . . . liked you. But now, *please*, I just want to go home and see my *kid*!"

She began to cry.

"OK, just a minute, I'm going to take a little walk," and as she began to protest, he raised his voice. "Just to get my bearings. I want to think, I just feel a little nervous now, Edith, I don't feel like driving." He put on his clothes and reached for his glasses. They hu : the bridge of his nose, they always did.

"Look, so you won't be afraid, I'll leave the car keys with you. So you won't think I'm going to run out on you or something. You'll have them right here."

"I don't even know you. I didn't even know what to say to you in the car coming here with you. I can remember it being like that before I got married, but I would have thought we would have been more . . . suave or something. Doesn't it get any easier as you get older?"

"I don't know," Ramirez said. "I doubt it." He felt in his jacket pocket for the camera.

I'll just walk around, he thought, and take whatever pictures I can. And leave the tape running. She won't touch it. That way I won't have to come back after I take her home. Unless I find something. Then I'll come back.

"I'm leaving for a minute or two, Edith. There's just something I have to think about. You keep the keys. But don't go outside! I . . . wouldn't want to have anything happen to you when you're with me. There're apt to be some weirdos around a place like this."

At the end of this speech (mumbled, said into his shirt as he crossed the room to hand her the keys) he looked down into her upturned face. She looked up at him, shook her head.

"Look who's talking." Her face broke into a prism of laughter. He shook his head to get her once more in focus.

"Sometimes, lately, when I'm talking to you I get the strangest sensation. . . ."

"I should hope so," she observed, and then giggled again. Even with all his worries, he could see she wasn't used to talking this way, and enjoyed it, even as she shocked herself.

"OK," he said, and held on for a moment to her upper arm, "I'm going." He wanted to say that if anything happened to him to tell Lorraine and watch out for the kids, when he remembered that he didn't know where Lorraine really was right now and that Edith would be bound to watch out for the kids anyway. "I'm going," he said again. "Just for a minute. You take care."

He turned and went outside. Once he'd shut the door behind him he stood alone on the miniature stoop. He was suddenly shaking with fear. I don't even have to do this, he thought, and reviewed every possibility of an alternative with that part of his mind which he could pull out like a drawer (and which, though it still checked out every variation on every new germ and its antibiotic enemy, had less and less to do with what was becoming his everyday life). No. They had him. Or he had himself. He'd been stupid enough to get into it, now he couldn't see a way out except this way. It comes from not knowing exactly what you want to do, he thought. There was no market for what he might want to do.

If I were a gardener right now, he thought, I'd weed the ice plant right under their windows. I'd turn the hose on the windowpane so hard that they'd come to complain. I'd take their picture and apologize. I'd put fertilizer all around. A stupid Mexican. He thought of Marlon Brando playing Zapata. Some people might choose to be what he'd been trying so hard all his life to get away from.

Ramirez pushed his glasses far up on his nose, moved away from the tiny porch and down the gravel driveway. At the end of the building he stopped, looked both ways, took out a handkerchief and polished his glasses. He put them back on and stared intently at the windows of the apartment next to where Edith waited for him. The shades were pulled tight, down below the sill. If they had been open the tiniest crack, Ramirez would have risked taking a picture even out there in the open, exposed to the possible gaze of the manager or Edith or anyone. But they were closed, closed tight.

Ramirez thought he saw a shade twitch, and quickly turned away. He blew his nose. He looked once more each way, every way, and then ducked back toward the ocean side of number eight. That would be, if it were like its neighbor, where the bathroom was. The window was high off the ground, perhaps made that way deliberately to inconvenience the average Peeping Tom, but Ramirez's chin was on a level with the sill. This shade was tightly shut too. It bothered Ramirez that it was so quiet inside; he began to have the strong, terrible feeling that someone (or several) was watching him, that he was being followed. He turned around, his breath coming in shallow gasps, but there was no one there, of course.

As quietly as he could, he continued around to the back of the house, standing at first in the squashy plants at the base of the veranda, then—after some hesitation—hoisting himself up on it. He lay with his ear to the wall, hearing at first only the ocean sound a wall makes when you put your ear to it, and then some voices in conversation; neutral, foreign.

He tried to see in the window; the shades were drawn here as well. But he hoped to see something of the shadows of his colleagues as they stood beside their own floor lamp. He did see shadows and they looked familiar, but he couldn't recognize anyone. He couldn't even recognize the language. He knew it wasn't Spanish or English, but beyond that it sounded even more obscure than when he and Edith had heard it on the balcony.

The shadows moved toward the back door, and Ramirez stopped breathing. If they came out, he thought. If they come out, I'll say my girl and I had a fight. I'll say I'm drunk. But the shadows remained where they were, chatting, standing up.

Ramirez could stand it no longer. He vaulted over the edge of the veranda and crashed into the underbrush. I'll say I'm out for a walk, he thought, and cut back rapidly the way he came. I don't care, I've got the tape to work with, and even though I was afraid, thank you, God, I had the courage to do it. I never thought I'd really do it. Why, I can do anything! I fooled those guards at AXEL, I made love to my friend's wife, I got my PhD in only four years when it takes most people seven.

The shade on number eight's bathroom window was up, and the window was open. Someone was humming inside. It was all to do over again. Ramirez could have gone back to his own veranda, climbed back on as he just had on number eight, surprised Edith, persuaded her to stay. They could try again. There had been that leisure, an intimation of a whole other style. It hadn't come from him or Edith either; it was a combination of them both, a point of view. But instead he went forward a few steps, and cautiously peered in the window.

An African stood in front of the mirror over the basin. He wore a western business suit of iridescent black, and was doing his hair with oil, a small jar of yellow oil. He dipped his fingers in the oil, then twisted each strand of his kinky hair into soft manageable curls. He hummed as he worked. Ramirez knew he had seen him somewhere but couldn't remember where. He reached for his camera, rested it on the sill for perfect focus, although his hands were by now perfectly steady.

He was out like a light. Lantana and geraniums cushioned his fall.

He woke up later tied to a tree. There were lengths and lengths of rope tied around him; he could hardly see his own skin or clothes. It was dark, cold, dusty, the moon had gone. He was alone.

He tried to work the knots; they had been badly tied, but there were too many of them. He kept trying and at the end of an hour had unraveled perhaps one or two.

Ramirez heard footsteps, heavy and relaxed. He thought immediately of Edith but it had to be someone much bigger, a man. Maybe the manager? Or was he in on it too?

The steps came closer. Shoes kicked lazily at the gravel of the driveway. A man slouched through the underbrush, came up behind Ramirez.

"Dummy," he said.

It was Walter Wong.

"Thank God," Ramirez said. "She told you then. Thank God you're here."

"She give you a pretty bad time?"

"Come on, come on," Ramirez said. "Can you get me loose? I've got to get out! We'll have a fight later, OK? I mean you're not exactly God's little lamb. You've got that girl, Lorraine told me, in sociology—"

"Actually, urban development. She'll be getting her MA in urban development. It's a new department."

"Hurry up, Walt, this is no joke."

"All tied up, aren't you?" Walter shook his head, smiled fondly at his old friend. He'd brought his gallon of wine; he held it hooked by the forefinger of his left hand, and brought it to his full, smiling lips for a drink. "The Red Mountain Club," he said reflectively. "If things go on like they are, I'll be the last surviving member. You never were one, were you? Too busy becoming rich and famous." Walter swayed, smiled benignly. "I think," he said, "you'd better take this." He pulled a thick pink capsule from his pocket. "Here."

"Look," Ramirez said. "Walt, look. It was wrong, I know. It was a mortal sin. It hurts people. I know it, I know that."

Walter listened, smiling. "Open up," he said, and held the capsule to Ramirez's mouth.

He took out a knife, held it to Ramirez's throat. "Take the fucking pill, Juan, or I'll kill you. How do you like that?"

"We have a saying in Spanish," Ramirez said desperately. "It means no woman on earth is worth the trouble."

"You bet," Walter agreed promptly. "But I'm afraid, I'm afraid, it's a little more serious than that."

XII

Ramirez was in a boat, rocking. It was a funny boat. Or it was an old man with asthma. It breathed and snored and turned over restlessly underneath him. Other times it laughed a lot. He was inside a boat painted blue and white. A lot of attention had been paid to certain brass fixtures; they winked at him when he opened his eyes. When they winked at him they disappeared (because their eyes were gone, of course). When they did that, Ramirez opened and shut his own eyes to do what the fixtures were doing. They figured out right away what he was up to and they couldn't stop laughing. After a while he gave up on them as being just too silly.

His bunk, the narrow hard bunk which was built against the inside of the boat, was asleep. He could hear it breathing too. Sometimes it turned over gently against him in its sleep. He moved quietly—when he moved at all—so as not to wake it up.

He was struck most of all by the fact that he didn't have to be frightened, that they were all taking care of him, and that God was taking care of them all. He had known it all along of course; they'd told him that often enough and he'd always believed it, but he saw now that it was perfectly, literally true.

Walt came in once to see how he was doing. "How's the boy?" Walter asked. He smiled his wino grin and his teeth flew straight out into the room, snickering as they bumped against each other.

With great effort Ramirez reminded him, "Put your hand on your mouth. They might not come back otherwise."

Then he saw himself as a boy on the dusty streets of the East Size or in summers walking the bluffs and meadows of New Mexico, and wept. Everyone was a child; everyone was taken care of.

"You're a boy," he said to Walter Wong, and the figure he addressed shrank to half its size; he saw Walter with slanting eyes, a sailboat in his hand and a skate key.

"You're all right, kid," his friend told him, and disappeared, leaving Ramirez to ponder the words ALL RIGHT which formed in his head in capital letters and moved with stately grandeur left to right while he read them slowly and with delight: ALL RIGHT, ALL RIGHT, ALL RIGHT.

He lay quietly and wept, it was so beautiful and true, but pretty soon the room told him to knock it off. It was true all right, but nothing to cry about. It began to do silly things to cheer him up again. The round portholes opened their mouths and then pursed themselves down to the size of raisins. They hummed and sang, it was a funny tune they kept on with; only one note, but with infinitely funny variations. They had some trouble breathing and singing at the same time but did their best.

Ramirez turned his attention to the wall beside his bed, it noticed him looking and blushed a deep melon orange. He put out his hand to touch it and touched the sweetest flesh, God's own flesh. He wept some more and spent an infinity, not talking asking beseeching only loving until he thought (if he thought) that his heart would burst with love.

Someone touched him on the back of the neck. His bunk was jarred awake, crossly muttered something and fell asleep again, snoring loudly.

"Turn it on its side," Ramirez told the presence and turned over himself to see who it was. Moving was the only thing he didn't like.

A dark-skinned girl sat on the edge of his bed. She wore a green silk robe and her brown arms were covered with thin gold bracelets.

"They thought you might like to eat," she said. "It's almost morning and they didn't think you had eaten."

In her lap she held a small white plate with several slices of cheese, some marinated artichoke hearts, sliced tomatoes and mushrooms. She put the plate on the bunk beside him and helped to raise him on one elbow where he could gaze down at his meal.

He tentatively touched an artichoke and it wiggled like a fox terrier and turned over on its back to be scratched.

"They're my friends," he told her. "I'm sorry, I don't mean to cry."

He slowly, slowly, ate. It was his first communion, and like Moses he discovered God had moods. He was vulnerable, the mushroom showed that. He was rich; oil was rich, riches, infinitely rich. Tomato told him God had nerves. He had a mean streak. Original Sin was mean. But why should He be better than we are? Ramirez thought. If He were better we'd be better. There was something beyond any Divine Person. Ramirez digressed to the Trinity for an endless second; but he dismissed it quickly as being too simple to bother with. What he cared about now was the problem of infinity. INFINITY spread out from his mind in flat blue waves.

"I want to look out the window," he said to the waiting girl. "I don't want to bother you."

She held his arm while he crossed the room. It was only four or five steps across but he was glad of her help. There was no question of staggering, but the difficulties were enormous. He had to duck his head under the low ceiling and duck even more to look out of the porthole. Bending his knees and rounding his shoulders, he pressed his face to the glass.

The boat was on water, flat green water; there was his infinity. He saw trees somewhere in the middle distance and realized that man puts up his own limits; that across there is land, down through the water there is more land yet, even up in the sky there are other lands. Not out but in, Ramirez thought. In! How obvious, how splendid.

He watched while the dark night dimmed and the stars faded, saw the flat graying of the sky's edge and studied the problems. Once or twice he was afraid, but he put his hand to the wall and its quiet breathing reassured him.

After the infinite he turned around and looked for the girl. He was sure she'd be there and she was, sitting in a tiny camp chair by his bunk, leafing through a magazine.

"What time is it?"

"About seven-thirty or eight. Almost time for breakfast."

"On the same *day*? Just from last night?"

"Yes. It's been about four hours, that's all."

"It's all over then."

"When you begin to think so the best is over, but you still have seven or eight more hours. Not so intense, but very nice."

As she said this her face was normal, just a beautiful girl's, but halfway through her sentence her face broke in two, he saw her profile, he saw her full face.

"If Picasso thought this way all the time, there isn't much credit in what he did," he told her.

"Oh, sure, there's credit," she said, and went back to her magazine.

"You stayed all night with me. Did you have to? Did they tell you to?"

"No," she said. "I just thought it might be nice. I couldn't sleep anyway. I have this paper to write and I couldn't get anywhere with it, so I came down here about midnight to see if anybody was around. They were all out, after you, I guess, and then everyone came back. Around three, I guess it was."

"So you haven't even slept."

"Oh, yes. I slept until three. In fact, I slept here until you came in. Let's get some breakfast. After that I'll take you to see Walter. Don't worry," she said as he gazed at her, "we'll come back here later, both of us."

He had been on a boat. (If that was true it was all true.) It was tied up to a bank, a dirt bank crowded with succulents, cactus, stunted trees. The early sun was hazy and there was no brightness about the day. Instead he felt a concentrated, precise, knowledgeable delight about the true colors of everything, and beneath that the texture; the weaving of it all together. Things had stopped breathing for him now. They stood quiet, not even smiling, but terrifically alive. (But it wasn't extreme really; he'd felt the same way walking to school on those hazy, expectant, dark, exciting mornings when he was ten; felt this extraordinary devotion to God not during any offertory or consecration—when kneeling upright made him faint and sick—but on his way to church on a narrow path—like this!—which crossed diagonally through a vacant lot of rye grass; bright green in April's sun but in May, touched with the gold of the sun and the sun's smell.)

"Come on," the girl said, "watch your step. They've been painting around here."

She led him across a narrow plank where tins of paint stood waiting for another day's work, their rags folded across their tops, more patches in God's quilt of Universal Order.

"It's always best to have someone with you," the girl went on, "even at this stage, because you just stop otherwise and someone has to come out and get you."

Once on land, Ramirez turned to look where he had been, ducking his head under and away from the intense overhanging branches. It was a boat all right. He had been on a boat. (If that was true it was all true.) It was a houseboat, parked maybe six feet from the land's edge. The lake was small; he guessed they were in some kind of park. The grounds were well cared for, even elegant. Land sloped up on every side from the lake like the sides of a small soup bowl.

The girl took his hand and led him down a narrow path by the lake. He read tiny signs which bore the names of species and another, longer sign which admonished: *This is God's house. Observe a reverent silence. Do not disturb your brothers.* They made their way perhaps halfway around the lake, Ramirez often stumbling in his attempts not to step off the narrow path, the girl exerting steady gentle pull.

"Where are we?"

"Don't you know? I thought everybody came here. Where do you go to school?"

"UCLA."

"I thought everybody came here. I've been coming here since I was fifteen. It was different then of course."

"Where are we?"

"The Self Realization Fellowship."

"They have the nutburgers over by Vermont Avenue?"

"Yes. They don't know we're here of course. I mean, they know we're here but not what we're doing. But it's a great place, great for afternoon dates, they let you do what you want. There's a wonderful feeling here."

"You people . . . are in charge of this place? What did you do with the regular people?"

"Gee, I don't know. They're still around. They love everyone. I know it's done me a lot of good to come here. I think Walter rents from them. I know we can use their rooms anytime we want to." They passed a tiny windmill and separate monuments to Jesus, Buddha and Mohammed, all no more than three feet high.

"These guys believe in everybody," the girl said. "They're getting ready for New Year's now, but they've got three or four of them in a year. It makes it nice."

They came to a large house set back from the lake. A young man sat out on the front porch attempting the lotus position. They went through the door down some steps, past a life-size photograph of a yoga in long hair caught in an immense mother-of-pearl frame—past a little counter of Indian curios, through a tiny museum (statues of ivory on large pedestals—spaced out—there weren't many of them, and an enormous snakeskin from India on the wall, so labeled).

"What's that smell?"

"Incense."

"I never smelled any like that."

"Well, it's incense. Walter likes it."

Through all this Ramirez had been thinking. Walter likes this, does that, lives here, goes there. *Walter?* His slack-jawed, bloodshot, good-natured neighbor? *Walter?*

"*Walter* likes it?"

"Oh, yes." She smiled with adolescent complacency. "He's a brilliant man. A sort of a genius really. Oh, he loves everything and he's so funny. He loves a joke. And his clothes, and oh," she smiled inwardly in the manner of bad movies and *True Confessions*, "he's more than all that."

"He's a married man," Ramirez said severely. "He's made his wife very unhappy in the past weeks." But inwardly he was saying to her smile, Are you kidding? *Walter?*

In an upstairs room with a view of the lake, Walter lay on an ottoman, a series of ottomans, some animal skins and a bear rug. He wore an expensive brocade smoking jacket and velvet pants which flared from the knee. His feet were bare and with one hand he scratched them as with the other he desultorily turned the pages of a large book of engravings. Ramirez stood respectfully looking down and saw that the book was full of engravings of people copulating in full Oriental dress, surrounded by delicate trees and art objects. On a low table before him Walter had spread an orderly pile of homemade cigarettes which Ramirez recognized from the East Side as marijuana, an engraved silver cup with a little wine still in it, another empty cup, a carved crystal flagon full of more wine, two packages of Pall Malls, a carton of colored pencils, an ashtray, a green plastic water pistol. The drapes were drawn against the morning light. Ramirez saw that Walter had been drinking but wasn't drunk. If he paced himself and was careful, he could stay that way all day until maybe nine or ten at night, when like a lump of Silly Putty or oil poured back into a vat, he would flatten and no amount of effort could reassemble him until the next morning. Ramirez had seen him that way often on Saturdays, docilely going through the day's errands against Edith's increasing hostility, smiling benignly, shooting her, when she turned her broad back, with his water pistol, carrying (to the store, the gas stations, the cleaners) his steady jug of Red Mountain which he pensively sipped and sipped, until sometimes after dinner and sometimes before, usually during Walter Cronkite's measured survey of the news, he slipped into an inert state. But this wine didn't look like Red Mountain.

"Sit down, kid. They say I'm clumsy but you're, uh, you're impossible. I guess they told you so often enough. They'd come to me and complain. They'd say Ramirez is a dummy. I'd say, no, some kind of a weirdo maybe, but a dummy, no. Why he got through graduate school in three years, I'd tell them. (Actually it was seven semesters, right?) He can't be a dummy, I'd tell them. Why it's taken me seven years and I haven't even got a dissertation topic, oh, Australian languages, yes, but that's not a topic. That's too *wide*. No, I told them, Ramirez is smart. He's a smart man."

Walter Wong delivered this speech with a strong Oriental accent. He pronounced smart as smaht, and wiggled his lips in imitation of a World War II Japanese villain they'd all recently seen on television.

"You knew about it all the time?"

"Who do you think got you the job? I knew you were up shit creek, Lorraine complaining to Edith all day long in that prissy way of hers—I tell you one thing, Juan baby, it was a good thing when Steve got hold of your wife. She's not nearly the pain in the ass she used to be. Boy! She used to be a terrific pain in the ass. In Europe! Boy! She'd say, What's Juan going to do? I don't want to push him but what's he going to do? Oh, Mother is just *livid*, but I don't want to tell him that. And all the time you were walking around with both thumbs jammed up your ass."

Ramirez, who had been standing, sat down, profoundly relieved that it was Walter after all. Because it was true that for all his drunkenness and bad habits (he might turn over from his evening torpor in Vets Housing, smile, open his mouth and throw up on you), still, you were at home in Walter's house.

"They say," Walter went on, "they say I'm clumsy. I run into doorjambs. I never change my handkerchiefs. You know something, Ramirez, I *drink*. But I got you your fucking job, *both* of them. If it weren't for me you'd be working right now in the children's room of some fucking public library. The old slant-eye here has put more students through school than the Mabel Wilson Richards Foundation." He considered this, poured Ramirez some wine, filled his own glass and lay back among the furs. "In fact, I've heard some rumors we own the Mabel Wilson Richards Foundation. Did you like that pill? I thought you deserved a treat after spending some time with Edith."

He lay back and laughed again but Ramirez knew enough of Walter (secret life or not) to hear the animal howling underneath. "They say it's something, they say in a few years it'll be all the rage. At meetings, they talk about giving it to students and addling their brains and putting it in the water supply for the parents, but shit! It'll catch on fast enough anyway. And it doesn't do any harm. It makes people easier to be around. Everyone's a lot nicer around here since they started fooling around with it. They want me to take it but they say it has an adverse effect on people who drink. It makes them want to stop."

The girl who had stayed with Ramirez came in with an enormous breakfast of chicken livers and sour cream, scrambled eggs and pancakes. She started to sit down to share it with them but Walter Wong said, "Beat it, kid," and she left.

"You got me *both* jobs?"

"Sure. I gave Jimmy your name and he checked you out and said OK after Ibi and Oku had said you were OK. Actually, you did OK. I was surprised if you want to know."

"Jimmy *Joyce*?"

"Yeah. He's big. Bigger than we know, I guess. But he doesn't do anything. That's a big test. He watches, you know? He runs all of it out here in California, maybe in the whole West. Or maybe he's not that big, I don't know. He's smart, I know that. He's been in it for years, as long as I have.''

"What is *it*? What is it I was doing?"

Walter scratched his toes. "One of the neatest, simplest businesses anybody around here ever thought up. You know those new stores they've got in town? Those discount houses, like import places? Cheap junk but you like to buy it? Well, what we're working for is like a discount spy outfit. Nothing big time, well, sometimes something pretty big, but usually small jobs for small countries, sort of a wholesale outfit. We fit the job to what they want. For instance, your job was to get that stuff on germs. They probably could have got the same thing by writing to the Health Education and Welfare guys, but they don't trust them, so we cashed in on it. And you did pretty well with the microdots from the QOL project. . . ."

"Microdots?"

"In the tea bags, dummy. Jimmy or somebody stuck them in the bags; you took them out. You could have got in trouble for that but you've got an honest face. Actually, you did all right. All I had to do was send them on to the Midwest office. I don't even know what country they're supposed to be for."

"Who's in charge of it? Who thought it up?"

"What do you want to know for? *I* don't know. There's a market for small jobs for small countries and there's very little risk involved. Jimmy knows more than I do, maybe, but maybe not. I think it might have been several independent outfits, doing a little work here and there and somebody, maybe one guy, decided to organize himself a chain. That part's no fun. It's just paper work."

"What's going to happen now? What are you going to do with me?"

"Nothing! What the fuck am I supposed to do with you? You just go home, I guess. There's something going on but I don't think you and I have to worry. We'll just work for whoever comes out on top. This isn't *dangerous*, you know, Juan. I wouldn't get either one of us involved in anything dangerous."

"What about that woman down in Chinatown? Wasn't that . . . something?"

Walter considered, hesitated. It occurred to Ramirez that

Walter Wong, maybe more than any of them, any of their friends, anyone he'd ever known, had what they all valued most, what made them different from the outside world and the same as each other; a secret intelligence, a brain that they'd early recognized and sometimes ignored like Lorraine, or made fun of like Steve, or took too seriously like Edith, or wanted to get famous with like Mr. Goodman, or to get rich by like countless others. Walter had intelligence; he knew the world.

"Yes. That was something, all right. But that was a different sort of thing. Solid merchandise. A solid deal. Loy wouldn't pay. They couldn't let him get away with that. The general feeling down there was that Loy didn't want his wife so much, he'd found himself a waitress from Bob's Big Boy Hamburgers, a Caucasian with blond hair, what did he want his wife for? Besides, she was a Communist as far as he could make out, and he still belongs to the local branch of the Kuomintang. But he had the family to please so he brought her over. This way, he's done the best he can, see? People suspect, but it's better than if he hadn't made the gesture."

"How big is this—organization?"

"It's big all right, pretty big. It takes in a lot of little operations. I don't know how important any of it is. But there's money in it."

"There's one thing."

"Yeah?"

"How'd you get into this? We were in school. You're an *anthropologist*. What happened?"

"You don't understand. I grew up with this stuff. You ought to understand. That's one reason I gave your name to Jimmy. My grandfather came over here when he was ten. He sold underwear door to door to whores in San Francisco. A kid who couldn't speak English. I must have told you how he stuffed the fake mermaid when he was fifteen and charged the boobs to see it. When he married my grandmother, she was the prettiest white girl in town. And his other wife, the Chinese one, was the prettiest girl in *her* town. When he died he was a hundred years old, worth a hundred thousand dollars, and had a son twelve years old. It was his all right, he kept track of those things. My best friend grew up with men in a furnished room over a gambling den across the border in Mexico. He never saw a Chinese woman until he came up here to high school. Do you understand me? My father has seven passports. I don't think he's ever used them, but they're there if he has to. My dad got me the job. I don't even take a salary. It goes into the family fund. Most of it goes into the business. We've got some of the best art objects in the country. The Chinese over here call this country the mountain of gold, and they want to be sure to get some of it."

"Are they Communists?"

"Are you *kidding*? They're better Americans than Eisenhower."

"Does Edith know about this?"

"You bastard, I ought to do something to you. I didn't think she'd ever pull a thing like this. You know I don't even remember the girl at the party. But she won't let me forget it. I've had women, with Edith you have to or go crazy, but I wouldn't want her to know."

"Does she know what you do?"

"She would if she kept her eyes open, but she doesn't care what I do. When I met her, I thought I saw something, you know? I thought I could tell her everything. Edith and I could have had a lot of fun. But to the Wongs, family is everything. We would never take a child into a store without buying him something. It would be bad manners. You just wouldn't do it. My father did that for me but I can't do that for China. Edith says I'm spoiling her if I buy her anything. The family cooks up a lot of great food—my mother and my aunt—and they give it to us and Edith throws it out. She won't talk to my mother, she won't talk to any of the women. She doesn't like to dress up. My uncle gave her some excellent jade earrings, she won't wear them. We could have had a whole life but it's not the one she wants. It happened the same way to a close friend of mine. He went on a buying trip to Tokyo. He met a girl who came to his room at night and when she left she took his socks with her and washed them and perfumed them and ironed them into ornamental shapes, butterflies and all that. He brought her back here and now she goes to City College and won't screw him."

"Do you," asked Juan, "do you think of divorce?"

"No. Edith is all right. And I have the little girl. I like them both, you know? I can't see it getting better, but I think Caucasians ask too much. I've got all this, I've got the girls here, and what I care about more than anything else is stability. To take care of my parents, my wife, my kids. And there are good times in the world, Juan. You've been working too hard to see them. Did Edith like it with you?''

"No. I'm almost sure she didn't."

"OK. I'm not sure what I'm supposed to do with you right now, I think you stay here for a few days. Maybe longer. You can be with Mei. Spelled M-e-i. She's a nice girl."

"Will Lorraine be all right?"

"How the fuck should I know?"

"Is she home?"

"I haven't the foggiest."

Mei led Juan back along the path to the boat. It was almost noon now; the sun was out, vapor rose from the damp patches of grass where isolated students practiced yoga, read, napped, necked.

While he had been gone, Mei had lit some incense, brought fruit, a bottle of wine. It made him terrifically happy to be back inside the little room. He recognized his feeling as part of the effects of the drug and tried to calm himself, but gave up almost immediately and floated on his happiness.

"Do you mind if we leave the top curtains open?" the girl asked. "I like to feel the sun." She sat him down on the narrow bunk. His ungainly body for once fit someplace perfectly. She slid her soft hand inside his shirt. Oh! Her perfume.

"Wait," he said. "You have to know." He took her hand and placed it on himself.

"That is not so important. If you studied the ancients they would teach you many things. I will teach you what I know. You will make me feel . . . every delight."

From somewhere the old Ramirez, violent and sad, gawky and with glasses, stood up. (He was in a dark garage, surrounded by stacks of comic books. Watch out! he signaled, and was gone, maybe forever.) Juan let the girl take off his shirt, lay back with a sigh and felt her beautiful hands begin to caress him.

XIII

As I seem to recall mentioning before, loneliness is my biggest hangup. Everything contributes to it; I don't see (well, maybe I begin to) how you can beat the rap. You sign up for a lover and feel worse than ever; your husband turns out to be a cardboard sign in front of a Chinese restaurant. Even friendship is a chancy thing. (In ten years more I'll probably have something to say on the Arctic Wastes of Motherhood but for now, let it lie.) Walter wasn't home when I got back, neither was Lorraine. The kids were gone, the sitter was gone. I called Walt's mother, Lorraine's mother, *my* mother. Nobody had seen anybody or left any notes. The sitter's phone was out of order. I called Steve Rader. He wasn't home or wasn't answering. I considered calling the police about the children but kidnapers don't usually take them in lots of three. Someone I knew had to have them somewhere. (By this time it had dawned on me that something was up, and that, once again, everyone in the world knew more about it than I did. I went next door to the empty Ramirez apartment and turned on the television. It showed me a series of test patterns.)

When it's late at night and I'm alone I'm afraid to read. The trouble is, I'm afraid of people breaking in. If I'm reading a book I won't hear them, I won't be ready with the proper thing to say. I once spent an entire evening typing up a list of right things to say to: (a) a burglar, (b) kidnaper, (c) sex molester. Can you see how much I want company?

Anyway, I was afraid to read, and didn't want to wake up the people upstairs, and our next-door neighbors on the other side weren't home either, so I sat in the Ramirez's house and watched the test patterns until a man finally came on and began in a dry, sad voice to explain some math problems to me and it began to be light outside and I sort of sank over on one side on the Ramirez bed and was able to go to sleep. I'd been through a lot.

I guess I didn't say how I got home. Juan ran out on me, can you imagine? I couldn't figure out why. In theory it might have been for guilt—his upbringing and all—but in practice he'd seemed pleased as punch with what had to be the worst screw of my entire life (and that really truly leaves out my own frigid state and gets to be, for the moment, objective).

I often wonder (and can't ask other women) if they feel the same as I. There is an attraction, a beauty, that men possess that may come from a tragic sense (like Walter), or a soul (like Juan), or a pair of lightly tanned fourteen-inch upper arms, or a spare chest in a blue workshirt. But that beauty's a mirage that emanates from skin, breath, moisture. Now, more advanced in time and age, I'm able with a little more ease to clasp that flesh, those sundry monuments of bone and blood. But that's not—as they say—where it's at. The men we love most are best when they're five feet away.

Ramirez had been quite pleased with himself until something I'd said gave it away. Then he seemed sad, all right. Sad, but not sad enough to run away.

I waited around in the motel for an hour or so. I drank up the rest of the champagne. It made me woozy for a while, then tired, then there was nothing but a splitting headache to show for it. I felt like Meg in *Little Women*; doubly, because besides the champagne headache I'd been on a debauch that Marmee wouldn't have liked very much. They'd put Meg to work making shirts after her taste of high life. Well, I wouldn't do that for anybody. I put my ear to the wall; if Juan had thought to get some strange and extra thrill I couldn't get the hang of it; it was more exciting, certainly more eventful, to listen through our walls at home. The tape recorder had run out and come to an automatic stop. They were still up next door, chatting in a foreign language, laughing.

I opened the front door and queried out into the dark, "Juan? Juan?" It silenced the folks next door, and there was nothing but the sound of the breeze blowing the weeds on the hill, some idle birds, the ocean. I went back inside, got dressed, washed my face, eyed the key on the dresser. I knew Juan would be angry when I left—if I left. I'd never driven anything but an old Volkswagen in my life. I went to the door again and called out in the false bravado voice I usually save for those theoretical burglars, "Juan, if you don't come back right away, I'm going home."

Silence, more profound than before. I grabbed the key and left the room. The door locked behind me. Once outside I became *absolutely sure* I was being watched. I would have run up the road to the manager and called a cab, but I knew that those bad things (half-bogeymen, half-bandits from *The Treasure of the Sierra Madre*) would get me, sure. My only chance at safety was to be cool, to drive Juan's car out of there.

I couldn't start the damn car. When I did start it and drove down to the end of the driveway toward the ocean, there was no place to turn. It took me twenty minutes to turn that tin monster around, all under the eyes of my imaginary friends out there. I would have cried a hundred times except that too would have given the whole show away.

I was stopped twice on the way home by policemen, once for not having my headlights turned on, another time for weaving—they thought I was drunk. Both times they were kind and accepted my explanation of a row with my husband, but in those days it was an unusual experience (as opposed to now, when we all know the cops a little better, and as a matter of course children get maced along with the faculty wives and finger sandwiches at your average mother-and-daughter tea).

I felt a good deal like a criminal type when I got home, or at least acquainted with the criminal element, which is another reason why it seemed foolhardy to go to sleep in the dark. They really were all out there.

So on one level I wasn't even surprised when after an hour or so of sleep, gritty-eyed and sour-stomached, I was awakened by official pounding on the door. I opened up, and it was the same old mistake, a little covey of officers and plainclothesmen were pounding next door, on *our* door. They asked me questions about myself, Lorraine, Juan, Walter, Steve, and also everyone any of us had ever known from our separate moments of birth until that morning. It was one of our worst bad dreams come true.

(Somewhat later than all this, during the long afternoons when teaching assistants in English gathered to gossip and exchange theories or read *Paradise Regained* aloud or plot our endless round of charades, home movies, mock-seminars, picnics, parties, and excursions, which are all the underground reasons why it takes seven years for the average graduate student to get his or her PhD; during, as I say, those long, deliciously idle afternoons when it always seemed to be springtime and the birds sang and the lawn outside was sweet and warm, we would scurrilously slander the faculty, the academic advisers on whom our futures must depend, although the present by that time had become so nice that we weren't in any hurry to get there. We called their scholarship into question, read their learned articles aloud and laughed until we choked, speculated upon their sex life, made fun of their speech impediments, sneered at the colors of their ties. Through it all we fancied ourselves at the mercy of an intercom system, since each of our offices was tied by wires to the large central office of the department of English. From time to time the boxes in our offices crackled; we would be summoned to the phone upstairs to answer one of those silly questions that people think up for themselves and then can't answer, and so phone a university: "What is the name of Ophelia's constant companion? No, not Hamlet! Her constant *companion*!" We'd never know the answer. Or we would be asked to run off a ditto, or give a final for a full professor, or take some papers over to the administration building. Once when the box called me upstairs they offered me a job teaching freshman English in Cairo; they wanted a lady, I didn't like to think why.

Anyway, if we could hear Dorothy crackling through that box, couldn't she hear us? And didn't they leave the box on, and listen? And wouldn't that sometime have some effect upon all of us? We decided that the only way to protect our privacy was to cheerfully give it up, that if everyone's secrets were known, then, as in algebra, it would all cancel itself out. We debated this question at the tops of our voices, glaring at our brown boxes, not even bothering to close our doors. And never knew if it hurt us or helped us to know or be known.)

Those cops were kings of gossip. They knew more about all of us than we knew; they'd held inverted glasses to all our walls. After the first hour or so of fear I admit I got interested. I filled them in on a few things they didn't know—roasted Lorraine's mother, defended Walter's mother, speculated about the Ramirez marriage, retold my several versions of the rape story, in return for their several versions of the rape story; complained about Walter's betrayal (they'd been at that first anthro party in elaborately sloppy plainclothes). But all the way through, they knew eighteen times more than I did; it was plain to see, it was monstrous.

Juan was in trouble, *Walter* was in trouble. Lorraine might be in trouble, Steve might be in trouble. They didn't think I was, they said, they had suspected me for some time but didn't now. (Once more I was left out of something big.) The Italian department was just then in an involved scrape about giving out good grades in return for amorous favors, and for the longest time, in spite of my earlier vague fears about what Juan was up to, I thought they were talking about a grading scandal. They kept talking about missing papers; I thought they meant term papers. I told the cops repeatedly I hadn't seen any papers around either of the two houses: "They wouldn't do anything like that," I kept saying helpfully but I knew perfectly well that Walter at least would *love* to do something like that; trade a screw for an A, or sell an old paper for a week's groceries.

When it finally dawned on me what they meant, I tried to ask them questions, but they, of course, weren't talking too much. I saw their gratification (I didn't know anything), their exasperation (they'd hoped for something from me), their suspicion (I couldn't have been so out of it). But the wife is traditionally the last to know, and I took some comfort from the fact that really, in the last analysis, nobody has the least notion of what's going on in the world outside. You can take anything from anyone; no one notices because, very simply, they're thinking about their own lives, period, end of report.

The officers were in a state; they had everybody under observation but they didn't know what to do with any of them. They gave me directions; I wasn't to leave the house for a while. They'd bring in meals from any restaurant I wanted as long as it was in Westwood. They were assigning a plainclothes policewoman to stay with me for a while (not that I was in trouble, understand, but I should stay close to home for my own good, etc.). This police lady would dress up like a co-ed, my cousin. We were not to talk about anything, anywhere. She'd audit my classes for me, bring home any tests I had to take. I was not to communicate with anyone for a while, even Walter, even Lorraine. (I never liked that lady cop, but at least she got our television set fixed.)

During the next few weeks the cops kept me more or less informed. Lorraine, they told me, was out in Gardena living in a motel with Steve. She'd decided, apparently by pure coincidence, to run off with her seedy lover the afternoon of my date with Ramirez. She'd left notes for her husband and for me, hidden under the pillows of our couch-beds, where we'd find them in the evening, giving the lovers a decent head start. I'll always believe she planned on being rescued, but since Juan and I weren't there to go to our respective beds, the cops found the notes and Lorraine was left for a longer while than she'd figured on with Steve and his visions.

Steve (and this is one of the parts the cops relished, just as malicious as any of the rest of us) had wanted to take his lady love to Mexico, thus beating out her gawky spouse on his own, his native ground. They'd gotten as far as Caborca, when a busted radiator and some flying cockroaches had made him revamp his vision of himself. He hated nature, he decided, he was an Urban Man. He came home and traded his crippled car for a motorcycle. Now, in Gardena (a South Side, white-trash suburb of LA) they lived some version of the ideal life he'd sketched out for me over the pastrami sandwiches: sex in the morning, so as to be pure for the day, a breakfast of chili dogs and beer so as to be part of the American Mainstream, motorcycle practice into the afternoon. Evening negotiations at the local stadium to see if he could break into the races. Lorraine was by his side at all times, together with her two children who they'd decided after all to take along. Steve encouraged this, it was part of his picture of a Southern Good Old Boy to have a couple of runny-nosed brats in tow. He dabbed their hair with peroxide at night to give them the proper Aryan cast, and any Mexican features they had he passed off gleefully as Cherokee. Their good health was against them, but he took them to the races every night and consistently forgot to bring their sweaters; soon their noses fell in with the general image. The nights were not so marvelous; Steve drank and socked them all around some. Lorraine had descended into a minor nightmare, but it had its rewards. There was some question about Lorraine's involvement in the general conspiracy; she and Steve were under strict surveillance, which the officers performed with tenacity and glee. Lorraine and Steve occupied one sordid room, David and Jennifer (at night) the room adjoining; on the other side, snuggled up, the cops.

So Lorraine had taken her kids that night, and my little girl was with my mother-in-law, in the immaculate apartment over their art store down in Chinatown, being stuffed with tea cakes, entertained with kites and firecrackers, learning to count on a special children's abacus. Walt's mother hadn't answered the phone that night because she too had been surrounded by police, who (she told me later) had eaten up quantities of Chinese noodles—after asking her at length how a nice Irish Lady came to be in a place like that. For days she fed them all her best goodies, delighted to have a flock of gawky boys once again around the house. My smooth father-in-law won away all their overtime pay in every card game he and they could think up, and even now they still go down to visit Walter's folks from time to time, and take their wives, and buy all their birthday and anniversary presents from the Wong's art store, which Mr. Wong spectacularly overprices, just for them.

It was a spy ring they were after; Juan a gentle novice in the work; Walter, *my* Walter, a junior executive. There were members from every concentric circle of our society; associate professors from UCLA in their first tentative adventure, a flock of technocrats from AXEL and those other glossy homes for our new intellectuals (which turn out to be, the more you think about it, nothing more than graduate-graduate schools), where espionage turned out to be as mild and expected as tax evasion.

It took me hours that first morning to get that much out of the police. By that time I was in your average state of hysteria: "What are you going to do to them?" I kept asking in indignation, terror, amazement, funk. "What are you going to *do*?"

The answer which came eventually, after a week or so—and tell me now if all human conduct isn't futile—was almost nothing.

The FBI, the CIA, whoever it was, was more interested in finding the head of the organization than punishing any underlings. And don't misunderstand, everything I ever heard about it, from my cop informants, from friends and passersby, seemed to indicate that they wanted the head man, not to hurt him but to hire him, the way Ford or CBS might snap up any bright young executive. But whoever it was they were after had covered his tracks so well they never did find him; it might have been anyone, any Korean kid over here working as a busboy while he made his way through English composition, anybody at all. Until they found The Fabled Man they couldn't afford to punish anybody, for fear of getting him by mistake.

Everyone would just have to go away for a while. While counterspies crept around and around that ring and looked for the chink (excuse me!) that held it together, it became evident that Juan, too, was to go away. He chose northern California and went on what everyone said was a retreat. (But he thought of it as an advance.) Lorraine and Steve were already gone so that question never came up. Some faculty members lost their tenure. The AXEL people that I learned about later dealt their way out: they knew so much, they argued, that a teensy bit of spying was certainly better than total defection. The ones who suffered most were the exchange students. The CIA (I guess it was) got to them by cutting off their grants, efficiently rehiring some of them as counterspies before they sent them back to the fun and games of exploding Africa, the Philippines, what have you. If they didn't make it as statesmen in their emerging governments, at least they had skills as ethnomusicologists, structural linguists, dulcimer makers, to tide them over. The government felt more strongly about Walter (they found names and addresses among his language cards); they were going to deport him. They didn't want him anywhere in Asia, which they figured would just compound their trouble, so they gave him a choice of the rest of the world. He chose Paris and they said no. He chose the South Seas, and they agreed. They thought it would encourage him in his work; he could still make it, if he wanted to, as a cultural anthropologist.

After six weeks of roundups and questionings, the authorities felt that they still didn't have enough evidence to pick up the ringleader (or if they did maybe they decided after all it wasn't worth the trouble). Like teachers in a rebellious high school class they continued to separate the troublemakers; there was a spate of grants in history, art, physics, to Finland and its counterparts, those few tiny countries with a minimum of social stress. During the semester break my teaching assistantship came through; for the next few years until I either got my PhD or left the university, I would be economically independent. There are some who might argue that it would have come through anyway. But folded in with my first (small) check I found a short note—actually a Xeroxed form—advising discretion in all things as a condition of my new employment.

No one ever was arrested, and most lives went on as usual, except that our gossip for a while sounded as though it came from the pages of _Newsweek_ instead of _True Confessions_. But some of our lives skidded off the turntable of our ordinary existence and over someplace else. They might have anyway, the decade breaking might have done it.

XIV

THERE WERE CHANGES, as I say, in our small lives, but the general cast of characters remained the same. There are only two hundred people in the world, a friend of mine says, the rest is done with mirrors. (We'll remember to make proverbs long after we've forgotten what those medieval guys wrote in their notebooks or on their jailhouse walls.) Do people from the East still think you can come west and be what you want? That you can forget your past out here and think up a neat future? Well, maybe so. You can go west from the West too. Most of us started from nothing and (after some confusion), I think we may have turned into what we wanted to be. The process goes on, hopefully. We watched our frog companions turn into princes—and we believe it. This is America, you know. (If some of it's true, it's all true.) But living out here it's nicer yet, because underneath the finery rented from Western Costumes, we recognize our same old friends.

In the middle of June, right after finals, Ottoline called and said she and Jimmy were giving a party to celebrate the beginning of summer. "Most of that awful spring fog is gone by now, and we have the whole beautiful vacation to look forward to." Well, OK, I went.

I'd been living alone for almost six months. At the end of January I'd put Walter on the plane, all dressed up in a new suit—a last present from his parents—carrying an Olympia portable typewriter and a thriftshop overcoat. We spent our last month together in a curious marriage-through-divorce; like prisoners in a snappy new jail we talked to each other by telephone and through bulletproof glass. We sat side by side in what was to be my car, and drove all over the city buying what was to be his luggage, and made last-minute familial but formal visits to Chinese widows, Eurasian merchants, Filipino waiters, Japanese landscape architects, importers and exporters, restaurateurs and entertainers, the whole network of Oriental society in this town. His parents took Walter's deportation in amazing style. Walter was never more their son than when he was thrown out of the country.

We collected a trunk here, a traveling iron there, left off a set of encyclopedias, picked up someone's antiquated book on the South Seas. We packed it all and laid it on the Railway Express people, where, for a large sum, they guaranteed to send it to Borneo, with no accidents. "I would have liked the Marquesas," Walter mourned, "or even Australia. They have restaurants and white people." But he wasn't unhappy. We found an apartment for me down in Venice; Walter paid three months' rent in advance. We moved in the furniture and painted, and I had money enough to get some plants for the living room. They always give economy as a reason for staying together, but separation seemed to dissolve a lot of our expenses.

It was quiet in my new house. You could hear the ocean far across the flat lonely beach, and, inland, some cars, and maybe a quarrel, and maybe not. Walter and I sat in the clean and pretty living room that we'd never share, and tried to talk; did talk in fact, with infinite interest and infinite caution. What we learned, what we said, may be irrelevant. I think of our marriage as a game of tag, a great rushing at each other (or someone) until we married, then a turn to run away. Apart, we longed again for each other.

Like picayune historians, as though marriage were our dissertation topic, we went over our common material.

"You ought never to have said I made our own hard time, that was a terrible thing to say."

"But you said that too, we *always* said that."

"No, but that time, after, when you were lying on the couch and I was playing solitaire and I tried to ask you about why—don't you remember?—and you said I always made my own hard time, don't you remember?''

Of course we would always remember: ''Did that get on your nerves? I honestly didn't even mean anything by it.''

So we parted and began again to pursue each other. It's all done with mirrors, believe me. My idea now of what Walter was is much more complicated than his bad imitations of Charlie Chan would have ever led me to believe, but if we were to get back together it would be the same; all that research would have gone for very little, because no research keeps you up to date on *now*.

The last afternoon we all went out to the airport to say good-bye. All the friends of his family, Oriental and motley. Loy was there, he didn't hold a grudge about his wife. (My father-in-law had gone to the funeral and wept aloud over the open coffin, and negotiations were already in progress for a new wife to be sent over by way of either Taiwan or Macao.) I was struck again by all their style compared to my Anglo-Saxon plainness, but I could see that I'd come some way in five years. And my beautiful baby girl, almost in the first grade now, thin and withdrawn in a beige, well-cut sunsuit carrying a striped ball, had what you'd have to call class.

Walter said good-bye in a dream. He was afraid of airplanes, he was all dressed up, he was wordless, he was a nice man. He kissed China—but with surprising casualness—he hugged his mother and me, laughed with all those inscrutable uncles and aunts and good-bye, he was dead gone. Alone, we all looked at each other. They'd wanted me to go to Borneo, but I have to say their Oriental sense of family was balanced by common sense about the world based on a couple of generations of getting the last plane or boat out of somewhere. Perhaps they figured that a Black wife with a dowry of shrunken heads would have just that much more to offer than me.

I drove up the coast to Malibu where Jimmy and Ottoline had their house. I'd left China with a divorced girl next door who had children of her own and a past married life which had had too much to do with the university. ''Isn't it wonderful here,'' she said, ''now?'' And she took China to play in the tall dried grass which grew in the sand beside her door.

Driving up the coast I thought how much the city had changed in the past ten years, but how the coast would be the last to change. There were spiffy beach houses, yes, but they'd been mostly built in the thirties and forties. And amusement parks are always old. Salt makes things old. The sun was out, the ocean glittered.

I'd never been to Jimmy's before, and it was hard to find. I turned left, inland, and drove up a steep hill which wound back and forth and around and down the same hill in some kind of crazy maze. Houses, in that great way they have in Los Angeles, appeared above in stucco cliffs, or I peered *down* at red tiled roofs, trying to find some house number among the jungle of walls and potted plants. This was one of the old beach sections, and the naturally barren cliff had been watered and tended for years until one home's bougainvillea twined with another's and walls of orange or purple blossoms obscured walls and garages and bicycles—you know what I'm saying—here was a wealth of all those things that anyone with style wants—but you know, the way they got them was with money.

Jimmy's house was one of those which rose straight up above the narrow street. All I saw of it from the street was a garage door, a stairwell and a passion flower vine. I walked up hundreds of stairs to a tiny deserted patio, to another patio, to a terrace, and finally to the broad veranda of the house itself. Out of breath, I waited a minute before going in and looked out to the sea. The ocean, which had been invisible from the street, was half the world up here. From Palos Verdes to Point Dume, dotted with Catalina and some islands I'd never heard of; it all spread out a half-mile below like the world's largest sequined bedspread, twinkling in the sun and mist.

The door was open and I went down a large white entry hall with a spiral staircase at the end. A breeze—no, a light wind—blew through this part of the house, combining salt from the sea with a heavy scent of orange blossoms. I found my way to the living room and had to laugh. It was beautiful, it was great. Imagine a large—oh, large—vaulted white stucco room, with that ocean at one end, and a grand piano, and square miles of polished floor, and gold velvet couches, and a Renaissance pulpit, and big, big golden paintings, and golden vases filled with burning yellow acacia blossoms, and air, all the air of the whole West Coast flowing across the sea through the room and through to the orchards and vines outside. When you have that clear in your mind, put what seemed like every friend I ever had—all dressed up!—in that room.

I don't know why (mind, I was a woman twice alone, bereft of my husband, by my country; I had a baby at home, and was still afraid of being single, and of possible reprisals, and worried about my phone being tapped, and that my mother didn't like me), anyway I had to laugh.

"How is Walter?" It was someone from the anthro department, owlish, gray, a plate of delicious goodies in one ink-stained hand, a drink in the other. "I didn't expect to see you here."

I smiled broadly. I was still nervous at parties alone.

"What do you hear from Walter?"

"Oh, he's still at that institute, they liked his work in Australian languages, so now he's setting up a team to transcribe the native dialects of Borneo, before they lose their culture or something."

"Are you kidding?"

"*No.* That's what he's doing." (And that, my God, was what he *was* doing.)

"What institute?"

I gave him a name, some name, one of those hundred dopey agencies the CIA runs, and the man nodded, doubtfully, cynically. No! What it was, he was envious. He wanted a grant for himself. "And," I said, in a burst of nostalgic loyalty, "his dissertation is almost done."

I found Ottoline in the kitchen talking to her Mexican maid, their language a charming combination of first year Spanish and greenhouse Jewish matron. (By which is meant—I don't know.) The sun streamed in a series of bay windows, and standing by the sink you could see part of that great slice of sea. The Mexican girl kept putting enormous trays of canapés into waist-high ovens and taking out trays from other ovens. While the two women excitedly talked the little morsels proliferated around them. And yet the mess which you think of connected with cooking or food or parties didn't pertain. There was smell without smoke, sight without sound—that's not quite true, but you get the picture. There was a cactus orchid on the kitchen sink, in bloom, of course.

Ottoline hadn't changed much since high school. She ran up and took my arm and told me about her dress; it was a caftan made out of pillow ticking and had Algerian trim. She told me it only cost ten dollars to have it made—outside of the dressmaker's fee. I don't know, it was like wonderland in that house. Ot didn't seem to notice, and I guessed it was because even though she'd spent some time being poor, she had always expected money. She gave me some cherry tomatoes to stuff and asked about Walter. I told the same old lie.

"A fellowship came through," I said. "You know, he passed his qualifyings and was having trouble finding a dissertation topic, but they let him go to Borneo, and he'll fool around there for a while, and just come back and write about it. Maybe a study of an economic system or something."

"But you didn't go with him."

"It isn't as if we hadn't had a lot of trouble. He's a nice man"—how complacent and kindly I felt to be able to say that and mean it—"but I don't think I could deal with Walter and Borneo, too."

"How long will he be out there?"

"I don't know. I think he wants to be quite thorough. I know one guy he always talks about stayed down in the Amazon Basin for twelve years."

"But if he really wants to get his degree . . ." Then she must have felt she hurt me because she rushed on. "It certainly is an honor for him to have got that money. I don't know, I think that it must be more fun to do that sort of thing than study a lot of laws someone else made up. I mean, it's just like writing about your trip, and then they make you a PhD."

She began to look harassed again, but I'd thought it and said just that often enough. It was one of the cheatier ways of getting a degree. It occurred to me suddenly that, story or not, Walter really *was* going to get his degree. Being a deportee and a subversive didn't make him an unclassified graduate student. Walter would have nothing else to do down there, he'd have to work on his dissertation. That explained why he'd been so serene, so pleased in those last days. That's what he'd wanted to do all along—poke around in some jungle and learn some goofy language and sit down by himself at night and count his language cards and get drunk. Neither one of us took to marriage very well, and with me he either would have stayed at home and felt awful, or I would have had to go out in the field, and then I would have felt awful. If it took treason as well as infidelity to cut him loose, well, anyway, there he was.

"I'm so happy," I said to Ot. She looked a little coldly at me, or looked at me some way, and said, "I'm glad someone is."

"What's wrong?"

"Nothing. Actually . . . nothing. Did you see what Jimmy was doing when you came in?"

"Playing the piano."

"Jesus."

"He sounded *nice*. I never knew he could do that. It was very elegant. Cole Porter, I think it was."

"Are you sure it was him?"

"I think so, why? What's wrong?"

"Jimmy's sick. There's something wrong with his spine. He's going in the hospital this week."

"Is it serious?"

"Well, he might not be able to walk, he might not be able to . . . They say he might not be able to carry on." Again, her face got hard, alert, basically crazy. "Can't you tell me anything about it? Don't you know what he's up to?"

Years of Vets Housing made me think of that one thing. She must be accusing me of dealing with Jimmy. *Jimmy?* I blushed and mumbled, "Ot, you're crazy. Why would *I* know anything about it? He's your husband."

She sighed, and looked around at that great airy kitchen, her docile maid. "OK, Edie, OK. Why don't you go out now and talk to some people? You shouldn't waste your time in here. I want to keep an eye on Lupe for a while longer. I'm sorry I said anything."

Out in that wide, breezy living room again, surrounded by elegant, elderly-young people and without the protection of a husband, I felt quite shy. On the other hand, that inward laughter kept starting up. I saw Mr. Goodman, in his baggy suit, waving a hot canapé, talking to an Indian girl in a sari. *Here I am.* I kept thinking, *here we are.*

I walked over to the piano. Jimmy Joyce was playing in

the lost style of the thirties; trills and little minor chords, and a few of those low notes that you hit with your little finger. Everything in that room seemed to remind me of something else. The bay windows which opened to that enormous, sunny ocean were a giant mock-up of the university's fake Tudor cafeteria; the flowers and flowering trees were the optimistic bloom of all those nasturtiums and zinnias that Juan Ramirez had planted. Jimmy, in this setting, looked goofy and sweet, and reminded me of when my mother would get a little zonked and rip through one of those trilling renditions of "Nola" or "Kitten on the Keys." Just one of the girls, she must have been. Jimmy looked tired but good. He nodded to me, and smiled, kept on playing.

"You look beautiful," he said.

I barely kept myself from saying, "Who, me?" but maybe I did say it, because he nodded again, and said, "In that dress."

It was yellow linen. I'd bought it that spring with some of Walter's going-away money. It was the first bright color I'd worn in years.

"Wait until I get a tan to go with it," I said, and then thought, *All Right!* Wait until I get a tan. I couldn't stop smiling.

Jimmy looked up and kept on playing. "Do you see much of Lorraine?"

"No, I haven't seen her since . . ." But that was part of what I shouldn't talk about. I began to see that keeping secrets for the rest of my life could be a drag. Jimmy didn't seem to notice. He went on softly playing, while behind us people talked and laughed, and out in front there was that inscrutable ocean.

"I have a friend who sees her often," he said.

"Well, where is she, what's she doing? Who's your friend?"

Jimmy smiled genially. There was something about him, he sure was a grown-up. And he was six months younger than I was.

"She stayed with that Steve character exactly two weeks." He said it with great satisfaction.

"What happened?"

"He *hit* her a lot, he beat her, she had bruises on her

ribs, every time you'd see her—my friend says—she'd be either laughing or crying, and she'd peel off her blouse, like for a conversation, to show those bruises.''

"My goodness." I tried to sound astounded, but I couldn't imagine that it bothered her very much. "What happened then?''

"He decided to get another girl. He said that he could only feel pure emotion for Lorraine if one or the other of them were married, that their relationship thrived on adversity.''

"So?''

"So he decided to get married.''

"He's kind of a pedant in a way.''

Jimmy went right on, there's a certain class of men who hate that way we talk.

"So he found a girl who looked just like Lorraine but never said anything and she was young, and they all had some fights over there, I don't know exactly." His fat hands wandered delicately over the keys of the piano. "Lorraine couldn't believe what was happening. Steve told her that she represented the alienation of the fifties to him, while his new girl was a symbol of the joyous sixties.''

"Goodness.''

"Well then, what happened, they kept getting into fights, every day, every night. Lorraine stabbed that girl in the wrist with a pair of scissors, that girl called the cops, Steve threw Lorraine through a plate-glass window and the neighbors complained. It was a weird situation.''

"How did it end up?''

"Steve found a third girl. The dialectic answer to his dilemma.''

"Is that what he *said*?''

"Of course.''

"Did he ever knock that other lady around?''

"He knocked her out cold one morning on her own front lawn.''

"What's Lorraine doing now? Why don't we ever see her?''

"She has a little studio down in Venice . . .''

"Why, I'm living down in Venice!''

". . . but she doesn't see many people. She's going back to work. She paints all the time.''

"Lorraine's working?"

"Yes."

"How do you know all this?" It had occurred to me by then to be really quite annoyed. Because Lorraine was my best friend. I couldn't see her now, which was bad enough, but who was this sinister upstart, anyway?

"She and my friend are quite close. She sees him often, she tells him everything."

"Who is he?"

"I don't think you'd know him."

If Lorraine had switched to Jimmy I couldn't believe it. You can . . . or she could . . . make a rapist laugh, but that Jimmy was out of the question. I had a vision of a Lorraine disconcertingly close to what her mother wanted her to be, scrubbed clean, in a bare room, with some kind of impressionistic good furniture around, churning out pictures all afternoon, with tonight's brownies baking in the oven. I thought of gentle Ot, her good-natured, hearty face twisted up in concern. What is it like to be bought? Lorraine and I had spent so much unacknowledged time allotting our poor moneys here and there, what would it be like to be bought? To fit in with his bright house, his Mediterranean chests, to be taken to Mazatlán and stay at the stately Bel Mar instead of the rat-infested Olas Altas? To be a thin foil to sturdy Ot? Let me say I saw Lorraine soon after that, and that's what she was, a thin, pretty woman, a little older, Jewish after all, painting picture after picture in her pretty house.

During our crisis, Lorraine told me later, Jimmy found out from his boys where she was. On impulse, just when things were worst with her, he drove down to the motel—eluding the police—and took her away from all that. Once he'd made the gesture he couldn't bear to give her up (although he tried, repeatedly, later). He put her in a house with her two children and he fished Lorraine's mother out of the hospital to help take care of the kids. (Mrs. Ross has almost recovered from the attack made on her by those crazy Blacks. They either gave her the wrong dose or used the wrong weapon. Anyway, she's well and happy now; whatever they put in that box did her good. She's become a gentle old thing, and spends hours playing games with her grandchildren.)

Lorraine ended up staying with Jimmy. She loves the free

time, and says he's not a bad ball, although she would have been happier if the operation turned out the other way. He's proud of his thing, she says, it's solid and big, as befits his grown-up position in the world. He's happy to have a mistress to practice on; he's happy still to be able to run a mile every day. He's good to her, Lorraine says, and very good to his wife. Beyond that, Lorraine doesn't talk about him the way she praised Steve or lovingly maligned Ramirez. She's kind of stately, if you can believe it, expensive paintings on her walls, and her studio like Jimmy's other home, filled with light and air. She's looking forward to her first show, and I imagine with Jimmy's influence she'll be a success. I wonder how long she'll stay with him. He's got a good arrangement, her kids have big rooms of their own and spend most of their time on the beach. But out in her kitchen, on the inside of a cupboard full of good china, she has pasted an old newspaper photo of Elvis Presley in a jumpsuit, goggles and crash helmet. Underneath, the caption reads: *Elvis went on a diet of mainly melons and is handsomer and even more appealing to women than he has ever been before.*

Later in the afternoon the guests would put on Fats Domino and the Hollywood Argyles, and try, ungraceful, happy and trying (don't misunderstand, me among them) the joyous new dances. But now, in charitable transition from Jimmy's elderly piano, the Modern Jazz Quartet played, clear and sweet. Jimmy got up and lounged in a corner. You couldn't like him, but there he was, glittery and personable, and forty-eight hours later, his back to be opened and inspected like a piece of flayed beef.

Which brings me, somehow, to the last. "I hear you're writing now." I got a terrible World War III feeling, and turned around and looked straight up to an unfamiliar face, a creature of some incredible beauty, you'll have to forgive me. I stared at a face I didn't know; kind, triangular, dazzling, crowned by endless halos of black, curly hair, slashed by an enormous Stalin mustache, an oyster mouth. I say oyster not because of mannerism, but because I remember in Mazatlán on a hot day, biting into one, and the firm flesh, the lemony delight . . . there are mouths, after all, that you wouldn't mind having on a plate.

I recognized my friend. He lowered his eyes, looked down

at me, his lashes lay long and thick on his cheeks, and that little extra chin he had from always looking down, there it was. He smiled, oh, I can't tell you.

"Where are your glasses?" I said, just like in those movies.

He turned his head to the side like a coquettish woman.

"Where've you *been*?"

"Learning to garden."

"Oh, of course."

"I've got some money. I'm going to buy a nursery. Either that or there's a convent up north I know about. They need a gardener."

"Are you, no, what about your job?"

"Well, I don't think I really liked to do that kind of work very much. What I really like is to be outdoors."

"But isn't that kind of a change?"

"Not really. I always liked to work with plants, and I think I can get a grant for something I've thought up." He hesitated. "It's difficult to explain, but if you introduce some . . . element into the plants themselves, the use of pesticides may become unnecessary, obsolete."

"But is there enough money? Will you be able to take care of your kids?"

He smiled. "God takes care of all of us." I fell down. It ordinarily embarrasses me when people talk like that, but he was just too great.

"What happened to your *hair*?"

He nodded. "I like your dress."

How much more can I say? There we were and there we were. I know what everyone could/would/might/did say about lengths and angles, about manias and maniacs, but there are, I'm ashamed to say in this enlightened world, more pleasures than the purely physical. Right in front of me there opened up a primrose path of good dinners and funny afternoons, of elliptical conversations I'd never understand and close evenings in wood houses with cats, Lorraine's paintings on the wall, and my little (I only say that) articles on the kitchen sink (magazines marked *Save* in his own clear hand), less a life than a wild-goose chase, with the colors and beautiful distortion of an acid trip, the smell of sherry and cake and the constant illusion that you're learning to make pure gold.

I left him, ate some, drank some, talked some more of our own favorite gossip about friends who, it seemed, were growing out instead of up, falling into funny jobs and second marriages. The sun slanted in so unbearably sweet. People began to go home; finally only eight or so of us were left. We sat on those brocaded couches, drinking, in some salute to our thirties parents, golden gin fizzes. Ramirez sat at one end of that opposite couch, and I sat at the opposite end of that other couch, and as we all talked and settled in among the cushions, I caught the glitter of his contact lenses, and got drunk and laughed at that incredible, self-conscious, ersatz beauty. There we were, you know, there we were.

About the Author

CAROLYN SEE was born and raised in Los Angeles, CA. She attended the University of California where she received her Ph.D. in American Literature. Ms. See has been published in *Esquire*, *McCalls*, *Atlantic* and other national magazines as well as having four other novels to her credit. She is a regular book reviewer for the *Los Angeles Times*.